THE GORILLA HUNTERS

BY R.M. BALLANTYNE.

CHAPTER ONE.

IN WHICH THE HUNTERS ARE INTRODUCED.

It was five o'clock in the afternoon. There can be no doubt whatever as to that. Old Agnes may say what she pleases--she has a habit of doing so--but I know for certain (because I looked at my watch not ten minutes before it happened) that it was exactly five o'clock in the afternoon when I received a most singular and every way remarkable visit--a visit which has left an indelible impression on my memory, as well it might; for, independent of its singularity and unexpectedness, one of its results was the series of strange adventures which are faithfully detailed in this volume.

It happened thus:--

I was seated in an armchair in my private study in a small town on the west coast of England. It was a splendid afternoon, and it was exactly five o'clock. Mark that. Not that there is anything singular about the mere fact, neither is it in any way mixed up with the thread of this tale; but old Agnes is very obstinate--singularly positive--and I have a special desire that she should see it in print, that I have not given in on that point. Yes, it was five precisely, and a beautiful evening. I was ruminating, as I frequently do, on the pleasant memories of bygone days, especially the happy days that I spent long ago among the coral islands of the Pacific, when a tap at the door aroused me.

"Come in."

"A veesiter, sir," said old Agnes (my landlady), "an' he'll no gie his name."

Old Agnes, I may remark, is a Scotchwoman.

"Show him in," said I.

"Maybe he's a pickpocket," suggested Agnes.

"I'll take my chance of that."

"Ay! that's like 'ee. Cares for naethin'. Losh, man, what if he cuts yer throat?"

"I'll take my chance of that too; only do show him in, my good woman," said I, with a gesture of impatience that caused the excellent (though obstinate) old creature to depart, grumbling.

In another moment a quick step was heard on the stair, and a stranger burst into the room, shut the door in my landlady's face as she followed him, and locked it.

I was naturally surprised, though not alarmed, by the abrupt and eccentric conduct of my visitor, who did not condescend to take off his hat, but stood with his arms folded on his breast, gazing at me and breathing hard.

"You are agitated, sir; pray be seated," said I, pointing to a chair.

The stranger, who was a little man and evidently a gentleman, made no reply, but, seizing a chair, placed it exactly before me, sat down on it as he would have seated himself on a horse, rested his arms on the back, and stared me in the face.

"You are disposed to be facetious," said I, smiling (for I never take offence without excessively good reason).

"Not at all, by no means," said he, taking off his hat and throwing it recklessly on the floor. "You are Mr Rover, I presume?"

"The same, sir, at your service."

"Are you? oh, that's yet to be seen! Pray, is your Christian name Ralph?"

"It is," said I, in some surprise at the coolness of my visitor.

"Ah! just so. Christian name Ralph, t'other name Rover--Ralph Rover. Very good. Age twenty-two yesterday, eh?"

"My birthday was yesterday, and my age is twenty-two. You appear to know more of my private history than I have the pleasure of knowing of yours. Pray, sir, may I--but, bless me! are you unwell?"

I asked this in some alarm, because the little man was rolling about in his seat, holding his sides, and growing very red in the face.

"Oh no! not at all; perfectly well--never was better in my life," he said, becoming all at once preternaturally grave. "You were once in the Pacific--lived on a coral island--"

"I did."

"Oh, don't trouble yourself to answer. Just shut up for a minute or two. You were rather a soft green youth then, and you don't seem to be much harder or less verdant now."

"Sir!" I exclaimed, getting angry.

"Just so," continued he, "and you knew a young rascal there--"

"I know a rascal here," I exclaimed, starting up, "whom I'll kick--"

"What!" cried the little stranger, also starting up and capsizing the chair; "Ralph Rover, has time and sunburning and war so changed my visage that you cannot recognise Peterkin?"

I almost gasped for breath.

"Peterkin--Peterkin Gay!" I exclaimed.

I am not prone to indulge in effeminate demonstration, but I am not ashamed to confess that when I gazed on the weather-beaten though ruddy countenance of my old companion, and observed the eager glance of his bright blue eyes, I was quite overcome, and rushed violently into his arms. I may also add that until that day I had had no idea of Peterkin's physical strength; for during the next five minutes he twisted me about and spun me round and round my own room until my brain began to reel, and I was fain to cry him mercy.

"So, you're all right--the same jolly, young old wiseacre in whiskers and long coat," cried Peterkin. "Come now, Ralph, sit down if you can. I mean to stay with you all evening, and all night, and all to-morrow, and all next day, so we'll have lots of time to fight our battles o'er again. Meanwhile compose yourself, and I'll tell you what I've come about. Of course, my first and chief reason was to see your face, old boy; but I have another reason too--a very peculiar reason. I've a proposal to make and a plan to unfold, both of 'em stunners; they'll shut you up and screw you down, and altogether flabbergast you when you hear 'em, so sit down and keep quiet--do."

I sat down accordingly, and tried to compose myself; but, to say truth, I was so much overjoyed and excited by the sight of my old friend and companion that I had some difficulty at first in fixing my attention on what he said, the more especially that he spoke with extreme volubility, and interrupted his discourse very frequently, in order to ask questions or to explain.

"Now, old fellow," he began, "here goes, and mind you don't interrupt me. Well, I mean to go, and I mean you to go with me, to--but, I forgot, perhaps you won't be able to go. What are you?"

"What am I?"

"Ay, your profession, your calling; lawyer, M.D., scrivener--which?"

"I am a naturalist."

"A what?"

"A naturalist."

"Ralph," said Peterkin slowly, "have you been long troubled with that complaint?"

"Yes," I replied, laughing; "I have suffered from it from my earliest infancy, more or less."

"I thought so," rejoined my companion, shaking his head gravely. "I fancied that I observed the development of that disease when we lived together on the coral island. It don't bring you in many thousands a year, does it?"

"No," said I, "it does not. I am only an amateur, having a sufficiency of this world's goods to live on without working for my bread. But although my dear father at his death left me a small fortune, which yields me three hundred a year, I do not feel entitled to lead the life of an idler in this busy world, where so many are obliged to toil night and day for the bare necessaries of life. I have therefore taken to my favourite studies as a sort of business, and flatter myself that I have made one or two not unimportant discoveries, and added a few mites to the sum of human knowledge. A good deal of my time is spent in scientific roving expeditions throughout the country, and in contributing papers to several magazines."

While I was thus speaking I observed that Peterkin's face was undergoing the most remarkable series of changes of expression, which, as I concluded, merged into a smile of beaming delight, as he said,--"Ralph, you're a trump!"

"Possibly," said I, "you are right; but, setting that question aside for the present, let me remind you that you have not yet told me where you mean to go to."

"I mean," said Peterkin slowly, placing both hands on his knees and looking me steadily in the face--"I mean to go a-hunting in--but I forgot. You don't know that I'm a hunter, a somewhat famous hunter?"

"Of course I don't. You are so full of your plans and proposals that you have not yet told me where you have been or what doing these six years. And you ye never written to me once all that time, shabby fellow. I thought you were dead."

"Did you go into mourning for me, Ralph?"

"No, of course not."

"A pretty fellow you are to find fault. You thought that I, your oldest and best friend, was dead, and you did not go into mourning. How could I write to you when you parted from me without giving me your address? It was a mere chance my finding you out even now. I was taking a quiet cup of coffee in the commercial room of a hotel not far distant, when I overheard a stranger speaking of his friend `Ralph Rover, the philosopher,' so I plunged at him promiscuously, and made him give me your address. But I've corresponded with Jack ever since we parted on the pier at Dover."

"What! Jack--Jack Martin?" I exclaimed, as a warm gush of feeling filled my heart at the sound of his well-remembered name. "Is Jack alive?"

"Alive! I should think so. If possible, he's more alive than ever; for I should suppose he must be full-grown now, which he was not when we last met. He and I have corresponded regularly. He lives in the north of England, and by good luck happens to be just now within thirty miles of this town. You don't mean to say, Ralph, that you have never met!"

"Never. The very same mistake that happened with you occurred between him and me. We parted vowing to correspond as long as we should live, and three hours after I remembered that we had neglected to exchange our addresses, so that we could not correspond. I have often, often made inquiries both for you and him, but have always failed. I never heard of Jack from the time we parted at Dover till to-day."

"Then no doubt you thought us both dead, and yet you did not go into mourning for either of us! O Ralph, Ralph, I had entertained too good an opinion of you."

"But tell me about Jack," said I, impatient to hear more concerning my dear old comrade.

"Not just now, my boy; more of him in a few minutes. First let us return to the point. What was it? Oh! a--about my being a celebrated hunter. A very Nimrod--at least a miniature copy. Well, Ralph, since we last met I have been all over the world, right round and round it. I'm a lieutenant in the navy now--at least I was a week ago. I've been fighting with the Kaffirs and the Chinamen, and been punishing the rascally sepoys in India, and been hunting elephants in Ceylon and tiger-shooting in the jungles, and harpooning whales in the polar seas, and shooting lions at the Cape; oh, you've no notion where all I've been. It's a perfect marvel I've turned up here alive. But there's one beast I've not yet seen, and I'm resolved to see him and shoot him too--"

"But," said I, interrupting, "what mean you by saying that you were a lieutenant in the navy a week ago?"

"I mean that I've given it up. I'm tired of the sea. I only value it as a means of getting from one country to another. The land, the land for me! You must know that an old uncle, a rich old uncle of mine, whom I never saw, died lately and left me his whole fortune. Of course he died in India. All old uncles who die suddenly and leave unexpected fortunes to unsuspecting nephews are old Indian uncles, and mine was no exception to the general rule. So I'm independent, like you, Ralph, only I've got three or four thousand a year instead of hundreds, I believe; but I'm not sure and don't care--and I'm determined now to go on a long hunting expedition. What think ye of all that, my boy?"

"In truth," said I, "it would puzzle me to say what I think, I am so filled with surprise by all you tell me. But you forget that you have not yet told me to which part of the world you mean to go, and what sort of beast it is you are so determined to see and shoot if you can."

"If I can!" echoed Peterkin, with a contemptuous curl of the lip. "Did not I tell you that I was a celebrated hunter? Without meaning to boast, I may tell you that there is no peradventure in my shooting. If I only get there and see the brute within long range, I'll--ha! won't I!"

"Get where, and see what?"

"Get to Africa and see the gorilla!" cried Peterkin, while a glow of enthusiasm lighted up his eyes. "You've heard of the gorilla, Ralph, of course--the great ape--the enormous puggy--the huge baboon--the man monkey, that we've been hearing so much of for some years back, and that the niggers on the African coast used to dilate about till they caused the very hair of my head to stand upon end? I'm determined to shoot a gorilla, or prove him to be a myth. And I mean you to come and help me, Ralph; he's quite in your way. A bit of natural history, I suppose, although he seems by all accounts to be a very unnatural monster. And Jack shall go too--I'm resolved on that; and we three shall roam the wild woods again, as we did in days of yore, and--"

"Hold, Peterkin," said I, interrupting. "How do you know that Jack will go?"

"How do I know? Intuitively, of course. I shall write to him to-night; the post does not leave till ten. He'll get it to-morrow at breakfast, and will catch the forenoon coach, which will bring him down here by two o'clock, and then we'll begin our preparations at once, and talk the matter over at dinner. So you see it's all cut and dry. Give me a sheet of paper and I'll write at once. Ah! here's a bit; now a pen. Bless me, Ralph, haven't you got a quill? Who ever heard of a philosophical naturalist writing with steel. Now, then, here goes:--`B'luv'd Jack,'--will that do to begin with, eh? I'm afraid it's too affectionate; he'll think it's from a lady friend. But it can't be altered,--`Here I am, and here's Ralph--Ralph Rover!!!!!! think of that,' (I say, Ralph, I've put six marks of admiration there); `I've found him out. Do come to see us. Excruciatingly important business. Ever thine--Peterkin Gay.' Will that bring him, d'ye think?"

"I think it will," said I, laughing.

"Then off with it, Ralph," cried my volatile friend, jumping up and looking hastily round for the bell-rope. Not being able to find it, my bell-pull being an unobtrusive knob and not a rope, he rushed to the door, unlocked it, darted out, and uttered a tremendous roar, which was followed by a clatter and a scream from old Agnes, whom he had upset and tumbled over.

It was curious to note the sudden change that took place in Peterkin's face, voice, and manner, as he lifted the poor old woman, who was very thin and light, in his arms, and carrying her into the room, placed her in my easy-chair. Real anxiety was depicted in his countenance, and he set her down with a degree of care and tenderness that quite amazed me. I was myself very much alarmed at first.

"My poor dear old woman," said Peterkin, supporting my landlady's head; "my stupid haste I fear you are hurt."

"Hech! it's nae hurt--it's deed I am, fair deed; killed be a whaumlskamerin' young blagyird. Oh, ma puir heed!"

The manner and tone in which this was said convinced me that old Agnes was more frightened than injured. In a few minutes the soothing tones and kind manner of my friend had such an effect upon her that she declared she was better, and believed after all that she was only a "wee bit frichtened." Nay, so completely was she conciliated, that she insisted on conveying the note to the post-office, despite Peterkin's assurance that he would not hear of it. Finally she hobbled out of the room with the letter in her hand.

It is interesting to note how that, in most of the affairs of humanity, things turn out very different, often totally different, from what we had expected or imagined. During the remainder of that evening Peterkin and I talked frequently and much of our old friend Jack Martin. We recalled his manly yet youthful countenance, his bold, lion-like courage, his broad shoulders and winning gentle smile, and although we knew that six years must have made an immense difference in his personal appearance--for he was not much more than eighteen when we last parted-- we could not think of him except as a hearty, strapping sailor-boy. We planned, too, how we would meet him at the coach; how we would stand aside in the crowd until he began to look about for us in surprise, and then one of us would step forward and ask if he wished to be directed to any particular part of the town, and so lead him on and talk to him as a stranger for some time before revealing who we were. And much more to the same effect. But when next day came our plans and our conceptions were utterly upset.

A little before two we sauntered down to the coach-office, and waited impatiently for nearly twenty minutes. Of course the coach was late; it always is on such occasions.

"Suppose he does not come," said I.

"What a fellow you are," cried Peterkin, "to make uncomfortable suppositions! Let us rather suppose that he does come."

"Oh, then, it would be all right; but if he does not come, what then?"

"Why, then, it would be all wrong, and we should have to return home and eat our dinner in the sulks, that's all."

As my companion spoke we observed the coach come sweeping round the turn of the road about half a mile distant. In a few seconds it dashed into the town at full gallop, and finally drew up abruptly opposite the door of the inn, where were assembled the usual group of hostlers and waiters and people who expected friends by the coach.

"He's not there," whispered Peterkin, in deep disappointment--"at least he's not on the outside, and Jack would never travel inside of a coach even in bad weather, much less in fine. That's not him on the back-seat beside the fat old woman with the blue bundle, surely! It's very like him, but too young, much too young. There's a great giant of a man on the box-seat with a beard like a grenadier's shako, and a stout old gentleman behind him with gold spectacles. That's all, except two boys farther aft, and three ladies in the cabin. Oh, what a bore!"

Although deeply disappointed at the non-arrival of Jack, I could with difficulty refrain from smiling at the rueful and woe-begone countenance of my poor companion. It was evident that he could not bear disappointment with equanimity, and I was on the point of offering some consolatory remarks, when my attention was attracted by the little old woman with the blue bundle, who went up to the gigantic man with the black beard, and in the gentlest possible tone of voice asked if he could direct her to the white house.

"No, madam," replied the big man hastily; "I'm a stranger here."

The little old woman was startled by his abrupt answer. "Deary me, sir, no offence, I hope."

She then turned to Peterkin and put the same question, possibly under a vague sort of impression that if a gigantic frame betokened a gruff nature, diminutive stature must necessarily imply extreme amiability. If so, she must have been much surprised as well as disappointed, for Peterkin, rendered irascible by disappointment, turned short round and said sharply, "Why, madam, how can I tell you where the white house is, unless you say which white house you want? Half the houses of the town are white--at least they're dirty white," he added bitterly, as he turned away.

"I think I can direct you, ma'am," said I, stepping quickly up with a bland smile, in order to counteract, if possible, my companion's rudeness.

"Thank you, sir, kindly," said the little old woman; "I'm glad to find some little civility in the town."

"Come with me, ma'am; I am going past the white house, and will show you the way."

"And pray, sir," said the big stranger, stepping up to me as I was about to move away, "can you recommend me to a good hotel?"

I replied that I could; that there was one in the immediate vicinity of the white house, and that if he would accompany me I would show him the way. All this I did purposely in a very affable and obliging tone and manner; for I hold that example is infinitely better than precept, and always endeavour, if possible, to overcome evil with good. I offered my arm to the old woman, who thanked me and took it.

"What!" whispered Peterkin, "you don't mean me to take this great ugly gorilla in tow?"

"Of course," replied I, laughing, as I led the way.

Immediately I entered into conversation with my companion, and I heard "the gorilla" attempt to do so with Peterkin; but from the few sharp cross replies that reached my ear, I became aware that he was unsuccessful. In the course of a few minutes, however, he appeared to have overcome his companion's ill-humour, for I overheard their voices growing louder and more animated as they walked behind me.

Suddenly I heard a shout, and turning hastily round, observed Peterkin struggling in the arms of the gorilla! Amazed beyond measure at the sight, and firmly persuaded that a cowardly assault had been made upon my friend, I seized the old woman's umbrella, as the only available weapon, and flew to the rescue.

"Jack, my boy! can it be possible?" gasped Peterkin.

"I believe it is," replied Jack, laughing.--"Ralph, my dear old fellow, how are you?"

I stood petrified. I believed that I was in a dream.

I know not what occurred during the next five minutes. All I could remember with anything like distinctness was a succession of violent screams from the little old woman, who fled shouting thieves and murder at the full pitch of her voice. We never saw that old woman again, but I made a point of returning her umbrella to the "white house."

Gradually we became collected and sane.

"Why, Jack, how did you find us out?" cried Peterkin, as we all hurried on to my lodgings, totally forgetful of the little old woman, whom, as I have said, we never saw again, but who, I sincerely trust, arrived at the white house in safety.

"Find you out! I knew you the moment I set eyes on you. Ralph puzzled me for a second, he has grown so much stouter; but I should know your nose, Peterkin, at a mile off."

"Well, Jack, I did not know you," retorted Peterkin, "but I'm safe never again to forget you. Such a great hairy Cossack as you have become! Why, what do you mean by it?"

"I couldn't help it, please," pleaded Jack; "I grew in spite of myself; but I think I've stopped now."

"It's time," remarked Peterkin.

Jack had indeed grown to a size that men seldom attain to without losing in grace infinitely more than they gain in bulk, but he had retained all the elegance of form and sturdy vigour of action that had characterised him as a boy. He was fully six feet two inches in his stockings, but so perfect were his proportions that his great height did not become apparent until you came close up to him. Full half of his handsome manly face was hid by a bushy black beard and moustache, and his curly hair had been allowed to grow luxuriantly, so that his whole aspect was more like to the descriptions we have of one of the old Scandinavian Vikings than a gentleman of the present time. In whatever company he chanced to be he towered high above every one else, and I am satisfied that, had he walked down Whitechapel, the Horse Guards would have appeared small beside him, for he possessed not only great length of limb but immense breadth of chest and shoulders.

During our walk to my lodgings Peterkin hurriedly stated his "plan and proposal," which caused Jack to laugh very much at first, but in a few minutes he became grave, and said slowly, "That will just suit--it will do exactly."

"What will do exactly? Do be more explicit, man," said Peterkin, with some impatience.

"I'll go with you, my boy."

"Will you?" cried Peterkin, seizing his hand and shaking it violently; "I knew you would. I said it; didn't I, Ralph? And now we shall be sure of a gorilla, if there's one in Africa, for I'll use you as a stalking-horse."

"Indeed!" exclaimed Jack.

"Yes; I'll put a bear-skin or some sort of fur on your shoulders, and tie a lady's boa to you for a tail, and send you into the woods. The gorillas will be sure to mistake you for a relative until you get quite close; then you'll take one pace to the left with the left foot (as the volunteers say), I'll take one to the front with the right--at fifty yards, ready--present--bang, and down goes the huge puggy with a bullet right between its two eyes! There. And Ralph's agreed to go too."

"O Peterkin, I've done nothing of the sort. You proposed it."

"Well, and isn't that the same thing? I wonder, Ralph that you can give way to such mean-spirited prevarication. What? `It's not prevarication!' Don't say that now; you know it is. Ah! you may laugh, my boy, but you have promised to go with me and Jack to Africa, and go you shall."

And so, reader, it was ultimately settled, and in the course of two weeks more we three were on our way to the land of the slave, the black savage, and the gorilla.

CHAPTER TWO.

LIFE IN THE WILD WOODS.

One night, about five or six weeks after our resolution to go to Africa on a hunting expedition was formed, I put to myself the question, "Can it be possible that we are actually here, in the midst of it?"

"Certainly, my boy, in the very thick of it," answered Peterkin, in a tone of voice which made Jack laugh, while I started and exclaimed--

"Why, Peterkin, how did you come to guess my thoughts?"

"Because, Ralph, you have got into a habit of thinking aloud, which may do very well as long as you have no secrets to keep but it may prove inconvenient some day, so I warn you in time."

Not feeling disposed at that time to enter into a bantering conversation with my volatile companion, I made no reply, but abandoned myself again to the pleasing fancies and feelings which were called up by the singular scene in the midst of which I found myself.

It seemed as if it were but yesterday when we drove about the crowded streets of London making the necessary purchases for our intended journey, and now, as I gazed around, every object that met my eye seemed strange, and wild, and foreign, and romantic. We three were reclining round an enormous wood fire in the midst of a great forest, the trees and plants of which were quite new to me, and totally unlike those of my native land. Rich luxuriance of vegetation was the feature that filled my mind most. Tall palms surrounded us, throwing their broad leaves overhead and partially concealing the starlit sky. Thick tough limbs of creeping plants and wild vines twisted and twined round everything and over everything, giving to the woods an appearance of tangled impenetrability; but the beautiful leaves of some, and the delicate tendrils of others, half concealed the sturdy limbs of the trees, and threw over the whole a certain air of wild grace, as might a semi-transparent and beautiful robe if thrown around the form of a savage.

The effect of a strong fire in the woods at night is to give to surrounding space an appearance of ebony blackness, against which dark ground the gnarled stems and branches and pendent foliage appear as if traced out in light and lovely colours, which are suffused with a rich warm tone from the blaze.

We were now in the wilds of Africa, although, as I have said, I found it difficult to believe the fact. Jack and I wore loose brown shooting coats and pantaloons; but we had made up our minds to give up waistcoats and neckcloths, so that our scarlet flannel shirts with turned-down collars gave to us quite a picturesque and brigand-like appearance as we encircled the blaze--Peterkin smoking vigorously, for he had acquired that bad and very absurd habit at sea. Jack smoked too, but he was not so inveterate as Peterkin.

Jack was essentially moderate in his nature. He did nothing violently or in a hurry; but this does not imply that he was slow or lazy. He was leisurely in disposition, and circumstances seldom required him to be otherwise. When Peterkin or I had to lift heavy weights, we were obliged to exert our utmost strength and agitate our whole frames; but Jack was so powerful that a comparatively slight effort was all that he was usually obliged to make. Again, when we two were in a hurry we walked quickly, but Jack's long limbs enabled him to keep up with us without effort. Nevertheless there were times when he was called upon to act quickly and with energy. On those occasions he was as active as Peterkin himself, but his movements were tremendous. It was, I may almost say, awful to behold Jack when acting under powerful excitement. He was indeed a splendid fellow, and not by any means deserving of the name of gorilla, which Peterkin had bestowed on him.

But to continue my description of our costume. We all wore homespun grey trousers of strong material. Peterkin and Jack wore leggings in addition, so that they seemed to have on what are now termed knickerbockers. Peterkin, however, had no coat. He preferred a stout grey flannel shirt hanging down to his knees and belted round his waist in the form of a tunic. Our tastes in headdress were varied. Jack wore a pork-pie cap; Peterkin and I had wide-awakes. My facetious little companion said that I had selected this species of hat because I was always more than half asleep! Being peculiar in everything, Peterkin wore his wide-awake in an unusual manner--namely, turned up at the back, down at the front, and curled very much up at the sides.

We were so filled with admiration of Jack's magnificent beard and moustache, that Peterkin and I had resolved to cultivate ours while in Africa; but I must say that, as I looked at Peterkin's face, the additional hair was not at that time an improvement, and I believe that much more could not have been said for myself. The effect on my little comrade was to cause the lower part of his otherwise good-looking face to appear extremely dirty.

"I wonder," said Peterkin, after a long silence, "if we shall reach the niggers' village in time for the hunt to-morrow. I fear that we have spent too much time in this wild-goose chase."

"Wild-goose chase, Peterkin!" I exclaimed. "Do you call hunting the gorilla by such a term?"

"Hunting the gorilla? no, certainly; but looking for the gorilla in a part of the woods where no such beast was ever heard of since Adam was a schoolboy--"

"Nay, Peterkin," interrupted Jack; "we are getting very near to the gorilla country, and you must make allowance for the enthusiasm of a naturalist."

"Ah! we shall see where the naturalist's enthusiasm will fly to when we actually do come face to face with the big puggy."

"Well," said I, apologetically, "I won't press you to go hunting again; I'll be content to follow."

"Press me, my dear Ralph!" exclaimed Peterkin hastily, fearing that he had hurt my feelings; "why, man, I do but jest with you--you are so horridly literal. I'm overjoyed to be pressed to go on the maddest wild-goose chase that ever was invented. My greatest delight would be to go gorilla-hunting down Fleet Street, if you were so disposed.--But to be serious, Jack, do you think we shall be in time for the elephant-hunt to-morrow?"

"Ay, in capital time, if you don't knock up."

"What! I knock up! I've a good mind to knock you down for suggesting such an egregious impossibility."

"That's an impossibility anyhow, Peterkin, because I'm down already," said Jack, yawning lazily and stretching out his limbs in a more comfortable and degage manner.

Peterkin seemed to ponder as he smoked his pipe for some time in silence.

"Ralph," said he, looking up suddenly, "I don't feel a bit sleepy, and yet I'm tired enough."

"You are smoking too much, perhaps," I suggested.

"It's not that," cried Jack; "he has eaten too much supper."

"Base insinuation!" retorted Peterkin.

"Then it must be the monkey. That's it. Roast monkey does not agree with you."

"Do you know, I shouldn't wonder if you were right; and it's a pity, too, for we shall have to live a good deal on such fare, I believe. However, I suppose we shall get used to it.--But I say, boys, isn't it jolly to be out here living like savages? I declare it seems to me like a dream or a romance.--Just look, Ralph, at the strange wild creepers that are festooned overhead, and the great tropical leaves behind us, and the clear sky above, with the moon--ah! the moon; yes, that's one comfort--the moon is unchanged. The same moon that smiles down upon us through a tangled mesh-work of palm-leaves and wild vines and monkeys' tails, is peeping down the chimney-pots of London and Edinburgh and Dublin!"

"Why, Peterkin, you must have studied hard in early life to be so good a geographer."

"Rather," observed Peterkin.

"Yes; and look at the strange character of the tree-stems," said I, unwilling to allow the subject to drop. "See those huge palmettoes like--like--"

"Overgrown cabbages," suggested Peterkin; and he continued, "Observe the quaint originality of form in the body and limbs of that bloated old spider that is crawling up your leg, Ralph!"

I started involuntarily, for there is no creature of which I have a greater abhorrence than a spider.

"Where is it? oh! I see," and the next moment I secured my prize and placed it with loathing, but interest, in my entomological box.

At that moment a hideous roar rang through the woods, seemingly close behind us. We all started to our feet, and seizing our rifles, which lay beside us ready loaded, cocked them and drew close together round the fire.

"This won't do, lads," said Jack, after a few minutes' breathless suspense, during which the only sound we could hear was the beating of our own hearts; "we have allowed the fire to get too low, and we've forgotten to adopt our friend the trader's advice, and make two fires."

So saying, Jack laid down his rifle, and kicking the logs with his heavy boot, sent up such a cloud of bright sparks as must certainly have scared the wild animal, whatever it was, away; for we heard no more of it that night.

"You're right, Jack," remarked Peterkin; "so let us get up a blaze as fast as we can, and I'll take the first watch, not being sleepy. Come along."

In a few minutes we cut down with our axes a sufficient quantity of dry wood to keep two large fires going all night; we then kindled our second fire at a few yards distant from the first, and made our camp between them. This precaution we took in order to scare away the wild animals whose cries we heard occasionally during the night. Peterkin, having proposed to take the first watch--for we had to watch by turns all the night through--lighted his pipe and sat down before the cheerful fire with his back against the stem of a palm-tree, and his rifle lying close to his hand, to be ready in case of a surprise. There were many natives wandering about in that neighbourhood, some of whom might be ignorant of our having arrived at their village on a peaceful errand. If these should have chanced to come upon us suddenly, there was no saying what they might do in their surprise and alarm, so it behoved us to be on our guard.

Jack and I unrolled the light blankets that we carried strapped to our shoulders through the day, and laying ourselves down side by side with our feet to the fire and our heads pillowed on a soft pile of sweet-scented grass, we addressed ourselves to sleep. But sleep did not come so soon as we expected. I have often noted with some surprise and much interest the curious phases of the phenomenon of sleep. When I have gone to bed excessively fatigued and expecting to fall asleep almost at once, I have been surprised and annoyed to find that the longer I wooed the drowsy god the longer he refused to come to me; and at last, when I have given up the attempt in despair, he has suddenly laid his gentle hand upon my eyes and carried me into the land of Nod. Again, when I have been exceedingly anxious to keep awake, I have been attacked by sleep with such irresistible energy that I have been utterly unable to keep my eyelids open or my head erect, and have sat with my eyes blinking like those of an owl in the sunshine, and my head nodding like that of a Chinese mandarin.

On this our first night in the African bush, at least our first night on a hunting expedition--we had been many nights in the woods on our journey to that spot--on this night, I say, Jack and I could by no means get to sleep for a very long time after we lay down, but continued to gaze up through the leafy screen overhead at the stars, which seemed to wink at us, I almost fancied, jocosely. We did not speak to each other, but purposely kept silence. After a time, however, Jack groaned, and said softly--

"Ralph, are you asleep?"

"No," said I, yawning.

"I'm quite sure that Peterkin is," added Jack, raising his head and looking across the fire at the half-recumbent form of our companion.

"Is he?" said Peterkin in a low tone. "Just about as sound as a weasel!"

"Jack," said I.

"Well?"

"I can't sleep a wink. Ye-a-ow! isn't it odd?"

"No more can I. Do you know, Ralph, I've been counting the red berries in that tree above me for half an hour, in the hope that the monotony of the thing would send me off; but I was interrupted by a small monkey who has been sitting up among the branches and making faces at me for full twenty minutes. There it is yet, I believe. Do you see it?"

"No; where?"

"Almost above your head."

I gazed upward intently for a few minutes, until I thought I saw the monkey, but it was very indistinct. Gradually, however, it became more defined; then to my surprise it turned out to be the head of an elephant! I was not only amazed but startled at this.

"Get your rifle, Jack!" said I, in a low whisper.

Jack made some sort of reply, but his voice sounded hollow and indistinct. Then I looked up again, and saw that it was the head of a hippopotamus, not that of an elephant, which was looking down at me. Curiously enough, I felt little or no surprise at this, and when in the course of a few minutes I observed a pair of horns growing out of the creature's eyes and a bushy tail standing erect on the apex of its head, I ceased to be astonished at the sight altogether, and regarded it as quite natural and commonplace. The object afterwards assumed the appearance of a lion with a crocodile's bail, and a serpent with a monkey's head, and lastly of a gorilla, without producing in me any other feeling than that of profound indifference. Gradually the whole scene vanished, and I became totally oblivious.

This state of happy unconsciousness had scarcely lasted--it seemed to me--two minutes, when I was awakened by Peterkin laying his hand on my shoulder and saying--

"Now then, Ralph, it's time to rouse up."

"O Peterkin," said I, in a tone of remonstrance, "how could you be so unkind as to waken me when I had just got to sleep? Shabby fellow!"

"Just got to sleep, say you? You've been snoring like an apoplectic alderman for exactly two hours."

"You don't say so!" I exclaimed, getting into a sitting posture.

"Indeed you have. I'm sorry to rouse you, but time's up, and I'm sleepy; so rub your eyes, man, and try to look a little less like an astonished owl if you can. I have just replenished both the fires, so you can lean your back against that palm-tree and take it easy for three-quarters of an hour or so. After that you'll have to heap on more wood."

I looked at Jack, who was now lying quite unconscious, breathing with the slow, deep regularity of profound slumber, and with his mouth wide open.

"What a chance for some waggish baboon to drop a nut or a berry in!" said Peterkin, winking at me with one eye as he lay down in the spot from which I had just risen.

He was very sleepy, poor fellow, and could hardly smile at his own absurd fancy. He was asleep almost instantly. In fact, I do not believe that he again opened the eye with which he had winked at me, but that he merely shut the other and began to slumber forthwith.

I now began to feel quite interested in my responsible position as guardian of the camp. I examined my rifle to see that it was in order and capped; then leaning against the palm-tree, which was, as it were, my sentry-box, I stood erect and rubbed my hands and took off my cap, so that the pleasant night air might play about my temples, and more effectually banish drowsiness.

In order to accomplish this more thoroughly I walked round both fires and readjusted the logs, sending up showers of sparks as I did so. Then I went to the edge of the circle of light, in the centre of which our camp lay, and peered into the gloom of the dark forest.

There was something inexpressibly delightful yet solemn in my feelings as I gazed into that profound obscurity where the great tree-stems and the wild gigantic foliage nearest to me appeared ghost-like and indistinct, and the deep solitudes of which were peopled, not only with the strange fantastic forms of my excited fancy, but, as I knew full well, with real wild creatures, both huge and small, such as my imagination at that time had not fully conceived. I felt awed, almost oppressed, with the deep silence around, and,

I must confess, looked somewhat nervously over my shoulder as I returned to the fire and sat down to keep watch at my post.

CHAPTER THREE.

WHEREIN I MOUNT GUARD, AND HOW I DID IT, ETCETERA.

Now it so happened that the battle which I had to fight with myself after taking my post was precisely the converse of that which I fought during the earlier part of that night. Then, it was a battle with wakefulness; now, it was a struggle with sleep; and of the two fights the latter was the more severe by far.

I began by laying down my rifle close by my side, leaning back in a sitting posture against the palm-tree, and resigning myself to the contemplation of the fire, which burned merrily before me, while I pondered with myself how I should best employ my thoughts during the three long hours of my watch. But I had not dwelt on that subject more than three minutes, when I was rudely startled by my own head falling suddenly and heavily forward on my chest. I immediately roused myself. "Ah! Ralph, Ralph," said I to myself in a whisper, "this won't do, lad. To sleep at your post! shame on you! Had you been a sentinel in time of war that nod would have cost you your life, supposing you to have been caught in the act."

Soliloquising thus, I arose and shook myself. Then I slapped my chest several times and pulled my nose and sat down again. Only a few minutes elapsed before the same thing occurred to me again, so I leaped up, and mended the fires, and walked to and fro, until I felt thoroughly awake, but in order to make sure that it should not occur again, I walked to the edge of the circle of light and gazed for some time into the dark forest, as I had done before. While standing thus I felt my knees give way, as if they had been suddenly paralysed, and I awoke just in time to prevent myself falling to the ground. I must confess I was much amazed at this, for although I had often read of soldiers falling asleep standing at their posts, I had never believed the thing possible.

I now became rather anxious, "for," thought I, "if I go to sleep and the fires die down, who knows but wild beasts may come upon us and kill us before we can seize our arms." For a moment or two I meditated awaking Jack and begging him to keep me company, but when I reflected that his watch was to come immediately after mine, I had not the heart to do it. "No!" said I (and I said it aloud for the purpose of preventing drowsiness)--"no; I will fight this battle alone! I will repeat some stanzas from my favourite authors. Yes, I will try to remember a portion of `A Midsummer-Night's Dream.' It will be somewhat appropriate to my present circumstances."

Big with this resolve, I sat down with my face to the fire and my back to the palm-tree, and--fell sound asleep instantly!

How long I lay in this condition I know not, but I was suddenly awakened by a yell so appalling that my heart leaped as if into my throat, and my nerves thrilled with horror. For one instant I was paralysed; then my blood seemed to rebound on its course. I sprang up and attempted to seize my rifle.

The reader may judge of my state of mind when I observed that it was gone! I leaped towards the fire, and grasping a lighted brand, turned round and glared into the woods in the direction whence the yell came.

It was grey dawn, and I could see things pretty distinctly; but the only living object that met my gaze was Peterkin, who stood with my rifle in his hand laughing heartily!

I immediately turned to look at Jack, who was sitting up in the spot where he had passed the night, with a sleepy smile on his countenance.

"Why, what's the meaning of this?" I inquired.

"The meaning of it?" cried Peterkin, as he advanced and restored the rifle to its place. "A pretty fellow you are to mount guard! we might have been all murdered in our sleep by niggers or eaten alive by gorillas, for all that you would have done to save us."

"But, Peterkin," said I gravely, "you ought not to have startled me so; you gave me a terrible fright. People have been driven mad before now, I assure you, by practical jokes."

"My dear fellow," cried Peterkin, with much earnestness, "I know that as well as you. But, in the first place, you were guilty of so heinous a crime that I determined to punish you, and at the same time to do it in a way that would impress it forcibly on your memory; and in the second place, I would not have done it at all had I not known that your nerves are as strong as those of a dray-horse. You ought to be taking shame to yourself on account of your fault rather than objecting to your punishment."

"Peterkin is right, my boy," said Jack, laughing, "though I must say he had need be sure of the nerves of any one to whom he intends to administer such a ferocious yell as that. Anyhow, I have no reason to complain; for you have given me a good long sleep, although I can't say exactly that you have taken my watch. It will be broad daylight in half an hour, so we must be stirring, comrades."

On considering the subject I admitted the force of these remarks, and felt somewhat crestfallen. No doubt, my companions had treated the thing jocularly, and, to say truth, there was much that was comical in the whole affair; but the more I thought of it, the more I came to perceive how terrible might have been the consequences of my unfaithfulness as a sentinel. I laid the lesson to heart, and I can truly say that from that day to this I have never again been guilty of the crime of sleeping at my post.

We now busied ourselves in collecting together the dying embers of our fire and in preparing breakfast, which consisted of tea, hard biscuit, and cold monkey. None of us liked the monkey; not that its flesh was bad--quite the contrary--but it looked so like a small roasted baby that we could not relish it at all. However, it was all we had; for we had set off on this hunting excursion intending to live by our rifles, but had been unfortunate, having seen nothing except a monkey or two.

The kettle was soon boiled, and we sat down to our meagre fare with hearty appetites. While we are thus engaged, I shall turn aside for a little and tell the reader, in one or two brief sentences, how we got to this place.

We shipped in a merchant ship at Liverpool, and sailed for the west coast of Africa. Arrived there we found a party, under the command of a Portuguese trader, about to set off to the interior. He could speak a little English; so we arranged to go with him as far as he intended to proceed, learn as much of the native language as possible while in his company, and then obtain a native guide to conduct us to the country in which the gorillas are found. To this native guide, we arranged, should be explained by the trader our object in visiting the country, so that he might tell the tribes whom we intended to visit. This, we found, was an absolutely needful precaution, on the following ground.

The natives of Africa have a singular and very bad style of carrying on trade with the white men who visit their shores. The traffic consists chiefly of ivory, barwood (a wood much used in dyeing), and indiarubber. The natives of the far interior are not allowed to convey these commodities directly to the coast, but by the law of the land (which means the law of the strongest, for they are absolute savages) are obliged to deliver their goods to the care of the tribe next to them; these pass them on to the next tribe; and so on they go from tribe to tribe till they reach the coast, where they are sold by the tribe there. The price obtained, which usually consists of guns, powder and shot, looking-glasses, cloth, and sundry other articles and trinkets useful to men in a savage state, is returned to the owners in the far interior through the same channel; but as each tribe deducts a percentage for its trouble, the price dwindles down as it goes, until a mere trifle, sometimes nothing at all, remains to be handed over to the unfortunate people of the tribe who originally sent off the goods for sale. Of course, such a system almost paralyses trade. But the intermediate tribes between the coast and the interior being the gainers by this system, are exceedingly jealous of anything like an attempt to carry on direct trade. They are ready to go to war with the tribes of the interior, should they attempt it, and they throw all the opposition they can in the way of the few white men who ever penetrate the interior for such a purpose.

It will thus be seen that our travels would be hindered very much, if not stopped altogether, and ourselves be regarded with jealousy, or perhaps murdered, if our motives in going inland were not fully and satisfactorily explained to the different tribes as we passed through their lands. And we therefore proposed to overcome the difficulty by taking a native guide with us from the tribe with which we should chance to be residing when obliged to separate from the Portuguese trader.

We had now reached this point. The day before that on which we encamped in the woods, as above related, we arrived at a native village, and had been received kindly by the king. Almost immediately after our arrival we heard so many stories about gorillas that I felt persuaded we should fall in with one if we went a-hunting, and being exceedingly anxious to add one to my collection of animals--for I had a small museum at home--I prevailed on Jack and Peterkin to go one day's journey into the bush to look for them. They laughed very much at me indeed, and said that we were still very far away from the gorilla country; but I had read in some work on Africa a remark to the effect that there is no cordillera, or mountain range, extending across the whole continent to limit the habitat of certain classes of animals, and I thought that if any animal in Africa would not consent to remain in one region when it wished to go to another, that animal must be the ferocious gorilla. The trader also laughed at me, and said that he had never seen any himself in that region, and that we would have to cross the desert before seeing them. Still, I felt a disposition to try; besides, I felt certain that we should at least fall in with some sort of animals or plants or minerals that would be worth collecting; so it was agreed that we should go out for a single day, and be back in time for a great elephant-hunt which was about to take place.

But to return from this digression. Having finished breakfast, we made three bundles or packages of our blankets, provisions, and camp equipage; strapped them on our backs; and then, shouldering our rifles, set out on our return to the negro village.

Of course we gave Jack the largest and heaviest bundle to carry. Peterkin's and mine were about equal, for although I was taller than Peterkin, I was not by any means so powerful or active. I often wondered at the great strength that lay in the little frame of my friend. To look at him, no one would believe that he was such a tough, wiry, hardy little fellow. He was the same hearty, jovial creature that I had lived with so pleasantly when he and Jack and I were cast away on the coral island. With the exception of a small scrap of whisker on each cheek, a scar over the right eye, and a certain air of manliness, there was little change in my old comrade.

"Ralph," said Jack, as we strode along through the forest, "do you remember how we three used to wander about together in the woods of our coral island?"

"Remember!" I cried with enthusiasm, for at that moment the thought occurred to my own mind; "how can I ever forget it, Jack? It seems to me just like yesterday. I can hardly believe that six long years have passed since we drank that delicious natural lemonade out of the green cocoa-nuts, and wandered on the coral beach, and visited Penguin Island, and dived into the cave to escape the pirates. The whole scene rises up before me so vividly that I could fancy we were still there. Ah! these were happy times."

"So they were," cried Peterkin; "but don't you go and become sentimentally sad, Ralph, when you talk of those happy days. If we were happy there, are we not happy here?--There's no change in us--except, indeed, that Jack has become a gorilla."

"Ay, and you a monkey," retorted Jack.

"True; and Ralph a naturalist, which is the strangest beast of all," added Peterkin.--"Can you tell me, Ralph, by the way, what tree that is?"

"I'm sure I cannot tell. Never saw or heard of one like it before," I replied, looking at the tree referred to with some interest. It was a fine tree, but the great beauty about it was the gorgeous fruit with which it was laden. It hung in the form of bunches of large grapes, and was of the brightest scarlet colour. The glowing bunches seemed like precious gems glittering amongst the green foliage, and I observed that a few monkeys and several parrots were peeping at us through the branches.

"It seems good for food," said Jack. "You'd better climb up, Peterkin, and pull a few bunches. The puggies won't mind you, of course, being one of themselves."

"Ralph," said Peterkin, turning to me, and deigning no reply to Jack, "you call yourself a naturalist; so I suppose you are acquainted with the habits of monkeys, and can turn your knowledge to practical account."

"Well," I replied, "I know something about the monkey tribes, but I cannot say that at this moment I remember any particular habit of which we might avail ourselves."

"Do you not? Well, now, that's odd. I'm a student of nature myself, and I have picked up a little useful knowledge in the course of my travels. Did you ever travel so far as the Zoological Gardens in London?"

"Of course I have done so, often."

"And did you ever observe a peculiar species of monkey, which, when you made a face at it, instantly flew into a towering passion, and shook the bars of its cage until you expected to see them broken?"

"Yes," said I, laughing; "what then?"

"Look here, you naturalist, and I'll put a wrinkle on your horn. Yonder hangs a magnificent bunch of fruit that I very much desire to possess."

"But it's too high to reach," said I.

"But there's a monkey sitting beside it," said Peterkin.

"I see. You don't expect him to pull it and throw it down, do you?"

"Oh no, certainly not; but--" Here Peterkin stepped up to the tree, and looking up at the monkey, said, "O-o-o-oo-o!" angrily.

"O-o-o-oo-oo!" replied the monkey, stretching out its neck and looking down with an expression of surprise and indignation, as if to say, "What on earth do you mean by that?"

"Oo-o-o-oo-o!" roared Peterkin.

Hereupon the monkey uttered a terrific shriek of passion, exposed all its teeth and gums, glared at its adversary like a little fiend, and seizing the branch with both hands, shook it with all its might. The result was, that not only did the coveted bunch of fruit fall to the ground, but a perfect shower of bunches came down, one of which hit Jack on the forehead, and, bursting there, sent its fragrant juice down his face and into his beard, while the parrots and all the other monkeys took to flight, shrieking with mingled terror and rage.

"You see I'm a practical man," observed Peterkin quietly, as he picked up the fruit and began to eat it. "Knowledge is power, my boy. A man with a philosophical turn of mind like yourself ought to have been up to a dodge of this sort. How capital this fruit is, to be sure!--Does it make good pomade, Jack?"

"Excellent; but as I'm not in the habit of using pomade, I shall wash this out of my beard as quickly as possible."

While Jack went to a brook that ran close to where we stood, I tasted the fruit, and found it most excellent, the pulp being juicy, with a very pleasant flavour.

While we were thus engaged a wild pig ran grunting past us.

"Doesn't that remind you of some of our doings on the coral island, Ralph?" said Peterkin.

Before I could reply a herd of lovely small gazelles flew past. Our rifles were lying on the ground, and before either of us could take aim the swift creatures were lost sight of in the thick underwood. Peterkin fired one shot at a venture, but without any result.

We were still deploring our stupidity in not having our rifles handy, when a strange sound was heard in the distance. By this time Jack had come up, so we all three seized our rifles and listened intently. The sound was evidently approaching. It was a low, dull, booming roar, which at one moment seemed to be distant thunder, at another the cry of some huge animal in rage or pain. Presently the beating of heavy hoofs on the turf and the crash of branches were heard. Each of us sprang instinctively towards a tree, feeling that if danger were near its trunk would afford us some protection.

Being ignorant, as yet, of the cries of the various wild beasts inhabiting those woods, we were greatly at a loss to determine what creature it could be that approached at such headlong speed. That its mad career was caused by fear soon became apparent, for the tones of terror either in man or beast, when distinctly heard, cannot be mistaken.

Immediately in front of the spot where we stood was an open space or glade of considerable extent. Towards this the animal approached, as was evident from the increasing loudness of its wild roar, which was almost continuous. In another moment the thick wall of underwood at its farther extremity was burst asunder with a crash, and a wild buffalo bull bounded into the plain and dashed madly across. On its neck was crouched a leopard, which had fixed its claws and teeth deep in the flesh of the agonised animal. In vain did the bull bound and rear, toss and plunge. At one moment it ran like the wind; the next it stopped with such violence as to tear up the turf and scatter it around. Then it reared, almost falling back; anon it plunged and rushed on again, with the foam flying from its mouth, and its bloodshot eyes glaring with the fire of rage and terror, while the woods seemed to tremble with its loud and deep-toned bellowing. Twice in its passage across the open glade it ran, in its blind fury, straight against a tree, almost beating in its skull, and for a moment arresting its progress; but it instantly recovered the shock and burst away again as madly as ever. But no effort that it was capable of making could relieve the poor creature from its deadly burden, or cause the leopard in the slightest degree to relax its fatal gripe.

It chanced that the wild bull's mad gallop was in a direction that brought it within a few yards of the spot where we stood, so we prepared to put an end to its misery. As it drew near, Jack, who was in advance, raised his rifle. I, being only a short distance from him, also made ready to fire, although I confess that in the agitation of the moment I could not make up my mind whether I should fire at the buffalo or the leopard. As far as I can recall my rapid and disjointed thoughts on that exciting occasion, I reasoned thus: "If I shoot the leopard the bull will escape, and if I shoot the bull the leopard will escape." It did not occur to me at that trying moment, when self-possession and decision were so necessary, that I might shoot the bull with one barrel, and the leopard with the other. Still less did it occur to me that I might miss bull and leopard altogether.

While I was engaged in this hurried train of troubled thought, Jack fired both barrels of his rifle, one after the other, as quickly as possible. The bull stumbled forward upon its knees. In order to make assurance doubly sure, I aimed at its head and fired both barrels at once. Instantly the bull rose, with a hideous bellow, and stood for one moment irresolute, glaring at its new enemies. The leopard, I observed, was no longer on its back. At this moment I heard an exclamation of anger, and looking round I observed Peterkin struggling violently in the grasp of one of the wild vines or thorny plants which abound in some parts of the African forests and render them almost impassable. It seems that as the bull drew near, Peterkin, who, like Jack and me, was preparing to shoot, found that a dense thicket came between him and the game, so as to prevent his firing. He leaped nimbly over a bush, intending to run to another spot, whence he could more conveniently take aim, but found himself, as I have related, suddenly entangled among the thorns in such a way that the more he struggled the more firmly he became ensnared. Being of an impatient disposition, he did struggle violently, and it was this, probably, that attracted the attention of the bull and decided its future course and its ultimate fate; for after remaining one moment, as I have stated, in an irresolute attitude, it turned suddenly to the left and rushed, with its head down and its tail up, straight at Peterkin.

I cannot describe the sensations that overwhelmed me on observing the imminent danger of my friend. Horror almost overwhelmed me as I gazed with a stare of fascination at the frightful brute, which with flashing eyes and bloody foam dripping from its mouth charged into the thicket, and crashed through the tough boughs and bushes as if they were grass. A film came over my eyes. I tried to reload my rifle, but my trembling hand refused to act, and I groaned with mingled shame and despair on finding myself thus incapable of action in the hour of extreme peril. At that moment I felt I would joyfully have given my own life to have saved that of Peterkin. It takes me long to describe it, but the whole scene passed with the rapidity almost of a flash of light.

Jack did not even attempt to load, but uttering a fearful cry, he sprang towards our friend with a bound like that of an enraged tiger. A gleam of hope flashed through my soul as I beheld his gigantic form dash through the underwood. It seemed to me as if no living creature could withstand such a furious onset. Alas for Peterkin, had his life depended on Jack, strong and lion-like though he was! His aid could not have been in time. A higher Power nerved his arm and steeled his heart at that terrible moment. As I gazed helplessly at Peterkin, I observed that he suddenly ceased his struggles to get free, and throwing forward the muzzle of his piece, stood boldly up and awaited the onset with calm self-possession. The bull was on him almost in an instant. One stride more and he would have been lost, but that stride was never taken. His rifle poured its deadly charge into the skull of the wild bull, which fell a mass of dead flesh, literally at his feet.

It were vain to attempt to describe the state of our feelings on this memorable occasion--the fervour with which we thanked our heavenly Father for our friend's deliverance--the delight with which we shook his hands, again and again, and embraced him. It was with considerable difficulty that we extricated Peterkin from his entanglement. When this was accomplished we proceeded to examine our prize.

We were not a little puzzled on discovering that only three bullets had struck the bull. For my part, I fired straight at its forehead, and had felt certain at the time that my shots had taken effect; yet there was but one ball in the animal's head, and that was undoubtedly Peterkin's, for the hair all round the hole was singed off, so near had it been to him when he fired. The other two shots were rather wide apart--one in the shoulder, the other in the neck. Both would have proved mortal in the long run, but neither was sufficiently near to a vital spot to kill speedily.

"Now, Ralph, my boy," said Jack, after our excitement was in some degree abated, "you and I must divide the honour of these two shots, for I fear we can't tell which of us fired them. Peterkin only fired once, and that was pretty effectual."

"Yes," I replied, "it is rather perplexing; for although I have no objection whatever to your having all the honour of those two shots, still one likes to know with certainty who actually made them."

"You'd better toss for them," suggested Peterkin, who was seated on the trunk of a fallen tree, examining, with a somewhat rueful countenance, the tattered condition of his garments.

"There would not be much satisfaction in that," replied Jack, laughing.

"It is probable," said I, "that each of us hit with one barrel and missed with the other."

"And it is possible," added Jack, "that one of us hit with both, and the other missed with both. All that I can positively affirm is that I fired both barrels at his shoulder--one after the other."

"And all that I am certain of," said I, "is that I fired both barrels at his forehead, and that I discharged them both at once."

"Did you?" said Peterkin, looking up quickly; "then, Ralph, I'm afraid you must give all the honour to Jack, for you have missed altogether."

"How do you know that?" I asked, in a somewhat piqued tone.

"Simply enough. If you fired both shots together at so short a distance, they would have been found close together wherever they had struck, whereas the two shots in the neck and shoulder are more than two feet apart."

I was compelled to admit that there was much truth in the observation, but still felt unwilling to give up all claim to having assisted in slaying our first buffalo. I pondered the subject a good deal during the remainder of the time we spent in cutting up and packing part of the buffalo meat, and in preparing to continue our journey, but could come at no satisfactory conclusion in my own mind, and, to say truth, I felt not a little crestfallen at my conduct in the whole affair.

While wandering in this mood near the spot where the buffalo had been first wounded, I received a sudden and severe start on observing the leopard crouching within a couple of yards of me. I saw it through the bushes quite distinctly, but could not make quite sure of its attitude. With a mingled cry of alarm and astonishment I sprang back to the place where I had left my rifle.

Jack and Peterkin instantly ran up with their pieces cocked.

"Where is it?" they cried in a breath.

"There, crouching just behind that bush."

Jack darted forward.

"Crouching!" he cried, with a loud laugh, seizing the animal by the tail and dragging it forth; "why, it's dead--stone dead."

"Dead as mutton," said Peterkin. "Hallo! what's this?" he added in surprise. "Two holes close together in its forehead, I do declare! Hooray! Ralph, my boy, give us your paw! You've missed the bull and hit the leopard! If you haven't been and put two bullets right between its two eyes, I'm a Dutchman!"

And so, in truth, it turned out. I had aimed at the bull and hit the leopard. So I left that spot not a little pleased with my bad aim and my good fortune.

CHAPTER FOUR.

WHEREIN WILL BE FOUND MUCH THAT IS PHILOSOPHICAL.

Having skinned the leopard and cut off as much of the buffalo meat as we could carry, we started for the negro village at a round pace, for we had already lost much time in our last adventure. As we walked along I could not help meditating on the uncertainty of this life, and the terrible suddenness with which we might at any unexpected moment be cut off. These thoughts led me naturally to reflect how important a matter it is that every one, no matter how young, should be in a state of preparedness to quit this world.

I also reflected, and not without a feeling of shame, on my want of nerve, and was deeply impressed with the importance of boys being inured from childhood to trifling risks and light dangers of every possible description, such as tumbling into ponds and off trees, etcetera, in order to strengthen their nervous system. I do not, of course, mean to say that boys ought deliberately to tumble into ponds or climb trees until they fall off; but they ought not to avoid the risk of such mishaps. They ought to encounter such risks and many others perpetually. They ought to practise leaping off heights into deep water. They ought never to hesitate to cross a stream on a narrow unsafe plank for fear of a ducking. They ought never to decline to climb up a tree to pull fruit merely because there is a possibility of their falling off and breaking their necks. I firmly believe that boys were intended to encounter all kinds of risks, in order to prepare them to meet and grapple with the risks and dangers incident to man's career with cool, cautious self-possession--a self-possession founded on experimental knowledge of the character and powers of their own spirits and muscles. I also concluded that this reasoning applies to some extent to girls as well as boys, for they too are liable through life to occasional encounters with danger--such as meeting with mad bulls, being run away with on horseback, being upset in boats, being set on fire by means of crinoline; in all of which cases those who have been trained to risk slight mishaps during early life will find their nerves equal to the shock, and their minds cool and collected enough to look around and take hasty advantage of any opportunity of escape that may exist; while those who have been unhappily nurtured in excessive delicacy, and advised from the earliest childhood to "take care of themselves and carefully avoid all risks," will probably fall victims to their nervous alarms and the kind but injudicious training of parents or guardians.

The more I pondered this subject the more deeply impressed did I become with its great importance to the well-being of mankind, and I was so profoundly engrossed with it that my companions utterly failed to engage me in general conversation as we walked briskly along through the forest. Jack again and again attempted to draw my attention to the splendour of the curious specimens of tropical foliage and vegetation through which we passed; but I could not rouse myself to take interest therein. In vain did Peterkin jest and rally me, and point out the monkeys that grinned at us ever and anon as we passed beneath them, or the serpents that glided more than once from our path, I was fascinated with my train of meditation, and as I could not then give it up until I had thought it out, so now I cannot pass from the subject until I have at least endeavoured to guard myself from misconception.

I beg, then, that it will be understood that I do not by any means inculcate hare-brained recklessness, or a course of training that will foster that state of mind. On the contrary, the course of training which I should like to see universally practised would naturally tend to counteract recklessness, for it would enable a boy to judge correctly as to what he could and could not do. Take an illustration. A naturally bold boy has been unwisely trained to be exceedingly careful of himself. He does not know the extent of his own courage, or the power and agility of his own muscles; he knows these things to some extent indeed, but owing to restraint he does not know them fully. Hence he is liable both to over and under estimate them.

This bold boy--we shall call him Tom--takes a walk into the country with a friend, whom we shall name Pat. Pat is a bad boy, but he has been permitted to train his muscles as he pleased, and his natural disposition has led him to do difficult and sometimes slightly dangerous things.

"You can't jump over that river, Tom," says Pat.

"Perhaps not," replies Tom: "I never tried such a jump, because my mother tells me never to go where I am likely to tumble into the water."

"Oh, your mother's a muff!" cries Pat.

"Pat," says Tom, flushing with indignation and confronting his friend, "don't you ever say that again, else the friendship between you and me will come to an end. I know you don't really mean what you say; but I won't allow you to speak disrespectfully of my mother."

"Well, I won't," says Pat, "but you're a muff, anyhow."

"Perhaps I am," replies Tom.

"Of course you are, because you're afraid to jump over that river, and I'm not. So here goes."

Pat thereupon jumps the river (he is a splendid leaper), and Tom hesitates.

"Come along, Tom; don't be a hen."

Tom gives way, alas! to a disobedient impulse, and dashing at the leap comes to the edge, when he finds, somehow, that he has not got the proper foot first for the spring--almost every boy knows the feeling I allude to; his heart fails, and he balks.

"O Tom, what a nimini-pimini muff you are, to be sure!"

Tom, as I have said, is a bold boy. His blood boils at this; he rushes wildly at the bank, hurls himself recklessly into the air, barely reaches the opposite side with a scramble, and falls souse into the river, from which he issues, as Pat says amid peals of laughter, "like a half-drowned rat."

Now, had Tom been permitted to follow the bent of his own bold impulses, he would have found out, years ago, how far and how high he could leap, and how far exactly he could depend on his own courage in certain circumstances; and he would either, on the one hand, have measured the leap with an accustomed eye, and declined to take it with a good-humoured admission that it was beyond his powers, or, on the other hand, he would calmly have collected his well and oft tried energies for the spring. The proper foot, from long experience, would have come to the ground at the right time. His mind, freed from all anxiety as to what he could accomplish, would have received a beneficial impulse from his friend's taunt. No nervous dread of a ducking would have checked the completeness of his bound, because he would have often been ducked before, and would have discovered that in most cases, if the clothes be changed at once, a ducking is not worth mentioning--from a hydropathic point of view is, in fact, beneficial--and he would have cleared the river with comfort to himself and confusion to his friend, and without a ducking or the uneasiness of conscience caused by the knowledge that he had disobeyed his mother. Had Peterkin not been trained to encounter danger, his natural boldness alone would never have enabled him to stand the charge of that buffalo bull.

There are muffs in this world. I do not refer to those hairy articles of female apparel in which ladies are wont to place their hands, handkerchiefs, and scent-bottles. Although not given to the use of slang, I avail myself of it on this occasion, the word "muff" being eminently expressive of a certain class of boys, big as well as little, old as well as young. There are three distinct classes of boys--namely, muffs, sensible fellows, and boasters. I say there are three distinct classes, but I do not say that every boy belongs to one or other of those classes. Those who have studied chemistry know that nature's elements are few. Nearly all kinds of matter, and certainly all varieties of mind, are composite. There are no pure and simple muffs. Most boasters have a good deal of the muff in them, and many muffs are boasters; while sensible fellows are occasionally tinged with a dash of both the bad qualities--they are, if I may be allowed to coin a word, sensible-boasto-muffers! Still, for the sake of lucidity, I will maintain that there are three distinct phases of character in boys.

The muff is a boy who from natural disposition, or early training, or both, is mild, diffident, and gentle. So far he is an estimable character. Were this all, he were not a muff. In order to deserve that title he must be timid and unenthusiastic. He must refuse to venture anything that will subject him to danger, however slight. He must be afraid of a shower of rain; afraid of dogs in general, good and bad alike; disinclined to try bold things; indifferent about learning to swim. He must object to the game called "dumps," because the blows from the ball are sometimes severe; and be a sworn enemy to single-stick, because the whacks are uncommonly painful. So feeling and acting, he will, when he becomes a man, find himself unable to act in the common emergencies of life--to protect a lady from insolence, to guard his house from robbery, or to save his own child should it chance to fall into the water. The muff is addicted to boasting sometimes, especially when in the company of girls; but when on the playground he hangs on the skirts of society, and sings very small. There are many boys, alas! who are made muffs by injudicious training, who would have grown up to be bold, manly fellows had they been otherwise treated. There are also many kinds of muffs. Some are good-hearted, amiable muffs; others are petty, sneaking muffs.

With many of the varieties I have a strong sympathy, and for their comfort I would say that muffs may cure themselves if they choose to try energetically.

Courage and cowardice are not two distinct and entirely antagonistic qualities. To a great extent those qualities are the result of training. Every courageous man has a slight amount of cowardice in his composition, and all cowards have a certain infusion of courage. The matador stands before the infuriated bull, and awaits its charge with unflinching firmness, not because he has more courage than his comrades in the ring who run away, but because long training has enabled him to make almost certain of killing the bull. He knows what he has done before, he feels that he can do it again, therefore he stands like a hero. Were a doubt of his capacity to cross his mind for an instant, his cheek would blanch, his hand would tremble, and, ten to one, he would turn and flee like the rest.

Let muffs, therefore, learn to swim, to leap, and to run. Let them wrestle with boys bigger than themselves, regardless of being thrown. Let them practise "jinking" with their companions, so that if even they be chased by a mad bull, they will, if unable to get out of his way by running, escape perhaps by jinking. Let them learn to leap off considerable heights into deep water, so that, if ever called on to leap off the end of a pier or the side of a ship to save a fellow-creature, they may do so with confidence and promptitude. Let them even put on "the gloves," and become regardless of a swelled nose, in order that they may be able to defend themselves or others from sudden assault. So doing they will become sensible fellows, whose character I have thus to some extent described. Of course, I speak of sensible fellows only with reference to this one subject of training the nerves and muscles. Let it never be forgotten that there are men who, although sensible in this respect, are uncommonly senseless in regard to other things of far higher moment.

As to boasters, I will dismiss them with a few words. They are too easily known to merit particular description. They are usually loud and bold in the drawing-room, but rather mild in the field. They are desperately egotistical, fond of exaggeration, and prone to depreciate the deeds of their comrades. They make bad soldiers and sailors, and are usually held in contempt by others, whatever they may think of themselves. I may wind up this digression--into which I have been tempted by an earnest desire to warn my fellow-men against the errors of nervous and muscular education, which, in my case, led to the weak conduct of which I had been guilty that day--I may wind up this digression, I say, by remarking that the boys who are most loved in this world are those who are lambs, almost muffs, in the drawing-room, but lions in the field.

How long I should have gone on pondering this subject I know not, but Peterkin somewhat rudely interrupted me by uttering a wild scream, and beginning to caper as if he were a madman. I was much alarmed as well as surprised at this course of conduct; for although my friend was an inveterate joker, he was the very reverse of what is termed a buffoon, and never indulged in personally grotesque actions with a view to make people laugh--such as making faces, a practice which, in ninety-nine cases out of a hundred, causes the face-makers to look idiotical rather than funny, and induces beholders to pity them, and to feel very uncomfortable sensations.

Peterkin's yells, instead of ceasing, continued and increased.

"Why, what's wrong?" I cried, in much alarm.

Instead of answering, Peterkin darted away through the wood like a maniac, tearing off his clothes as he went. At the same moment Jack began to roar like a bull, and became similarly distracted. It now flashed across me that they must have been attacked by an army of the Bashikouay ant, a species of ant which is so ferocious as to prove a perfect scourge to the parts of the country over which it travels. The thought had scarcely occurred to me when I was painfully convinced of its accuracy. The ants suddenly came to me, and in an instant I was covered from head to foot by the passionate creatures, which hit me so severely that I also began to scream and to tear off my garments; for I had been told by the trader who accompanied us to this part of the country that this was the quickest method of getting rid of them.

We all three fled, and soon left the army of Bashikouay ants behind us, undressing, as we ran, in the best way we could; and when we at length came to a halt we found ourselves almost in a state of nudity. Hastily divesting ourselves of the remainder of our apparel, we assisted each other to clear away the ants, though we could not rid ourselves of the painful effects of the bites with which we were covered.

"What dreadful villains!" gasped Peterkin, as he busied himself in hastily picking off the furious creatures from his person.

"It would be curious to observe the effect of an army of soldiers stepping into an army of Bashikouays," said Jack. "They would be routed instantly. No discipline or courage could hold them together for two minutes after they were attacked."

I was about to make some reply, when our attention was attracted by a shout at no great distance, and in a few seconds we observed, to our confusion, the trader and a band of negroes approaching us. We hurried on our clothes as rapidly as possible, and were a little more presentable when they arrived. They had a good laugh at us, of course, and the naked blacks seemed to be much tickled with the idea that we had been compelled to divest ourselves, even for a short time, of what they considered our unnecessary covering.

"We thought you were lost," said the trader, "and I began to blame myself for letting you away into the woods, where so many dangers may be encountered, without a guide. But what have you got there? meat of some kind? Your guns seem to have done service on this your first expedition."

"Ay, that they have," answered Jack. "We've killed a buffalo bull, and if you send your black fellows back on our track for some hours they'll come to the carcass, of which we could not, of course, bring very much away on our shoulders, which are not accustomed yet to heavy loads."

"Besides," added Peterkin, "we were anxious to get back in time for your elephant-hunt, else we should have brought more meat with us. But Jack has not mentioned what I consider our chief prize, the honour of shooting which belongs to my friend Ralph Rover.--Come, Ralph, unfasten your pack and let them see it."

Although unwilling to put off more time, I threw down my pack, and untying it, displayed my leopard skin. The shout of delight and surprise which the sight of it drew from the negroes was so enthusiastic that I at once perceived I was considered to have secured a great prize.

"Why, Mr Rover, you're in luck," said the trader, examining the skin; "it's not every day that one falls in with such a fine leopard as that. And you have already made a reputation as a daring hunter, for the niggers consider it a bold and dangerous thing to attack these critters; they're so uncommon fierce."

"Indeed I do not by any means deserve such a reputation," said I, refastening my pack, "for the shot was entirely accidental; so I pray you, good sir, to let the negroes know that, as I have no desire to go under a false flag, as my friend Peterkin would say--"

"Go under a false flag!" exclaimed Peterkin, in contempt. "Sail under false colours, man! That's what you should have said. Whatever you do, Ralph, never misquote a man. Go under a false flag! ha, ha! Why, you might just as well have said, `progress beneath assumed bunting.'"

"Well, accidental or otherwise," said the trader, "you've got credit for the deed, and your fame will be spread among the tribe whether you will or not; for these fellows are such incorrigible liars themselves that they will never believe you if you tell them the shot was accidental. They will only give you credit for some strange though unknown motive in telling such a falsehood."

While the trader was speaking I observed that the negroes were talking with the eager looks and gesticulations that are peculiar to the Africans when excited, and presently two or three of them came forward and asked several questions, while their eyes sparkled eagerly and their black faces shone with animation as they pointed into the woods in the direction whence we had come.

"They want to know where you have left the carcass of the leopard, and if you have taken away the brains," said the trader, turning to me. "I daresay you know--if not you'll soon come to find out--that all the nigger tribes in

Africa are sunk in gross and cruel superstitions. They have more fetishes, and greegrees, and amulets, and wooden gods, and charms, than they know what to do with, and have surrounded themselves with spiritual mysteries that neither themselves nor anybody else can understand. Among other things, they attach a very high value to the brains of the leopard, because they imagine that he who possesses them will be rendered extraordinarily bold and successful in hunting. These fellows are in hopes that, being ignorant of the value of leopard brains, you have left them in the carcass, and are burning with anxiety to be off after them."

"Poor creatures!" said I, "they are heartily welcome to the brains; and the carcass lies not more than four hours' march from this spot, I should think,-- Is it not so, Jack?"

My friend nodded assent, and the trader, turning to the expectant crowd of natives, gave them the information they desired. No sooner had he finished than with loud cries they turned and darted away, tossing their arms wildly in the air, and looking more like to a band of scared monkeys than to human beings.

"They're queer fellows," remarked Peterkin.

"So they are," replied the trader, "and they're kindly fellows too-- jovial and good-humoured, except when under the influence of their abominable superstitions. Then they become incarnate fiends, and commit deeds of cruelty that make one's blood run cold to think of."

I felt much saddened by these remarks, and asked the trader if the missionaries accomplished any good among them.

"Oh yes," he replied, "they do much good, such of them at least as really are missionaries; for it does not follow that every one who wears a black coat and white neck-cloth, and goes abroad, is a missionary. But what can a few men scattered along the coast here and there, however earnest they be, do among the thousands upon thousands of savages that wander about in the interior of Africa? No good will ever be done in this land, to any great extent, until traders and missionaries go hand in hand into the interior, and the system of trade is entirely remodelled."

"From what you remark," said I, feeling much interested, "I should suppose that you have given this subject a good deal of attention."

"I have. But there are people in this world who, supposing that because I am a trader I am therefore prone to exalt trade to an equality with religion, do not give me credit for disinterestedness when I speak. Perhaps you are one of these."

"Not I, in truth," said I, earnestly. "My chief desire in conversing with mankind is to acquire knowledge; I therefore listen with attention and respect to the opinions of others, instead of endeavouring to assert my own. In the present instance, being ignorant, I have no opinions to assert."

"I wish there were more people in your country," replied the trader, "who felt as you do. I would tell them that, although a trader, I regard the salvation of men's souls as the most important work in this world. I would argue that until you get men to listen, you cannot preach the gospel to them; that the present system of trade in Africa is in itself antagonistic to religion, being based upon dishonesty, and that, therefore, the natives will not listen to missionaries--of course, in some cases they will; for I believe that the gospel, when truly preached, is never preached in vain--but they will throw every possible impediment in their way. I would tell them that in order to make the path of the missionary practicable, the system of trade must be inverted, the trader and the missionary must go hand in hand, and commerce and religion--although incomparably different in their nature and ends--must act the part of brother and sister if anything great is to be done for the poor natives of Africa."

Conversing thus we beguiled the time pleasantly while we proceeded rapidly on our way, for the day was drawing to a close, and we were still at a considerable distance from the native village.

CHAPTER FIVE.

PREPARATIONS FOR A GRAND HUNT.

All was bustle, noise, and activity in the village, or, more correctly speaking, in the native town of his Majesty King Jambai, early in the morning after our arrival. A great elephant-hunt had been resolved on. The hunters were brushing up their spears and old guns--all of which latter were flint-locks that had been procured from traders, and were not worth more than a few shillings. The women were busy preparing breakfast, and the children were playing around their huts.

These huts were of the simplest construction--made of bamboo, roofed with large palm-leaves, and open in front. The wants of savages are generally few; their household furniture is very plain, and there is little of it. A large hut near to that of his sable majesty had been set apart for the trader and his party during our residence at the town. In this we had spent the night as pleasantly as we could, but the mosquitoes kept up an unceasing warfare upon us, so that daylight was welcomed gladly when it came.

On going to the hut of King Jambai, who had invited us to breakfast with him, we found the Princess Oninga alone, seated in the king's armchair and smoking her pipe with uncommon gusto. She had spent the early part of the morning in preparing breakfast for her father and ourselves, and was now resting from her labours.

"You are early astir, Princess Oninga," said the trader as we entered and took our seats round the fire, for at that hour the air felt chilly.

The princess took her pipe from her lips and admitted that she was, blowing a long thin cloud of smoke into the air with a sigh of satisfaction.

"We are ready for breakfast," added the trader. "Is the king at home?"

"He is in the woods, but will be back quickly." With this remark the princess rose, and knocking the ashes out of her pipe, left the tent.

"Upon my word, she's a cool beauty," said Peterkin.

"I should rather say a black one," remarked Jack.

"Perhaps an odd one would be the most appropriate term," said I. "Did you ever see such a headdress?"

The manner in which the Princess Oninga had seen fit to dress her head was indeed peculiar, I may say ludicrous. Her woolly hair had been arranged in the form of a cocked hat, with a horn projecting in front, and at a short distance off it might easily have been mistaken for the headpiece of a general officer minus the feathers. There was little in the way of artificial ornament about it, but the princess wore a number of heavy brass rings on her arms and ankles. Those on the latter reached half-way up to her knees, and they were so heavy that her walk was little better than a clumsy waddle. Before we could pass further comment on her appearance, King Jambai entered, and saluted us by taking us each separately and rubbing noses with us. This done, he ordered in breakfast, which consisted of roast and boiled plantains, ground nuts, roast fowl, and roast pig; so we fell to at once, and being exceedingly hungry after our long walk of the day before, made a hearty meal.

"Now, sir," said Jack, when our repast was about concluded, "as you are going to leave us soon, you had better arrange with the king about getting us an interpreter and supplying us with a few men to carry our goods. I think you said there was once a man in the tribe who spoke a little English. Have you found out whether he is alive?"

"Yes; I have heard that he is alive and well, and is expected in every day from a hunting expedition. He is a splendid hunter and a capital fellow. His name is Makarooroo, and if you get him you will be fortunate."

"Then ask his black majesty," said Peterkin, "as quick as you please, for, to say truth, I'm rather anxious on this point. I feel that we should never get on without a good interpreter."

To our satisfaction we found that the king was quite willing to do all that we wished and a great deal more. In fact, we soon perceived that he felt highly honoured by our visit, and had boasted not a little of "his white men" to the chiefs of neighbouring tribes, some of whom had come a considerable distance to see us.

"You have made quite a conquest, gentlemen, of worthy Jambai," said the trader, after translating the king's favourable reply. "The fact is he is pleased with the liberality you have shown towards him in the way of gifts, and is proud of the confidence you have placed in him. Had you been bent on a trading expedition, he would have opposed your further progress; but knowing that you are simply hunters, he is anxious to assist you by all the means at his command. He is surprised, indeed, at your taking so much trouble and coming so far merely to kill wild animals, for he cannot understand the idea of sporting. He himself hunts for the sake of procuring meat."

"Can he not understand," said Peterkin, "that we hunt for fun?"

"No, he don't quite see through that. He said to me a few minutes ago, `Have these men no meat at home, that they come all this long way to get it?' I told him that you had plenty, and then endeavoured to explain your idea of hunting `for fun.' But he shook his head, and I think he does not believe you."

At this point in our conversation the king rose and gave the signal to set out on the hunting expedition. Instantly the whole population of the town turned out and rushed to the banks of the river, near which it stood, where canoes were prepared for us. Suddenly there arose a great shout, and the name "Makarooroo, Makarooroo," passed from mouth to mouth. Presently a fine, tall, deep-chested and broad-shouldered negro stepped up to the king and laid a leopard skin at his feet, while the people shouted and danced with delight at the success of their companion; for, as I have already stated, it is deemed a bold feat to attack and slay a leopard single-handed.

While the commotion caused by this event was going on, I said to the trader--

"How comes it that Makarooroo can speak English?"

"He spent a couple of years on the coast, in the service of a missionary, and during that time attended the missionary school, where he picked up a smattering of English and a trifle of geography and arithmetic; but although a stout, sturdy hunter, and an intelligent man, he was a lazy student, and gave the good missionary much trouble to hammer the little he knows into his thick skull. At last he grew tired of it, and returned to his tribe; but he brought his Bible with him, and I am told is very diligent in the study of it. His education has gained for him a great reputation as a fetishman, or doctor of mysteries, among his people. I used often to see him at school hammering away at m-a, ma-b-a, ba, and so on, amid a group of children. He used to sit beside the king--"

"The king!" said I, in surprise.

"Ay; the king of that district became a Christian, and he and the queen, with one or two others of the royal household, used to attend school with the children every day, and their diligence in studying the A B C was beyond all praise. But they were terribly stupid. The children beat them easily, showing how true is the saying that `youth is the time to learn.' The king was always booby, and Makarooroo was always beside him."

As the trader spoke, Makarooroo came forward and shook hands with him in the English fashion. He was then introduced to us, and expressed his willingness to become our interpreter in somewhat curious but quite comprehensible English. As I looked at his intelligent, good-natured countenance, I could not help thinking that the trader had underrated his intellectual powers.

"He's a funny dog that Makarooroo," said Peterkin, as our interpreter hastened away to fetch his rusty old gun and spears; for he meant to join our hunting expedition, although he had only that moment arrived from a long and fatiguing chase.

"Do you think so?" said Jack.

"I don't agree with you," said I; "to me he seems rather of a grave and quiet disposition."

"O Ralph, what a bat you are! He was grave enough just now, truly; but did you not observe the twinkle in his eye when he spoke to us in English? Depend on it he's a funny dog."

"There must be freemasonry, then, among funny dogs," I retorted, "for Jack and I don't perceive it."

"Is this our canoe?" inquired Jack of the trader.

"It is."

"Then let's jump in."

In a few seconds the river was crowded with a fleet of small canoes, and we all paddled quickly up the stream, which was sluggish at that part. We did not intend to proceed more than a few miles by water, as the place where game was expected was at some distance from the river. I felt some regret at this, for the trip up the river was to me most enchanting.

Every yard we advanced new beauties of scenery were revealed to view.

The richness of the tropical vegetation seemed in this place to culminate, it was so rank and gorgeous. The day was fine, too, and all the strange-looking creatures--ugly and beautiful, large and small-- peculiar to those regions, seemed to have resolved on a general peace in order to bask in the sunshine and enjoy the glorious weather. Man alone was bent on war, and our track, alas! was marked with blood wherever we passed along. I pondered much on this subject, and wondered at the bloodthirsty spirit which seems to be natural to man in all conditions and climes. Then I thought of the difficulty these poor Africans have at times in procuring food, the frequency with which they are reduced almost to a state of starvation, and I ceased to wonder that they shot and speared everything that came in their way.

We proceeded up the left bank of the river, keeping close in to the shore in order to obtain the protection of the overhanging boughs and foliage; for the sun soon began to grow hot, and in the middle of the day became so intense that I sometimes feared that I or my companions would receive a sunstroke. I confess that the subject of health often caused me much anxiety; for although I knew that we were all old experienced travellers--though young in years--and had become in a great degree inured to hardships, I feared that the deadly climate of Central Africa might prove too much for our European constitutions. By the free use of quinine, however, and careful attention to the roles of health as far as circumstances would permit, we were fortunate enough to keep in excellent health and spirits during the whole course of our sojourn there; for which, when I thought of the hundreds of Europeans who had perished on that deadly coast without even venturing into the interior, I felt very thankful. One of our chief delights, to which I in a great degree attribute our uninterrupted health, was bathing daily in the streams and ponds with which we fell in, or on which we paddled during our travels. On these occasions we were fain, however, to be exceeding careful in the selection of our bathing-pool, as crocodiles and alligators, and I know not what other hideous animals, were constantly on the lookout for prey, and I make no doubt would have been very ready to try the flavour of a morsel of English food had we given them the chance.

On these occasions, when we had made sure of our pool, we were wont to paddle about in the cool refreshing stream, and recall to mind the splendid dips we had had together six years before in the clear waters of the coral island. Since that time Peterkin had learned to swim well, which was not only a source of much satisfaction and gratification to himself now, but, he told me, had been the means of preserving not only his own life on more than one occasion, but the life of a little child which he had the good fortune to rescue from drowning when cruising off the island of Madagascar.

Peterkin used to speak very strongly when talking on this subject, and I observed, from the unusual seriousness of his manner, that he felt deeply too.

"Ralph," he said to me one day, "half the world is mad--I am not sure that I might not say three-quarters of the world is mad--and I'm quite certain that all the ladies in the world are mad with the exception of the brown ladies of the South Seas, and a few rare specimens elsewhere; they're all mad together in reference to the matter of swimming. Now that I have learned it nothing is so easy, and any one who is not as blind as a rheumatic owl must see that nothing is more important; for every one almost is subject to being pitched now and then into deep water, and if he can't swim it's all up with him. Why, every time an angler goes out to fish he runs the chance of slipping and being swept into a deep hole, where, if he cannot swim, he is certain to be drowned. And yet five strokes would save his life. Good swimming is by no means what is wanted; swimming of any kind, however poor, is all that is desiderated. Every time a lady goes to have a row on a lake she is liable to be upset by the clumsiness of those who accompany her, and although it may be close to shore, if she cannot swim, down she goes to the bottom. And floating won't do. Some ladies delude themselves with the idea that floating is of great value. In nine cases out of ten it is of no value at all; for unless water be perfectly smooth and still, a person cannot float so as to keep the waves from washing over the face, in which case choking is the certain result. There is no excuse for not learning to swim. In most large cities there are swimming-baths; if the sea is not available, a river is, everywhere. I tell you what it is, Ralph: people who don't learn to swim are--are--I was going to say asses, but that would be an insult to the much-maligned long-eared animal; and parents who don't teach their offspring to swim deserve to be drowned in butter-milk; and I wish I saw--no, I don't quite wish I saw them all drowned in that way, but I do wish that I could impress upon mankind over the length and breadth of this rotund world the great, the immense, the intense importance of boys and girls being taught to swim."

"You make use of strong language," said I.

"Quite a powerful orator," added Jack, laughing.

"Bah!" exclaimed Peterkin; "your reception of this grand truth is but a type of the manner in which it will be received by the pig-headed world. What's the use of preaching common sense? I'm a perfect donkey!"

"Nay, Peterkin," said Jack; "I appreciate what you say, and have no doubt whatever that your remarks, if made public, would create quite a revolution in the juvenile world, and convert them speedily into aquatic animals. Did you ever think of sending your views on that subject to the Times?"

"The Times!" cried Peterkin.

"Yes, the Times; why not?"

"Because," said Peterkin slowly, "I once sent a letter to that great but insolent periodical, and what do you think it did?"

"Can't tell, I'm sure."

"Took no notice of it whatever!" said Peterkin, with a look of ineffable disgust.

But to return from this digression. I was much struck with the splendid contrast of colours that met my eye everywhere here. The rich variety of greens in the different trees harmonised with the bright pink plums and scarlet berries, and these latter were almost dimmed in their lustre by the bright plumage of the birds, which I felt intense longing to procure, many of them being quite new to me, and, I am certain, totally unknown to naturalists, while others I recognised with delight as belonging to several of the species of which I had read in ornithological works. I tried hard to shoot several of these lovely creatures, intending to stuff them, but, to my regret, was utterly unable to hit them. Seeing this, Peterkin took pity on me, and sitting down in the bow of our canoe, picked off all the birds I pointed out to him as we passed, with unerring precision. Most of them fell into the water, and were easily secured, while one or two toppled off the branches into the canoe. Several of them he shot on the wing--a feat which even filled Jack with surprise, and so astounded the natives that they surrounded our canoe at last, and gazed open-mouthed at my friend, whom they evidently regarded as the greatest fetishman that had ever come amongst them.

He was obliged to stop at last and lay down his gun in order to make the natives cease from crowding round us and delaying our voyage. A number of iguanas were observed on the branches of the trees that overhung the stream. They dropped into the water as we approached; but the natives succeeded in spearing a good many, and I afterwards found that they considered them excellent food.

If I was charmed with the birds, Peterkin was no less delighted with the monkeys that chattered at us as we passed along. I never saw a man laugh as he did that day. He almost became hysterical, so much was he tickled with their antics; and the natives, who have a keen sense of the ludicrous, seemed quite to sympathise with his spirit, although, of course, what amused him could not have similarly affected them, seeing that they were used to monkeys from infancy.

"There's something new!" exclaimed Jack, as we rounded a bend in the river and came in view of an open flat where it assumed somewhat the aspect of a pond or small lake. He pointed to a flock of birds standing on a low rock, which I instantly recognised to be pelicans.

"Surely," said I, "pelicans are not new to you!"

"Certainly not; but if you look a little more attentively, I think you will find material for your note-book."

Jack was right. I observed a very fine fish-hawk circling over the head of one of the pelicans. Its head and neck were white, and its body was of a reddish chocolate colour. Just as we came in sight, the pelican caught a fine fish, which it stowed away safe in the pouch under its chin. The sly hawk, which had been watching for this, immediately made a descent towards its victim, making a considerable noise with its wings as it came down. Hearing this, the pelican looked hastily up, and supposing that a terrible and deadly assault was about to be made, opened its mouth and screamed in terror. This was just what the hawk wanted. The open bill revealed the fish in the pouch. Down he swooped, snatched it out, and then soared away with his ill-gotten gains in his talons.

"Oh, what a thief!" exclaimed Peterkin.

"And the pelican seems to take his loss in a remarkably philosophical manner," observed Jack.

To my surprise the great stupid bird, instead of flying away, as I had expected, quietly resumed his fishing as if nothing had happened. No doubt he was well pleased to find himself still alive, and it is not improbable that the hawk made several more meals at the expense of his long-beaked friend after we had passed by.

We soon put him to flight, however, by landing near the spot where he stood, this being the place where we were to quit our canoes and pass through the jungle on foot. The hunters now prepared themselves for action, for the recent tracks of elephants were seen on the bank of the stream, and the natives said they could not be far off. Jack and Peterkin were armed with immensely heavy rifles, which carried balls of the weight of six-ounces. I carried my trusty, double-barrelled fowling-piece, which is of the largest size, and which I preferred to a rifle, because, not being a good shot, I resolved, on all occasions, to reserve my fire until we should come to close quarters with game, leaving my more expert comrades to take the longer shots. We had also two natives--one being our guide, Makarooroo, who carried Jack and Peterkin's double-barrelled guns as a reserve. These were loaded, of course, with ball.

"This looks something like business," said Jack, as he leaned on his heavy rifle and looked at the natives, who were selecting their spears and otherwise making preparations.

"It does," replied Peterkin. "Are you loaded?"

"Ay, and I have just examined the caps to see that they are dry; for it's not like grouse-shooting on the Scottish hills this African hunting, depend upon it. A snapping cap might cost us our lives,-- Ralph, my boy, you must keep well in rear. I don't want to hurt your feelings, but it won't do to go in front when you cannot depend on your nerves."

I experienced a feeling of sadness not unmingled with shame as my friend said this, but I could not question the justness of his remark, and I knew well that he would not have made it at all, but for his anxiety lest I should run recklessly into danger, which I might find myself, when too late, unable to cope with. I was careful, however, to conceal my feelings as I replied with a smile--

"You are right, Jack. I shall act the part of a support, while you and Peterkin skirmish in advance."

"And be careful," said Peterkin, solemnly, "that you don't fire into us by mistake."

Somewhat of Peterkin's own spirit came over me as I replied, "Indeed, I have been thinking of that, and I'm not sure that I can restrain myself when I see a chimpanzee monkey and a gorilla walking through the woods before me."

"I think we'd better take his gun from him," suggested Jack.

At this moment the king gave the signal to advance, so we shouldered our weapons and joined him. As we walked rapidly along, Jack suggested that we should allow the natives to kill any elephants we might fall in with in their own way, so as to observe how they managed it, rather than try to push ourselves forward on this our first expedition. We all agreed to this, and shortly after we came to the place which elephants were known to frequent.

Here great preparations had evidently been made for them. A space of more than a mile was partially enclosed by what might be termed a vine wall. The huge, thorny, creeping vines had been torn down from the trees and woven into a rude sort of network, through which it was almost impossible for any animal except an elephant to break. This was intended--not to stop the elephant altogether, but to entangle and retard him in his flight, until the hunters could kill him with their spears. The work, we were given to understand, was attended with considerable danger, for some of the natives were occasionally caught by the thorny vines when flying from the charge of the infuriated animal, and were instantly stamped to death by his ponderous feet.

I felt a new and powerful excitement creep over me as I saw the natives extend themselves in a wide semicircle of nearly two miles in extent, and begin to advance with loud shouts and cries, in order to drive the game towards the vines, and the flashing eyes and compressed lips of my two companions showed that they were similarly affected. We determined to keep together and follow close on that part of the line where the king was.

"You no be 'fraid?" said Makarooroo, looking down at Peterkin, who, he evidently supposed, was neither mentally nor physically adapted for an African hunter.

Peterkin was so tickled with the question that he suddenly began to tremble like an aspen leaf, and to chatter with his teeth and display all the symptoms of abject terror. Pointing over Makarooroo's shoulder into the bush behind him, he gasped, "The leopard!"

The negro uttered a hideous yell, and springing nearly his own height into the air, darted behind a tree with the agility of a wild-cat.

Instantly Peterkin resumed his composure, and turning round with a look of cool surprise, said--

"What! you're not afraid, Makarooroo?" The good-humoured fellow burst into a loud laugh on perceiving the practical joke that had been passed on him, and it was evident that the incident, trifling though it was, had suddenly raised his estimation of Peterkin to a very exalted pitch.

We now began to draw near to the enclosure, and I was beginning to fear that our hunt was to prove unsuccessful that day. A considerable quantity of small game had passed us, alarmed by the cries of the natives; but we purposely withheld our fire, although I saw that Jack was sorely tempted once or twice, when several beautiful gazelles and one or two wild pigs ran past within shot. Presently we heard a shrill trumpeting sound, which Peterkin, who had hunted in the forests of Ceylon, told us, in an excited voice, was the cry of the elephant. We hastened forward with our utmost speed, when suddenly we were brought to a stand by hearing a tremendous roar close in front of us. Immediately after, a large male lion bounded from among the bushes, and with one stroke of his enormous paw struck down a negro who stood not twenty yards from us. The terrible brute stood for an instant or two, lashing his sides with his tail and glaring defiance. It chanced that I happened to be nearest to him, and that the position of the tangled underwood prevented my companions from taking good aim; so without waiting for them, being anxious to save, if possible, the life of the prostrate negro, I fired both barrels into the lion's side. Giving utterance to another terrible roar, he bounded away into the bush, scattering the negroes who came in his way, and made his escape, to our great disappointment.

We found, to our horror, on going up to the fallen hunter, that he was quite dead. His skull had been literally smashed in, as if it had received a blow from a sledge-hammer.

I cannot describe my feelings on beholding thus, for the first time, the king of beasts in all the savage majesty of strength and freedom, coupled with the terrible death of a human being. My brain was in a whirl of excitement; I scarce knew what I was doing. But I had no time to think, for almost immediately after firing the shots at the lion, two elephants came crashing through the bushes. One was between ten and eleven feet high, the other could not have been less than twelve feet. I had never seen anything like this in the menageries of England, and their appearance, as they burst thus suddenly on my vision, was something absolutely appalling.

Those who have only seen the comparatively small and sluggish animals that are wont to ring their bells to attract attention, and to feed on gingerbread nuts from the hands of little boys, can form no idea of the terrible appearance of the gigantic monsters of Africa as they go tearing in mad fury through the forests with their enormous ears, and tails, and trunks erect, their ponderous tusks glistening in the sunshine, and their wicked little eyes flashing like balls of fire as they knock down, rend asunder, and overturn all that comes in their way.

The two that now approached us in full career were flying before a crowd of negroes who had already fixed a number of spears in their sides, from which the blood was flowing copiously. To say that the bushes went down before them like grass would not give a correct idea of the ponderous rush of these creatures. Trees of three and four inches diameter were run against and snapped off like twigs, without proving in any degree obstructive.

By this time the negroes had crowded in from all sides, and as the elephants approached the place where we stood, a perfect cloud of spears and javelins descended on their devoted sides. I observed that many of the active natives had leaped up into the trees and discharged their spears from above, while others, crouching behind fallen trees or bushes, threw them from below, so that in a few seconds dozens of spears entered their bodies at every conceivable angle, and they appeared as if suddenly transformed into monstrous porcupines or hedgehogs. There was something almost ludicrous in this, but the magnitude and aspect of the animals were too terrible, and our danger was too imminent, to permit anything like comic ideas to enter our brains. I observed, too, that the natives were perfectly wild with excitement. Their black faces worked convulsively, and their white eyes and teeth glittered as they leaped and darted about in a state of almost perfect nudity, so that their aspect was quite demoniacal.

The suddenness and violence of the attack made near to us had the effect of turning the elephants aside, and the next instant they were tearing and wrenching themselves through the meshes of the tough and thorny vines. The natives closed in with wild cries and with redoubled energy. Nothing surprised me so much as to observe the incredible number of spears that were sticking all over these creatures, and the amount of blood that they lost, without any apparent diminution of strength resulting. It seemed as if no human power could kill them, and at that moment I almost doubted Peterkin's assertion that he had, while in Ceylon, actually killed elephants with a single ball.

While Jack and Peterkin and I were gazing in deep interest and surprise at the curious struggle going on before us, and holding ourselves in readiness to act, should there be any chance of our game escaping, the larger of the two elephants succeeded in disentangling himself by backing out of the snare. He then wheeled round and charged straight at King Jambai, who stood close to us, with incredible fury. The beast, as it came on with the bristling spears all over it, the blood spirting from its innumerable wounds, and trumpeting shrill with rage, seemed to me like some huge unearthly phantom. It was with difficulty I could believe the whole scene other than a hideous dream. Jambai launched his javelin into the animal's chest, and then turned and fled. The other natives also darted and scattered hither and thither, so that the elephant could not make up its mind on which of its enemies to wreak its vengeance. We, too, turned and took to our heels at once with right good will. All at once I heard Jack utter a wild shout or yell, very unlike to anything I ever heard from him before. I looked back, and saw that his foot had got entangled in a thorny shrub, and that the elephant was making at him.

To this day I have never been able to account for the remarkable condition of mind and body that ensued on this occasion. Instead of being paralysed as I had been when Peterkin was in imminent danger, all sensation of fear or hesitancy seemed to vanish on thine instant. I felt my nerves and muscles strung, as it were, and rendered firm as a rock, and with calm deliberation, yet with the utmost rapidity of which I was capable, I turned round, sprang between Jack and the enraged beast, and presented my piece at his head.

"Right in the centre of his forehead," gasped Jack, as he endeavoured to wrench his foot from the entanglement.

At that moment I observed Peterkin leap to my side; the next instant the report of both our guns rang through the woods; the elephant bounded completely over Jack, as Peterkin and I leaped to either side to let it pass, and fell to the ground with such violence that a tree about six inches thick, against which it struck, went down before it like a willow wand.

We immediately assisted Jack to extricate himself; but we had no time to congratulate ourselves on our narrow escape, for mingled shouts and yells from the men in the bushes ahead apprised us that some new danger menaced them in that direction.

Reloading as fast as we could, we hastened forward, and soon gained the new scene of battle. Here stood the other elephant, trying to break down a small tree up which King Jambai had climbed, partly for safety and partly in order to dart a javelin down on the brute as it passed.

This was a common custom of the natives; but the king, who was a bold, reckless man, had neglected to take the very necessary precaution of selecting a strong tree. The elephant seemed actually to have observed this, for instead of passing on, it suddenly rushed headlong against the tree and began to break it down. When we came up the beast was heaving and straining with all its might, the stout tree was cracking and rending fearfully, so that the king could scarcely retain his position on it. The natives were plying their spears with the utmost vigour; but although mortally wounded, it was evident that in a few more seconds the elephant would succeed in throwing down the tree and trample the king to death.

Peterkin instantly sprang forward, but Jack laid his hand on his shoulder.

"It's my turn this time, lad," he cried, and leaping towards the monster, he placed the muzzle of his rifle close to its shoulder and sent a six-ounce ball right through its heart.

The effect was instantaneous. The elephant fell to the ground, a mountain of dead flesh.

The delight of the negroes at this happy termination of the battle was excessive. They leaped and laughed and danced like insane men, and we had much ado to prevent them seizing us in their arms and rubbing noses with us.

As we had not commenced the hunt until well on in the day, evening was now closing in; so the king gave orders to encamp on a dry rising ground not far distant, where the jungle was less dense, and thither we all repaired, the natives bringing in all the game, and cutting up the elephants in a very short space of time.

"Your shot was not such a bad one this time, Ralph," observed Peterkin, as we three stood looking at the large elephant which the natives were cutting up. "There they are, just above the proboscis. But let me warn you never again to venture on such a foolhardy thing as to fire in the face of a charging elephant unless you are a dead shot."

"Thank you, Peterkin, for your advice, which, however, I will not take when a comrade's life may depend on my doing so."

"I give you full credit for the excellence of your intention," rejoined my friend; "but if Jack's life had depended on those two shots from your double-barrel, he would have been but a dead man now. There is only one vulnerable spot in the front of an elephant's head; that is, exactly in the centre of the forehead. The spot is not bigger than a saucer, and the bone is comparatively thin there. If you cannot make sure of hitting that, you simply face certain death. I would not have tried it on any account whatever, had I not seen that both you and Jack would have been killed had I not done so."

On examination we found that the heavy ball from Peterkin's rifle had indeed penetrated the exact spot referred to, and had been the means of killing the elephant, while my two bullets were found embedded in the bone.

The tusks of this animal were magnificent. I do not know what their exact weight was, not having the means wherewith to weigh them. They were probably worth a considerable sum of money in the British market. Of course we did not lay claim to any part of the spoil of that day, with the exception of a few of the beautiful birds shot on the voyage up the river, which were of no value to the natives, although priceless to me. Alas! when I came to examine them next morning, I found that those destructive creatures the white ants had totally destroyed the greater part of them, and the few that were worth stuffing were very much damaged.

Experience is a good though sometimes a severe teacher. Never again did I, after that, put off the stuffing of any valuable creature till the next day. I always stuffed it in the evening of the day on which it was killed; and thus, although the practice cost me many a sleepless night, I preserved, and ultimately brought home, many specimens of rare and beautiful birds and beasts, which would otherwise have been destroyed by those rapacious insects.

That night the scene of our camp was indescribably romantic and wild. Numerous huge fires were lighted, and round these the negroes circled and cooked elephant and venison steaks, while they talked over the events of the day or recounted the adventures of former hunts with noisy volubility and gesticulation.

The negro has a particular love for a fire. The nights in his warm climate are chill to him, though not so to Europeans, and he luxuriates in the heat of a fire as a cat does in the rays of the sun. The warm blaze seems to draw out his whole soul, and causes his eyes to sparkle with delight. A good supper and a warm fire render him almost perfectly happy. There is but one thing wanting to render him supremely so, and that is--a pipe! No doubt, under similar circumstances, the white man also is in a state of enviable felicity, but he does not show his joy like the negro, who seems to forget his cares and sorrows, the miseries which his gross superstitions entail on him, the frequency with which he is exposed to sudden destruction; everything, in short, is forgotten save the present, and he enjoys himself with unmitigated fervour.

It really did my heart good as I sat with my comrades beside our fire and looked around me on their happy faces, which were rendered still happier by the gift from us of a small quantity of tobacco, with which we had taken care to provide ourselves for this very purpose.

I could scarcely believe that the jovial, kindly, hearty fellows were the very men who are well-known to be such cruel, bloodthirsty fiends when under the influence of their dreadful superstitions, and who, but a few hours before, had been darting through the woods besmeared with blood and yelling like maniacs or demons. In fact, the whole scene before me, and the day's proceedings, seemed to me, at that time, like a vivid dream instead of a reality. Moreover, after I lay down, the reality became a dream, and I spent that night, as I had spent the day, shooting gazelles, lions, wild pigs, and elephants in imagination.

CHAPTER SIX.

DREAMING AND FEEDING AND BLOODY WORK ENLARGED UPON.

The first object of which my senses became cognisant on awaking next morning was my friend Peterkin, who had evidently awakened just a moment or two before me, for he was in the act of yawning and rubbing his eyes.

I have all my life been a student of character, and the most interesting yet inexplicable character which I have ever studied has been that of my friend Peterkin, whose eccentricities I have never been able fully to understand or account for. I have observed that, on first awaking in the mornings, he has been wont to exhibit several of his most eccentric and peculiar traits, so I resolved to feign myself asleep and watch him.

"Heigh-ho!" he exclaimed, after the yawn I have just referred to. Having said this, he stretched out both arms to the utmost above his head, and then flung himself back at full length on his couch, where he lay still for about half a minute. Then he started up suddenly into a sitting posture and looked slowly from one to another of the recumbent forms around him. Satisfied, apparently, that they were asleep, he gave vent to a long yawn which terminated in a gasp, and then he looked up contemplatively at the sky, which was at that hour beginning to warm with the red rays of the rising sun. While thus engaged, he caressed with his right hand the very small scrap of whisker that grew on his right cheek. At first it seemed as if this were an unconscious action, but he suddenly appeared to become absorbed in it, and stared straight before him as one does when only half awake, mumbling the while in an undertone. I could not make out distinctly what he said, but I think I caught the words, "Yes, a little--a very little thicker--six new hairs, I think--umph! slow, very slow." Here he looked at Jack's bushy beard and sighed.

Suddenly he thrust both hands deep into his breeches pockets and stared at the black embers of the extinct fire; then as suddenly he pulled out his hands, and placing the forefinger of his right hand on the end of the thumb of his left, said slowly--

"Let me see--I'll recall it."

He spoke with intense gravity. Most persons do when talking to themselves.

"Yes, I remember now. There were two elephants and four--or three, was it?--no, it must have been four lions. The biggest elephant had on a false front of fair curls and a marriage-ring on its tail. Stay; was it not the other one had that? No, it was the biggest. I remember now, for it was just above the marriage-ring I grasped it when I pulled its tail out. I didn't pull it off, for it wouldn't come off; it came out like a telescope or a long piece of indiarubber. Ha! and I remember thinking how painful it must be. That was odd, now, to think of that. The other elephant had on crinoline. That was odder still; for of all animals in the world it least required it. Well, let me see. What did I do? Oh yes, I shot them both. Of course, that was natural; but it wasn't quite so natural that the big one should vomit up a live lion, which attacked me with incredible fury. But I killed it cleverly. Yes, it was a clever thing, undoubtedly, to split a lion in two, from the tip of its nose to the extremity of its tail, with one stroke of a penknife--"

At this climax I could contain myself no longer, and burst into a loud laugh as I perceived that Peterkin had spent the night, as I myself had done, in hunting--though, I confess, there was a considerable difference in the nature of our achievements, and in the manner of their accomplishment.

"Why, what are you laughing at?" said Jack, sitting up and gazing at me with a stupid stare.

"At Peterkin's dreams," said I.

"Ah!" said Jack, with a smiling yawn, "that's it, is it? Been hunting elephants and lions, eh?"

"Why, how did you guess that?" I asked, in surprise; "were you not asleep just now?"

"Of course I was, and dreaming too, like yourself, I make no doubt. I had just bagged my fifteenth elephant and my tenth lion when your laugh awoke me. And the best of it is that I was carrying the whole bagful on my back at once, and did not feel much oppressed by the weight."

"That beats my dream hollow," observed Peterkin; "so its my opinion we'd better have breakfast.--Makarooroo, hy! d'ye hear? rouse up, you junk of ebony."

"Yis, massa, comin'," said our guide, rising slowly from his lair on the opposite side of our fireplace.

"D'you hear?"

"Yis, massa."

"You're a nigger!"

"Dat am a fact."

"Well, being a nigger you're a brick, so look sharp with that splendid breakfast you promised us last night. I'll wager a million pounds that you had forgotten all about it."

"No, massa, me no forgit. Me up in centre ob de night and put 'im in de hole. Wat you call 'im--oben?"

"Ay, oven, that's it."

"Yis. Well, me git 'im d'rec'ly."

"And, I say, hold on," added Peterkin. "Don't you suppose I'm going to stand on ceremony with you. Your name's too long by half. Too many rooroos about it, so I'm going to call you Mak in future, d'ye understand?"

The negro nodded and grinned from ear to ear as he left us. Presently he returned with a huge round, or lump of meat, at which we looked inquisitively. The odour from it was delightful, and the tender, juicy appearance of the meat when Makarooroo, who carved it for us, cut the first slice, was quite appetising to behold.

"What is it?" inquired Peterkin.

"Elephant's foot," replied the guide.

"Gammon," remarked Peterkin.

"It's true, massa. Don't you see him's toe?"

"So it is," said Jack.

"And it's first-rate," cried I, tasting a morsel.

With that we fell to and made a hearty meal, after which we, along with the king and all his people, retraced our steps to the river and returned to the native town, where we spent another day in making preparations to continue our journey towards the land of the gorilla.

During the hunt which I have just described I was very much amused as well as amazed at the reckless manner in which the negroes loaded their rusty old trade-guns. They put in a whole handful of powder each time, and above that as much shot and bits of old iron of all kinds as they dared; some I saw charged thus to within a few inches of the muzzle, and the owners seemed actually afraid to put them to their shoulders, as well they might be, for the recoil was tremendous, and had the powder been good their guns must have been blown to pieces and themselves killed.

On our return to the village we found the people on the eve of one of those terrible outbursts of superstitious passion which rarely if ever pass away without some wretched human creature perishing under the hands of murderers.

"There is something wrong with the fetishman, I think," remarked Jack, as we disembarked at the landing. "He seems excited. Do you know what it can be at, Makarooroo?"

"Jack," interposed Peterkin, "I have changed his name to Mak, so you and Ralph will please to remember that.--Mak, my boy, what's wrong with your doctor?"

The negro looked very grave and shook his head as he replied, "Don' know, massa. Him's be goin' to rizz de peepil wid him norrible doin's. Dere will be death in the camp mos' bery quick--p'raps dis night."

"That is terrible," said I. "Are you sure of what you say?"

"Sartin sure," replied the negro, with another shake of the head.

"Then, Mak," said Jack, "it behoves us to look to ourselves. You look like an honest fellow, and I believe we may trust you. We cannot expect you to help us to fight against your own kith and kin, but I do expect that you will assist us to escape if any foul play is intended. Whatever betides, it is as well that you should know that white men are not easily conquered. Our guns are good--they never miss fire. We will sell our lives dearly, you may depend on it."

"Ay," added Peterkin, "it is well that you should know that; moreover, it is well that the rascally niggers of your tribe should know it too; so you can take occasion to give them a hint that we shall keep ourselves prepared for them, with my compliments."

"De mans ob my peepil," replied the negro, with some dignity of manner, "be not wuss dan oder mans. But dem is bad enuff. But you no hab need for be fraid. Dey no touch de white mans. Dem bery much glad you com' here. If any bodies be killed it be black mans or 'oomans."

We felt somewhat relieved on hearing this, for, to say truth, we knew well enough that three men, no matter how well-armed or resolute they might be, could not hope to defend themselves against a whole tribe of savages in their own country. Nevertheless we resolved to keep a sharp lookout, and be prepared for the worst. Meanwhile we did all in our power to expedite our departure.

That evening the trader started on his return journey to the coast, leaving us in charge of King Jambai, who promised earnestly to take good care of us. We immediately put his willingness to fulfil his promise to the test by begging him to furnish us with men to carry our goods into the interior. He tried very hard to induce us to change our minds and remain hunting with his tribe, telling us that the gorilla country was far far away from his lands; that we should never reach it alive, or that if we did we should certainly be killed by the natives, who, besides being cruel and warlike, were cannibals; and that if we did meet in with gorillas we should all be certainly slain, for no one could combat successfully with that ferocious giant of the monkey tribe.

To this we replied that we were quite aware of the dangers we should have to encounter in our travels, but added that we had come there for the very purpose of encountering such dangers, and especially to pay a visit to the giant monkeys in their native land, so that it was in vain his attempting to dissuade us, as we were resolved to go.

Seeing that we were immovable, the king eventually gave in, and ordered some of his best men to hold themselves in readiness to start with us on the following morning. We then proceeded to his majesty's house, where we had supper, and afterwards retired to our own hut to rest.

But we were destined to have little or no rest that night. The doctor or fetishman of the tribe had stirred up the passions of the people in a manner that was quite incomprehensible to us. King Jambai, it seems, had been for some weeks suffering from illness--possibly from indigestion, for he was fond of gorging himself--and the medicine-man had stated that his majesty was bewitched by some of the members of his own tribe, and that unless these sorcerers were slain there was no possibility of his getting well.

We never could ascertain why the fetishman should fix upon certain persons to be slain, unless it was that he had a personal enmity against them; but this seemed unlikely, for two of the persons selected were old female slaves, who could never, of course, have injured the doctor in any way. But the doings of Africans, especially in regard to religious superstitions, I afterwards found were so mysterious that no one could or would explain the meaning of them to us. And I am inclined to believe that in reference to the meaning of many things they were themselves utterly ignorant.

Towards midnight the people had wrought themselves up to a frenzied condition, and made so much noise that we could not sleep. In the midst of the uproar Makarooroo, who we observed had been very restless all the evening, rushed into our hut, exclaiming, "Massa! massa! come, save my Okandaga! come quick!"

The poor fellow was trembling with anxiety, and was actually pale in the face; for a distinctly discernible pallor overspreads the countenance of the negro when under the influence of excessive terror.

Okandaga we had previously heard of and seen. She was, according to African notions, an exceedingly pretty young girl, with whom our worthy guide had fallen desperately in love. Makarooroo's education had done much for him, and especially in regard to females. Having observed the kind, respectful consideration with which the missionaries treated their wives, and the happiness that seemed to be the result of that course of conduct, he resolved in his own mind to try the experiment with one of the girls of his own tribe, and soon after rejoining it paid his attentions to Okandaga, who seemed to him the most modest and lovable girl in the village.

Poor Okandaga was first amazed and then terrified at the strangely gentle conduct of her lover, and thought that he meant to bewitch her; for having never before been accustomed to other than harsh and contemptuous treatment from men, she could not believe that Makarooroo meant her any good. Gradually, however, she began to like this respectful wooer, and finally she agreed to elope with him to the sea-coast and live near the missionaries. It was necessary, however, to arrange their plans with great caution. There was no difficulty in their getting married. A handsome present to the girl's father was all that was necessary to effect that end, and a good hunter like Makarooroo knew he could speedily obtain possession of his bride, but to get her removed from her tribe and carried to the coast was quite a different affair. While the perplexed negro was pondering this subject and racking his brains to discover a way of getting over the difficulty,` our arrival at the village occurred. At once he jumped to the conclusion that somehow or other he should accomplish his object through our assistance; and holding this in view, he the more willingly agreed to accompany us to the gorilla country, intending first to make our acquaintance, and afterwards to turn us to account in furthering his plans. All this we learned long afterwards. At the period of which I am now writing, we were profoundly ignorant of everything save the fact that Okandaga was his affianced bride, and that the poor fellow was now almost beside himself with horror because the fetishman had condemned her, among others, to drink the poisoned cup.

This drinking of the poisoned cup is an ordeal through which the unhappy victims to whom suspicion has been attached are compelled to pass. Each one drinks the poison, and several executioners stand by, with heavy knives, to watch the result. If the poison acts so as to cause the supposed criminal to fall down, he is hacked in pieces instantly; but if, through unusual strength or peculiarity of constitution, he is enabled to resist the effects of the poison, his life is spared, and he is declared innocent.

Jack and Peterkin and I seized our weapons, and hurrying out, followed our guide to the spot where this terrible tragedy was enacting.

"Don't fear, Mak," said Peterkin, as we ran along; "we'll save her somehow. I'm certain of that."

The negro made no reply, but I observed a more hopeful expression on his countenance after the remark. He evidently had immense faith in Peterkin; which I must say was more than I had, for when I considered our small numbers, my hope of influencing savages was very slight.

The scene that met our eyes was indescribably horrible. In the centre of a dense circle of negroes, who had wrought themselves up to a pitch of ferocity that caused them to look more like wild beasts than men, stood the king, and beside him the doctor or fetishman. This latter was ornamented with a towering headdress of feathers. His face was painted white, which had the effect of imparting to him an infinitely more hideous and ghastly aspect than is produced in the white man when he is painted black. A stripe of red passed round his head, and another down his forehead and nose. His naked body was decked with sundry fantastic ornaments, and altogether he looked more like a fiend than I had believed it possible for man to appear.

The ground all round him was saturated with blood and strewn with arms, fingers, cleft skulls, and masses of flesh that had been hewn from the victims who had already fallen, one of whom, we afterwards learned, had belonged to the royal family. Two still remained--a young female and an old man. The emaciated frame and white woolly head of the latter showed that in the course of nature his earthly career must soon terminate. It is probable that the poor old man had become a burden to his relations, and the doctor took this opportunity of ridding the tribe of him. The girl was Okandaga, who stood weeping and trembling as she gazed upon the butchery that had already taken place.

The old man had swallowed the poison shortly before we arrived, and he was now struggling to maintain an erect position. But he failed, his quivering limbs sank beneath him, and before we could interfere the bloody executioners had cut off his head, and then, in a transport of passion, they literally hacked his body to pieces.

We rushed hastily forward to the king, and Jack, in an earnest voice, implored him to spare the last victim.

"Surely," said he, "enough have been sacrificed already.--Tell him,

Makarooroo, that I will quit his village and never see him more if he does not spare the life of that young girl."

The king appeared much perplexed by this unlooked-for interference on our part.

"I cannot check the spirits of my people now," he replied. "They are roused. The girl has bewitched me and many others. She must die. It is our custom. Let not my white men be offended. Let them go to their hut and sleep."

"We cannot sleep while injustice is done in the village," answered Jack, in a lofty tone. "Let not King Jambai do that which will make his visitors ashamed of him. Let the girl live till to-morrow at midnight. Let the case be investigated, and if she be proved guilty then let her die."

The king commenced a long reply in the same dignified manner and tone which Jack had assumed. While he was thus engaged Peterkin touched our guide on the shoulder and whispered--

"I say, Mak, tell the doctor to back up Jack's request, and I'll give him a gun."

The negro slipped at once to the side of the doctor, who had begun to frown fiercely on Jack, and whispered a few words in his ear. Instantly his face assumed a calmer aspect, and presently he stepped up to the king, and a whispering conversation ensued, in which the doctor, carefully refraining from making any mention of the gun, commended the wise advice of the white man, and suggested that the proposal should be agreed to, adding, however, that he knew for certain that the girl was a witch, but that the investigation would do good in the way of proving that he, the doctor, was correct, and thus the girl should perish on the following night, and the white men would be satisfied.

Having announced this to the multitude, the king ordered Okandaga to be conducted back to her prison and carefully guarded; and we returned to our hut--not, however, to sleep, but to consult as to what was to be done next.

"I knew that you wanted a respite for her," said Peterkin, as we sat round our fire, "that you might have time to consider how to act, and I backed up your request accordingly, as you know. But now, I confess, I'm very much at a loss what to suggest. It seems to me we have only purchased a brief delay."

"True," answered Jack. "The delay is not so brief, however, but that we may plan some method of getting the poor girl out of this scrape.--What say you, Mak?"

"If you no can tink 'pon someting, I gib up all hope," replied our guide sorrowfully.

"Come, Mak, cheer up," cried Peterkin. "If the worst comes to the worst, you can, at any rate, fight for your bride."

"Fight!" exclaimed the negro, displaying his white teeth like a mastiff, rolling his eyes and clinching his fists convulsively. Then in a calmer tone he continued, "Ay, me can fight. Me could kill all de guards an' take Okandaga by de hand, an' run troo de bushes for eber. But guards no dic widout hollerin' an' yellerin' like de gorilla; an' nigger mans can run fasterer dan womans. No, no, dat am dumpossobable."

"Nothing's `dumpossobable' to brave hearts and stout arms," replied Jack. "There are only four guards put over her, I believe. Well, there are just four of us--not that we require to be equal, by any means. Peterkin and I could settle them easily; but we require to be equal in numbers, in order to do it quietly. I have a plan in my head, but there's one hitch in it that I cannot unravel."

"And what may that be?" If asked.

"Why, I don't see how, after getting clear off with Okandaga, we are to avoid being pursued on suspicion and captured."

"Dere is one cave," remarked the guide, "not far off to here. P'raps we be safe if we git into 'im. But I 'fraid it not do, cause him be peepiled by fiends an' dead man's spirits."

"That's a grave objection," said Peterkin, laughing.

"Yes, an' de tribe neber go near dere; dey is most drefful terrorfied to be cotched dere."

"Then, that will just do," cried Jack, with animation. "The very thing. And now I'll tell you what my plan is. To-morrow morning early we will tell the king that we wish to be off at once--that we have put off too much time already, and wish to make no further delay. Then we'll pack up and start. At night we will encamp in a quiet, out-of-the-way part of the woods, and slip back to the village in the dark a short time before midnight. The whole village will at that time be assembled, probably, at the spot where the execution is to take place; so we can rush in, overpower the guard, free Okandaga, and make our escape to the cave, where they will never think of looking for us."

Peterkin shook his head. "There are two difficulties in your plan, Jack. First, what if the natives are not assembled on the place of execution, and we find it impossible to make our entrance into or exit from the village quietly?"

"I propose," replied Jack, "that we shall undress ourselves, rub ourselves entirely over with charcoal and grease, so that they shall not recognise us, and dash in and carry the girl off by a coup de main. In which case it will, of course, be neck or nothing, and a tremendous race to the cave, where, if they follow us, we will keep them at bay with our rifles."

"Umph! dashing, no doubt, but risky," said Peterkin--"extremely risky. Yet it's worth trying. Well, my second difficulty is--what if they don't stick to their promise after we quit, and kill the poor thing before midnight?"

"We must take our chance of that. But I shall put the king on his honour before leaving, and say that I will make particular inquiry into the way in which the trial has been conducted on my return."

"Put the king on his honour!" observed Peterkin. "I'm afraid that you'll put his majesty on an extremely unstable foundation. However, I see nothing better that can be done."

"Have you any more difficulties?"

"Yes," said I. "There is one other. What do you propose to do with the men who are to be supplied us by the king during these extremely delicate and difficult manoeuvres?"

The countenances of my comrades fell at this question.

"I never thought of them," said Jack.

"Nor I," said Peterkin.

Makarooroo groaned.

"Well," said I, "if you will allow me to suggest, I would recommend that we should, towards the close of the day, send them on ahead of us, and bid them encamp at a certain place, saying that we shall spend the night in hunting, and return to them in the morning."

"The very thing," said Jack. "Now, comrades, to rest. I will occupy myself until I fall asleep in maturing my plans and thinking out the details. Do you the same, and if anything should occur to you let us consult over it in the morning."

We were all glad to agree to this, being wearied more perhaps by excitement than want of rest; so bidding each other good-night, we lay down side by side to meditate, and for my part to dream of the difficult and dangerous work that awaited us on the morrow.

CHAPTER SEVEN.

WE CIRCUMVENT THE NATIVES.

We arose on the following morning with the dawn of day, and began to make preparation for our departure.

To our satisfaction we found the king quite willing that we should go; so embarking our goods in one of the native canoes, we ordered our negroes to embark, and commenced our journey amid the firing of guns and the good wishes of the natives. I must confess that I felt some probings of conscience at the thought of the double part we were compelled to play; but the recollection of the horrid fate that awaited the poor negro girl put to flight such feelings, and induced a longing for the time of action to arrive.

I have more than once referred to our goods. Perhaps it may be as well to explain that, when we first landed on the African coast, we made inquiries of those who were best acquainted with the nature and requirements of the country we were about to explore, as to what goods we ought to purchase of the traders, in order to be in a position to pay our way as we went along; for we could not, of course, expect the savages to feed us and lodge us and help us on our way for nothing. After mature consideration, we provided ourselves with a supply of such things as were most necessary and suitable--such as tobacco, powder, and shot, and ball, a few trade-guns, several pieces of brightly-coloured cloth, packages of beads (some white enamelled, others of coloured glass), coffee and tea, knives, scissors, rings, and a variety of other knick-knacks. These, with a little brandy to be used medicinally, our blankets and camp cooking utensils, formed a heavy load for ten men; but, of course, as we advanced, the load was lightened by the consumption of our provisions and the giving away of goods. The additions which I made, however, in the shape of stuffed specimens, began in the course of time to more than counterbalance this advantage.

Being resolved to impress the natives with a respect for our physical powers, we made a point of each carrying a pretty heavy load on our journeys--excepting, of course, when we went out a-hunting. But to return.

Our crew worked willingly and well, so that ere night closed in upon us we were a considerable distance away from the village. As the sun set we landed, and ordering our men to advance in the canoe to a certain bend in the river, and there encamp and await our return, we landed and went off into the woods as if to search for game.

"Now, Makarooroo, quick march, and don't draw rein till we reach the cave," said Jack when we were out of sight of the canoe.

Our guide obeyed in silence, and for the next two hours we travelled through the woods at a sort of half trot that must have carried us over the ground at the rate of five miles in hour. The pace was indeed tremendous, and I now reaped the benefit of those long pedestrian excursions which for years past I had been taking, with scientific ends in view, over the fields and hills of my native land. Jack and Peterkin seemed both to be made of iron, and incapable of suffering from fatigue. But I have no doubt that the exciting and hazardous nature of the expedition on which we had embarked had much to do with our powers of endurance.

After running and doubling, gliding and leaping through the dense woods, as I have said, for two hours, we arrived at a broken, rocky piece of ground, over which we passed, and eventually came upon a thick jungle that concealed a vast cliff almost entirely from view. The cracking of the bushes as we approached showed that we had disturbed the slumbers of more than one of the wild beasts that inhabited the spot. Here Makarooroo paused, and although it was intensely dark I could observe that he was trembling violently.

"Come, Mak," said I in a whisper, "surely you, who have received a Christian education, do not really believe that devils inhabit this spot?"

"Me don know, massa. Eber since me was be a pikaniny me 'fraid--horrobably 'fraid ob dat cave."

"Come, come," said Jack impatiently; "we have no time for fears of any kind this night. Think of Okandaga, Mak, and be a man."

This was sufficient. The guide pushed boldly forward, and led us to the mouth of a large cavern, at which he halted and pointed to the gloomy interior.

"You have the matches, Peterkin; quick, strike a light. It is getting late," said Jack.

In another moment a light was struck, and with it we kindled three goodly-sized torches with which we had provided ourselves. Holding these high over our heads, we entered the cavern--Jack first, Peterkin second, I next, and the terrified negro in rear.

We had scarcely entered, and were peering upwards at the black vault overhead, when an indescribable rushing sound filled the air of the cavern, and caused the flame of our torches to flicker with such violence that we could not see any object distinctly. We all came to a sudden pause, and I confess that at that moment a feeling of superstitious dread chilled the blood in my veins. Before we could discover the cause of this strange effect, several large black objects passed through the air near our heads with a peculiar muffled noise. Next instant the three torches were extinguished.

Unable to command himself any longer, the negro uttered a cry of terror and turned to fly; but Jack, whose wits seemed always prepared for any emergency, had foreseen the probability of this, and springing quickly after him, threw his arms round his neck and effectually prevented his running away.

The noise caused by the scuffle seemed to arouse the fury of all the evil spirits of the place, for a perfect hurricane of whirring sounds raged around us for a few seconds.

"It's only bats," cried Jack.--"Look alive, Peterkin; another light."

In a few seconds the torches were rekindled, and we advanced into the cavern; and Mak, after recovering from his fright and learning the cause thereof, became much bolder. The cave was about a hundred yards deep by about fifty wide; but we could not ascertain its height, for the light of our torches failed to penetrate the deep gloom overhead. It was divided into two natural chambers, the outer being large, the inner small--a mere recess, in fact. In this latter we planted our torches, and proceeded with our hasty preparations. Peterkin was ready first. We endeavoured to make ourselves as like to the natives in all respects as possible; and when I looked at my companions, I was obliged to confess that, except in the full blaze of the torch-light, I could not discern any point of difference between them and our guide.

"Now then, Jack," said Peterkin, "as you're not quite ready and I am, I shall employ myself in preparing a little plan of my own which I intend to put in force if the savages dare to venture into the cavern after us."

"Very good; but see that you finish it in less than five minutes, for I'll be ready in that time."

Peterkin immediately poured out a large quantity of powder on a flat rock, and mingling with it a little water from a pool near by, converted it into a semi-moist ball. This he divided into three parts, and forming each part into the shape of a tall cone, laid the whole carefully aside.

"There!" said he, "lie you there until you are wanted."

At this moment, while Jack and I were bending down fastening the latchet of our shoes, our ears were saluted with one of the most appalling yells I ever listened to. Makarooroo fell flat to the earth in his fright, and my own heart chilled with horror, while Jack sprang up and instinctively grasped the handle of his hunting-knife.

"Very good," said Peterkin, as he stood laughing at us quietly, and we immediately perceived that it was he who uttered the cry.

"Why, what mean you?" said Jack, almost angrily. "Surely this is no time for foolish jesting."

"I am anything but jesting, Jack. I'm only rehearsing another part of my plan."

"But you ought to give us warning when you are about to do such startling things," said I remonstratively.

"Nay, that would not have done at all, because then I should not have known what effect my cry is likely to produce on unexpectant ears."

"Well, now, are you all ready?" inquired Jack. "Then let us go."

Issuing forth armed only with our double-barrelled guns and heavy hunting-knives, we hastened towards the native village. When within a hundred yards of the edge of the wood that skirted it we stopped to pull off our shoes, for it was necessary that we should have nothing about our persons to tell who we were should any one chance to see us as we ran. We also left our rifles beside the shoes at a spot where we could find them in an instant in passing, and then slowly approached the outskirts of the village.

Presently we heard the hum of distant voices shouting, and the fear that the scene of bloodshed had already begun induced us to quicken our pace to a smart run. I never saw a man so deeply affected as was our poor guide, and when I looked at him I felt extremely anxious lest his state of mind should unfit him for acting with needful caution.

We gained the first cottages--they were empty. The village having been recently built, no stockade had yet been thrown round it, so our progress was unimpeded.

"We must be very cautious now," observed Jack in a whisper.--"Restrain yourself, Makarooroo; Okandaga's life depends on our coolness."

On reaching the back of the next hut, which was also empty. Jack motioned to us to halt, and coming close to us looked earnestly in each of our faces without saying a word. I supposed that, like a wise general, he was reviewing his troops--seeing whether the men he was about to lead into battle were fit for their work.

"Now," said he rapidly, "it's evident from the shouting that's going on that they won't waste much time with their palaver. The hut in which she is confined is not fifty yards off; I took care to ascertain its position before leaving this morning. What we have to do is simple. Spring on the guards and knock them down with our fists or the hilts of our hunting-knives, or with bits of stick, as suits us best. But mind"--here he looked pointedly at our guide--"no shedding of blood if it can be avoided. These men are not our enemies. Follow me in single file; when I halt, come up into line; let each single out the man nearest to him, and when I hold up my hand spring like wild-cats. If there happen to be five or six guards instead of four, leave the additional ones to me." We merely nodded assent, and in another minute were close upon the prison. Peterkin, Mak, and I had provided us with short heavy bludgeons on our way. These we held in our right hands; our left hands we kept free either to grasp our opponents with, or to draw our knives if necessary. Jack carried his long knife--it might almost have been termed a short sword--in his left hand, and from the manner in which he clinched his right I saw that he meant to make use of it as his principal weapon.

On gaining the back of the house we heard voices within, but could see nothing, so we moved softly round to the front, keeping, however, well behind the screen of bushes. Here Jack halted, and we ranged up alongside of him and peeped through the bushes. The hut was quite open in front and the interior was brightly lighted by a strong fire, round which the four guards--stout fellows all of them--were seated with their spears beside them on the ground. They were conversing in an excited tone, and taking no notice of Okandaga, who sat behind them, partially in the shade, with her face buried in her hands. She was not tied in any way, as the guards knew well enough that she could not hope to escape them by mere running way.

One rapid glance showed us all this, and enabled us to select our men. Then Jack gave the signal, and without an instant's hesitation we darted upon them. I know not in what manner my comrades acted their part. From the moment I set eyes on the negro nearest to me, my blood began to boil. Somehow or other I saw Jack give the signal without taking my eyes off my intended victim, then I sprang forward, and he had barely time to look up in alarm when I struck him with all my force on the right temple. He fell without a groan. I looked round instantly, and there lay the other three, with my companions standing over them. Our plan had been so well concerted and so promptly executed that the four men fell almost at the same instant, and without a cry.

Poor Okandaga leaped up and uttered a faint scream of alarm, but Makarooroo's voice instantly reassured her, and with an exclamation of joy she sprang into his arms. There was no time for delay. While the scene I have described was being enacted the shouts in the centre of the village had been increasing, and we guessed that in a few minutes more the bloodthirsty executioners would come for their helpless victim. We therefore left the hut at once, and ran as fast as we could towards the place where our guns and shoes had been left. Our guide seized Okandaga by the wrist and dragged her along; but indeed she was so nimble that at first she required no assistance. In a short time, however, we were obliged to slacken our pace in order to enable her to keep up. We reached the guns in safety; but while we were in the act of lifting them a burst of wild cries, that grew louder and fiercer as they approached, told that the natives were rushing tumultuously towards the prison.

"Now, lads," said Jack, "we must put on full speed.--Mak, take her right hand.--Here, Okandaga, your left."

At that instant there was a shout in the village, so loud that we knew the escape was discovered. An indescribable hubbub ensued, but we soon lost it in the crackling of the underwood as we burst through it in our headlong flight towards the cave. The poor girl, feeling that her life depended on it, exerted herself to the utmost, and with the aid of Jack and her lover kept well up.

"She'll never hold out to the end," said Peterkin, glancing over his shoulder as he ran.

The cries of the savages filled the woods in all directions, showing that they had instantly scattered themselves in the pursuit, in order to increase their chances of intercepting us. We had already traversed the greater part of the wood that lay between the village and the haunted cavern, when two negroes, who must have taken a shorter route, descried us. They instantly uttered a yell of triumph and followed us at full speed, while from the cries closing in upon us we could tell that the others had heard and understood the shout. Just then Okandaga's strength began to fail, and her extreme terror, as the pursuers gained on us, tended still further to increase her weakness. This was all the more unfortunate that we were now almost within a couple of hundred yards of the mouth of the cave.

Makarooroo spoke encouragingly to her, but she was unable to reply, and it became evident that she was about to sink down altogether. Jack glanced over his shoulder. The two negroes were within fifty yards of us, but no others were in sight.

"Hold my gun," said Jack to me sharply.

I seized it. He instantly stooped down, grasped Okandaga round the waist, and without stopping, swung her, with an exertion of strength that seemed to me incredible, into his arms. We gained the mouth of the cavern; Jack dropped Okandaga, who immediately ran in, while the rest of us stopped abruptly and faced about.

"Back, all of you," cried Jack, "else they will be afraid to come on."

The words had scarcely passed his lips when the two negroes came up, but halted a few yards from the mouth of the cave on seeing such a giant form guarding the entrance.

To let those men escape and reveal the place of our concealment was not to be thought of. Jack darted out upon them. They separated from each other as they turned to fly. I was peeping out of the cave, and saw that Jack could not secure them both; I therefore darted out, and quickly overtaking one, seized him by the hair of the head and dragged him into the cave with the aid of Peterkin. Jack lifted the other savage completely from the ground, and carried him in struggling in his gripe like a child in its nurse's arms.

This last episode was enacted so quickly that the two negroes were carried into the cavern and gagged before the other pursuers came up. At the cave's mouth the whole of the men of the village shortly assembled with the king at their head. Thus far the excitement of the chase had led them; but now that the first burst of their rage was over, and they found themselves on the threshold of that haunted cavern, the fear of which had been an element in their training from infancy, they felt, no doubt, overawed by superstitious dread, and hesitated to enter, although most of them must have been convinced that the fugitives were there. Their fears increased as their anger abated, and they crowded round King Jambai, who seemed loath to take upon himself the honour of leader.

"They must have sought shelter here," said the king, pointing to the cavern and looking round with an assumption of boldness which he was evidently far from feeling. "Who among my warriors will follow me?"

"Perhaps the evil spirits have carried them away," suggested one of the sable crew.

"That is the word of a coward," cried the king, who, although somewhat timorous about spirits, was in reality a bold, brave man, and felt nettled that any of his warriors should show the white feather. "If evil spirits are there, our fetishman will drive them away. Let the doctor stand forth."

At that moment the doctor, worthy knave, must have wished in his inmost soul that he had remained quietly at home and left to warriors the task of capturing the fugitives, but there was no resisting the mandate of the king; besides, his honour and credit as a fetishman was at stake; moreover, no doubt he felt somewhat emboldened by the presence of such a large number of men--there were certainly several hundreds on the ground--so, all things considered, he thought it best to accept the post of leader with a good grace. Stepping quickly forward, he cried, "Let torches be brought, and I will lead the way."

A murmur of approbation ran through the crowd of blacks, who, like a flock of sheep, felt bold enough to follow a leader blindly.

While the consultation was going on outside, we were making hasty preparation for defending ourselves to the last extremity. Peterkin, in particular, was extremely active, and, to say truth, his actions surprised us not a little. I once or twice fancied that excitement had turned his brain. He first dressed up his head in a species of wild turban made of dried grass and tall sedgy leaves; then he put several patches of red and white earth on his black face, as well as on his body in various places, and fastened a number of loose pieces of rag, torn from a handkerchief, and bits of tattered leaves to his arms and legs in such a manner as to give him an extremely wild and dishevelled appearance. I must say that when his hasty toilet was completed he seemed to me the most horrible-looking demon I had ever conceived of. He next poured out nearly a whole flask of gunpowder on a ledge of rock, the edge of which was visible from the entrance to the cave, while the rock itself concealed him from view. Last of all, he took up the three cones of moistened gunpowder which the reader will remember he had made before we left the cave to attack the village. One of these he placed among the grass and branches on his head, the other two he held in his hands.

"Now, boys," he said, when all was ready, "all I have to ask of you is that you will stand by with matches, and when I give the word light the points of those three cones of gunpowder simultaneously and instantly, and leave me to finish the remainder of my part. Of course you will be prepared to back me up with your rifles if need be, but keep well out of sight at first."

We now saw the drift of our eccentric friend's intention, but for my part I felt little confidence in his success. The plan seemed altogether too wild and absurd. But our danger was imminent. No way of escape seemed possible, and it is wonderful how readily men will grasp at anything in the shape of a ruse or stratagem, no matter how silly or wild, that affords the most distant chance of escape from danger. Jack, too, I could see from the look of his face, put little faith in the plan; and I observed an expression on the countenance of our negro guide which seemed to indicate that his respect for Peterkin's wisdom was on the wane.

We had not to wait long. The doctor, with several torch-bearers, suddenly darted in with a shout, followed closely by the warriors, who yelled furiously, in order, no doubt, to keep up their courage.

Alarmed by such an unusual hubbub in their usually quiet domain, the bats came swooping from their holes in the walls by hundreds, and the torches were extinguished almost instantly. The savages who were near the entrance drew back in haste; those who had entered stood rooted to the spot in terror.

"Now!" whispered Peterkin eagerly.

We struck our lights at once and applied them to the points of the gunpowder cones, which instantly began to spout forth a shower of sparks with great violence. Peterkin darted out from behind the rock with a yell so appalling that we ourselves were startled by it, having forgotten that it formed an element in his plan. In passing he allowed a few sparks to fall on the heap of powder, which exploded with so bright a flame that the whole cavern was illuminated for an instant. It also set fire to the ragged scraps with which Peterkin had decked himself out--a result which had neither been intended nor anticipated-- so that he rushed towards the mouth of the cave howling with pain as well as with a desire to scare the savages.

The effect of this apparition was tremendous. The negroes turned and crushed through the narrow entrance screaming and shrieking with terror. The bats, no less alarmed than the men, and half suffocated with smoke, fled out of the cave like a whirlwind, flapping their wings on the heads of the negroes in their flight, and adding, if that were possible, to their consternation. The negroes ran as never men ran before, tumbling over each other in their mad haste, dashing against trees and crashing through bushes in their terror, while Peterkin stood leaping in the cave's mouth, smoking and blazing and spurting, and unable to contain himself, giving vent to prolonged peals of demoniacal laughter. Had the laugh been that of negroes it might have been recognised; but Peterkin's was the loud, violent, British guffaw, which, I make no doubt, was deemed by them worthy of the fiends of the haunted cave, and served to spur them on to still greater rapidity in their wild career.

Returning into the cave's innermost recess, we lighted one of the torches dropped by the savages, and placing it in a sort of natural niche, seated ourselves on several pieces of rock to rest.

Our first act was to look earnestly in each other's faces; our next to burst into peals of laughter.

"I say, comrades," I exclaimed, checking myself, "don't we run some risk in giving vent to our feelings so freely?"

"No fear," cried Peterkin, who was still smoking a little from unextinguished sparks. "There is not a man in the whole crew who will draw rein till he is sitting, with the teeth still chattering in his head, at his own fireside. I never saw men in such a fright since I was born. Depend upon it, we are safe enough here from this day forth.-- Don't you think so, Mak?"

Our guide, who was now trying to reassure his trembling bride, turned, with a broad grin on his sable countenance, and said--

"Safe? ho! yis, massa. Dere not be a man as'll come to dis yere cuvern for de nix tree hun'r year or more. Massa Peterkin be de most horriboble ghost dey ever did saw, an' no mistake. But, massas, we mus' go 'way quick an' git to our camp, for de king sure to go dere an' see if you no hab someting to do wid it all. Him's a bery clebber king, am Jambai--bery clebber; him's no be bughummed bery easy."

"Humbugged, you mean," said Jack, laughing. "You're right, Mak; we must set off at once. But what are we to do with poor Okandaga, now that we have got her?"

This was indeed a puzzling question. It was impossible to take her to our camp and account to the negroes for her appearance in a satisfactory manner; besides, if Jambai took it into his head to pursue us, in order to ascertain whether we had had anything to do with the rescue, our case would be hopeless. It was equally impossible to leave her where she was, and to let her try to make her escape through the woods alone was not to be thought of. While we pondered this dilemma an idea occurred to me.

"It seems to me," said I, "that men are seldom, perhaps never, thrown into a danger or difficulty in this world without some way of escape being opened up, which, if they will but grasp at it promptly, will conduct them at last out of their perplexities. Now, it has just occurred to me that, since everything else seems to be impossible, we might send Okandaga into the woods, with Makarooroo to guide and defend her and to hunt for her. Let them travel in a line parallel with the river route which we intend to follow. Each night Mak will make a secure shelter for her, and then return to our camp as if he had come in from hunting. Each morning he will set off again into the woods as if to hunt, rejoin Okandaga; and thus we will journey together, as it were, and when we reach the next tribe of natives we will leave the girl in their charge until we return from the gorilla country. What do you think of that plan?"

"Not a bad one," replied Jack; "but if Mak is away all day, what are we to do for an interpreter?"

"Make him describe to us and to the men the day's route before leaving us," suggested Peterkin; "and as for the talking, we can manage that well enough for all needful purposes by a mixture of the few phrases we know with signs."

In the excitement of this whole affair we had totally forgotten our two prisoners, who lay not far from us on the ground, gagged and pinioned. We were now reminded of their presence rather abruptly. We must have secured their fastenings badly, for during the time we were conversing they managed to free themselves, and made a sudden dash past us. Jack's eye fortunately caught sight of them in time. He sprang up, rushed at the one nearest him, and throwing out his foot as he passed, tripped him up. It chanced that at that spot there was a deep hole in the floor of the cavern. Into this the poor wretch plunged head first, and he was killed on the spot. Meanwhile, the other gained the outlet of the cave, and had almost escaped into the forest, when Makarooroo darted after him with the speed of an antelope. In a few seconds we heard a cry, and shortly after our guide returned with his knife clotted with blood. He had overtaken and slain the other negro.

I cannot convey to the reader the horror that filled me and my two companions at this unexpected and melancholy termination of the affair. Yet we felt that we were guiltless of rashly spilling human blood, for Jack had no intention of killing the poor negro whom he tripped up; and as to the other, we could not have prevented our guide from doing what he did. He himself deemed it justifiable, and said that if that man had escaped to the village, and told who it was that frightened them out of the cave, they would certainly have come back and murdered us all. There was truth in this. Still we could not but feel overwhelmed with sadness at the incident.

We were now doubly anxious to get away from this cave, so we rapidly finished the discussion of our plan, and Jack arranged that he should accompany what may be termed the overland part of our expedition. This settled, we washed the charcoal off our persons, with the exception of that on our faces, having been advised by King Jambai himself to hunt with black faces, as wild animals were quicker to perceive our white skins than their black ones. Then we resumed our garments, and quitting the haunted cavern, set out on our return journey to the camp.

CHAPTER EIGHT.

PETERKIN DISTINGUISHES HIMSELF, AND OKANDAGA IS DISPOSED OF, ETCETERA.

When within about three miles of the place where our men had been ordered to haul the canoe out of the water and make the camp, we came to a halt and prepared a spot for Okandaga to spend an hour or two in sleep. The poor creature was terribly exhausted. We selected a very sequestered place in a rocky piece of ground, where the light of the small fire we kindled, in order to cook her some supper, could not be seen by any one who might chance to pass by that way.

Jack remained with her, but the guide went on with us, in order to give instructions to our men, who, when we arrived, seemed much surprised that we had made such a bad hunt during the night. Having pointed out our route, Makarooroo then left us, and we lay down to obtain a few hours' repose.

We had not lain more than an hour when one of our men awoke us, saying that it was time to start; so we rose, very unwillingly, and embarked.

"I say, Ralph," observed Peterkin, as we glided up the stream, which in this place was narrow and sluggish, "isn't it strange that mankind, as a rule, with very few exceptions, should so greatly dislike getting up in the morning?"

"It is rather curious, no doubt. But I suspect we have ourselves to thank for the disinclination. If we did not sit up so late at night we should not feel the indisposition to rise so strong upon us in the morning."

"There you are quite wrong, Ralph. I always find that the sooner I go to bed the later I am in getting up. The fact is, I've tried every method of rousing myself, and without success. And yet I can say conscientiously that I am desirous of improving; for when at sea I used to have my cot slung at the head with a block-tackle, and I got one of the middies to come when the watch was changed and lower me, so that my head lay on the deck below, and my feet pointed to the beams above. And would you believe it, I got so accustomed to this at last that, when desperately sleepy, I used to hold on in that position for a few minutes, and secure a short nap during the process of suffocation with blood to the head."

"You must indeed have been incorrigible," said I, laughing. "Nevertheless, I feel assured that the want of will lies at the root of the evil."

"Of course you do," retorted Peterkin testily; "people always say that when I try to defend myself."

"Is it not probable that people always say that just because they feel that there is truth in the remark?"

"Humph!" ejaculated my friend.

"Besides," I continued, "our success in battling with the evil tendencies of our natures depends often very much on the manner in which we make the attack. I have pondered this subject deeply, and have come to the conclusion that there is a certain moment in the awaking hour of each day which if seized and improved gains for us the victory. You know Shakespeare's judicious remark--`There is a tide in the affairs of men which, taken at the flood, leads on to fortune,' or something to that effect. I never feel quite sure of the literal correctness of my quotations, although I am generally certain as to the substance. Well, there is a tide also in the affair of getting up in the morning, and its flood-point is the precise instant when you recover consciousness. At that moment every one, I believe, has moral courage to leap violently out of bed; but let that moment pass, and you sink supinely back, if not to sleep, at least into a desperate condition of unconquerable lethargy."

"You may be very correct in your reasoning," returned Peterkin; "but not having pondered that subject quite so deeply as you seem to have done, I shall modestly refrain from discussing it. Meanwhile I will go ashore, and stalk yonder duck which floats so comfortably and lazily in the cove just beyond the point ahead of us, that I think it must be in the condition of one who, having missed the flood-tide you have just referred to, is revelling in the luxury of its second nap.--Ho, you ebony-faced scoundrel!" he added, turning to the negro who steered our canoe; "shove ashore, like a good fellow.--Come, Ralph, lend me your fowling-piece, and do you carry my big rifle. There is nothing so good for breakfast as a fat duck killed and roasted before it has had time to cool."

"And here is a capital spot on which to breakfast," said I, as we landed.

"First-rate. Now then, follow me, and mind your muzzle. Better put the rifle over your shoulder, Ralph, so that if it does go off it may hit the sun or one of the stars. A six-ounce ball in one's spine is not a pleasant companion in a hunting expedition."

"But," retorted I, "you forget that I am particularly careful. I always carry my piece on half-cock, and never put my finger on the trigger."

"Indeed: not even when you pull it?"

"Of course when I am about to fire; but you know well enough what I mean."

"Hush, Ralph! we must keep silence now and step lightly."

In a few minutes we had gained the clump of bushes close behind which the duck lay; and Peterkin, going down on all fours, crept forward to get a shot. I followed him in the same manner, and when he stopped to take a deliberate aim, I crept up alongside. The duck had heard our approach, and was swimming about in a somewhat agitated manner among the tall reeds, so that my companion made one or two unsuccessful attempts to take aim.

"What an aggravating thing!" exclaimed Peterkin in a whisper.

At that moment I happened to cast my eyes across the river, and the reader may judge of my surprise when I beheld two elephants standing among the trees. They stood so silently and so motionless, and were so like in colour to the surrounding foliage, that we had actually approached to within about thirty yards without observing them. I touched Peterkin on the shoulder, and pointed to them without saying a word. The expression of amazement that instantly overspread his features showed that he also saw them.

"The rifle, Ralph," he said, in a low, excited whisper.

I handed it to him. With careful deliberation he took aim, and fired at the animal nearest to us. The heavy ball entered its huge body just behind the shoulder. Both elephants tossed up their trunks, and elevating their great ears they dashed furiously into the bush; but the one that had been hit, after plunging head foremost down a low bank fell to the ground with a heavy crash, quite dead.

It was a splendid shot. The natives, who almost immediately after came up screaming with delight, could scarcely believe their eyes. They dashed across the river in the canoe, while some of them, regardless of the alligators that might be hidden there, sprang into the water and swam over.

"I'm sorry we did not get the duck, however," observed Peterkin, as we returned to the place where we had left the canoe. "Elephant meat is coarse, nasty stuff, and totally unfit for civilised mouths, though these niggers seem to relish it amazingly."

"You forget the baked foot," said I.

"Well, so I did. It was pretty good, certainly; but that's the only part o' the brute that's fit to eat."

Soon after this the canoe came back and took us over the river; and we breakfasted on the side where the elephant had fallen, in order to allow the natives to cut off such portions of the meat as they required, and to secure the tusks. Then we continued our journey, and at night encamped near a grove of palm-trees which Makarooroo had described to us, and where we were soon joined by him and Jack, who told us that he had got on well, during the day--that he had shot an antelope, and had seen a zebra and a rhinoceros, besides a variety of smaller game. He also told us that Okandaga was encamped in a place of safety a few miles to the right of our position, and that she had stood the journey well.

I was much interested by Jack's account of the zebra and the rhinoceros, specimens of both of which animals I had seen in menageries, and felt disposed to change places with him on the march; but reflecting that he was much more likely than I successfully to hunt anything he might pursue, I made up my mind to remain by the canoe.

Thus we travelled for several days without anything particular occurring, and at length arrived at a native village which lay on the banks of a noble stream.

Here Makarooroo introduced us to Mbango the chief, a fine-looking and good-natured negro, who received us most hospitably, supplied us with food, and urged us to remain and hunt with his people. This, however, we declined to do, telling our entertainer that we had come to his country for the purpose of shooting that wonderful animal the gorilla, but assuring him that we would come back without fail if we should be spared. We further assured him on this head by proposing to leave in his charge a woman for whom we had a great respect and love, and whom we made him promise faithfully to take care of till we returned.

Peterkin, who soon gave them a specimen of his powers as a marksman, and contrived in other ways to fill the minds of the chief and his people with a very exalted idea of his powers both of body and intellect, endeavoured to make assurance doubly sure by working on their superstitious fears.

"Tell Mbango," said he to our guide, "that though we be small in numbers we are very powerful; that we can do deeds" (here he became awfully solemn and mysterious) "such as no black man ever conceived of; and that if a hair of the head of Okandaga is hurt, we will on our return--"

Instead of completing the sentence, Peterkin started up, threw himself into violent contortions, rolled his eyes in a fearful manner, and, in short, gave the chief and his people to understand that something quite indescribable and unutterably terrible would be the result of their playing us false.

"Send for Njamie," said Mbango to one of his retainers.

Njamie, who was the chief's principal wife, soon appeared. She led a sturdy little boy by the hand. He was her only son, and a very fine little fellow, despite the blackness of his skin and his almost total want of clothing.

To this woman Mbango gave Okandaga in charge, directing her in our presence how to care for her, and assuring her of the most terrible punishment should anything befall the woman committed to her care.

Njamie was a mild, agreeable woman. She had more modesty of demeanour and humility of aspect than the most of the women of her tribe whom we happened to see, so that we felt disposed to believe that Okandaga was placed in as safe keeping as it was possible for us to provide for her in our circumstances. Even Makarooroo appeared to be quite at ease in his mind; and it was evidently with a relieved breast and a light heart that he bade adieu to his bride, and started along with us on the following day on our journey into the deeper recesses of the wilderness.

Before entering upon these transactions with the people of this village, we took care to keep our crew in total ignorance of what passed by sending them on in advance with the canoe under Jack's care, a few hours before we brought Okandaga into the village, or even made mention of her existence; and we secured their ready obedience to our orders, and total indifference as to our motives in these incomprehensible actions, by giving them each a few inches of tobacco--a gift which rendered them supremely happy.

One day, about a week after the events above narrated, we met with an adventure which well-nigh cost Jack his life, but which ultimately resulted in an important change in our manner of travelling. We were traversing an extremely beautiful country with the goods on our shoulders, having, in consequence of the increasing turbulence of the river as well as its change of direction, been compelled to abandon our canoe, and cut across the country in as straight a line as its nature would permit. But this was not easy, for the grass, which was bright green, was so long as to reach sometimes higher than our shoulders.

In this species of country Jack's towering height really became of great use, enabling him frequently to walk along with his head above the surrounding herbage, while we were compelled to grope along, ignorant of all that was around us save the tall grass at our sides. Occasionally, however, we came upon more open ground, where the grass was short, and then we enjoyed the lovely scenery to the full. We met with a great variety of new plants and trees in this region. Many of the latter were festooned with wild vines and other climbing plants. Among others, I saw several specimens of that curious and interesting tree the banyan, with its drop-shoots in every state of growth--some beginning to point towards the earth, in which they were ultimately destined to take root; some more than half-way down; while others were already fixed, forming stout pillars to their parent branches-- thus, as it were, on reaching maturity, rendering that support which it is the glory as well as the privilege of youth to accord to age. Besides these, there were wild dates and palmyra trees, and many others too numerous to mention, but the peculiar characteristics of which I carefully jotted down in my note-book. Many small water-courses were crossed, in some of which Mak pointed out a number of holes, which he said were made by elephants wading in them. He also told us that several mud-pools, which seemed to have been recently and violently stirred up, were caused by the wallowing of the rhinoceros; so we kept at all times a sharp lookout for a shot.

Lions were also numerous in this neighbourhood, and we constantly heard them roaring at night, but seldom saw them during our march.

Well, as I have already remarked, one day we were travelling somewhat slowly through the long grass of this country, when, feeling oppressed by the heat, as well as somewhat fatigued with my load, I called to Jack, who was in advance, to stop for a few minutes to rest.

"Most willingly," he replied, throwing down his load, and wiping away the perspiration which stood in large drops on his brow. "I was on the point of calling a halt when you spoke.--How do you get on down there, Peterkin?"

Our friend, who had seated himself on the bale he had been carrying, and seemed to be excessively hot, looked up with a comical expression of countenance, and replied--

"Pretty well, thank'ee. How do you get on up there?"

"Oh, capitally. There's such a nice cool breeze blowing, I'm quite sorry that I cannot send a little of it down."

"Don't distress yourself, my dear fellow; I'll come up to snuff it."

So saying, Peterkin sprang nimbly upon Jack's shoulders, and began to gaze round him.

"I say, Peterkin," said Jack, "why are you a very clever fellow just now?"

"Don't know," replied Peterkin. "I give it up at once. Always do. Never could guess a riddle in all my life."

"Because," said Jack, "you're `up to snuff.'"

"Oh, oh! that certainly deserves a pinch; so there's for you."

Jack uttered a roar, and tossed Peterkin off his shoulders, on receiving the punishment.

"Shabby fellow!" cried Peterkin, rubbing his head. "But, I say, do let me up again. I thought, just as you dropped me, that I saw a place where the grass is short. Ay, there it is, fifty yards or so ahead of us, with a palmyra tree on it. Come, let us go rest there, for I confess that I feel somewhat smothered in this long grass."

We took up our packs immediately, and carried them to the spot indicated, which we found almost free from long grass. Here we lay down to enjoy the delightful shade of the tree, and the magnificent view of the country around us. Our negroes also seemed to enjoy the shade, but they were evidently not nearly so much oppressed with the heat as we were, which was very natural. They seemed to have no perception of the beautiful in nature, however, although they appreciated fully the agreeable influences by which they were surrounded.

While I lay at the foot of that tree, pondering this subject, I observed a very strange-looking insect engaged in a very curious kind of occupation. Peterkin's eye caught sight of it at the same instant with mine.

"Hollo! Jack, look here!" he cried in a whisper. "I declare, here's a beast been and shoved its head into a hole, and converted its tail into a trap!"

We all three lay down as quietly as possible, and I could not but smile when I thought of the literal correctness of my friend's quaint description of what we saw.

The insect was a species of ant-eater. It was about an inch and a quarter long, as thick as a crow-quill, and covered with black hair. It put its head into a little hole in the ground, and quivered its tail rapidly. The ants, which seemed to be filled with curiosity at this peculiar sight, went near to see what the strange thing could be; and no sooner did one come within the range of the forceps on the insect's tail, than it was snapped up.

"Now, that is the most original trapper I ever did see or hear of," remarked Peterkin, with a broad grin. "I've seen many things in my travels, but I never expected to meet with a beast that could catch others by merely wagging its tail."

"You forget the hunters of North America," said Jack, "who entice little antelopes towards them by merely wagging a bit of rag on the end of a ramrod."

"I forget nothing of the sort," retorted Peterkin. "Wagging a ramrod is not wagging a tail. Besides, I spoke of beasts doing it; men are not beasts."

"Then I hold you self-convicted, my boy," exclaimed Jack; "for you have often called me a beast."

"By no means, Jack. I am not self-convicted, but quite correct, as I can prove to the satisfaction of any one who isn't a philosopher. You never can prove anything to a philosopher."

"Prove it, then."

"I will. Isn't a monkey a beast?"

"Certainly."

"Isn't a gorilla a monkey?"

"No doubt it is."

"And aren't you a gorilla?"

"I say, lads, it's time to be going," cried Jack, with a laugh, as he rose and resumed his load.

At that moment Mak uttered an exclamation, and pointed towards a particular spot in the plain before us, where, close by a clump of trees, we saw the graceful head and neck and part of the shoulders of a giraffe. We were naturally much excited at the sight, this being the first we had fallen in with.

"You'd better go after it," said Jack to Peterkin, "and take Mak with you."

"I'd rather you'd go yourself," replied Peterkin; "for, to say truth, I'm pretty well knocked up to-day. I don't know how it is--one day one feels made of iron, as if nothing could tire one; and the next, one feels quite weak and spiritless."

"Well, I'll go; but I shall not take any one with me.--Take observation of the sun, Mak, and keep a straight course as you are now going until night. D'ye see yonder ridge?"

"Yes, massa."

"Then hold on direct for that, and encamp there. I'll not be long behind you, and hope to bring you a giraffe steak for supper."

We endeavoured to dissuade Jack from going out alone, but he said truly that his load distributed among us all was quite sufficient, without adding to it by taking away another member of the party. Thus we parted; but I felt a strange feeling of depression, a kind of foreboding of evil, which I could not shake off, despite my utmost efforts. Peterkin, too, was unusually silent, and I could not avoid seeing that he felt more anxiety on account of Jack's rashness than he was willing to allow. Our friend took with him one of our large-bore rifles, and a double-barrel of smaller bore slung at his back.

Shortly after parting with him, we descried an ostrich feeding in the plain before us. I had long desired to meet with a specimen of this gigantic bird in its native wilds, and Peterkin was equally anxious to get a shot at it; so we called a halt, and prepared to stalk it. We were aware that the ostrich is a very silly and very timid bird, but not being aware of the best method of hunting it, we asked Makarooroo to explain how he was in the habit of doing it.

"You mus' know," he began, "dat bird hims be a mos' ex'roroninary beast. When hims run hims go fasterer dan--oh! it be dumpossobable for say how much fast hims go. You no can see him's legs; dey go same as legs ob leetle bird. But hims be horrobably stupid. Suppose he see you far, far away, goin' to de wind'ard ob him, he no run 'way to leeward; hims tink you wants to get round him, so off him start to git past you, and before hims pass he sometimes come close 'nuff to be shooted or speared. Me hab spear him dat way, but him's awful differcult to git at for all dat."

"Well then, Mak, after that lucid explanation, what d'you propose that we should do?" inquired Peterkin, examining the locks of his rifle.

"Me pruppose dat you go far ober dere, Massa Ralph go not jist so far, and me go to de wind'ard and gib him fright."

Acting upon this advice, we proceeded cautiously to the several spots indicated, and our guide set off towards an exposed place, where he intended to show himself. In a few minutes we observed the gigantic bird look up in alarm, and then we saw Makarooroo running like a deer over the plain. The ostrich instantly rushed off madly at full speed, not, as might have been expected, in a contrary direction, or towards any place of shelter, but simply, as it appeared to me, with no other end in view than that of getting to windward of his supposed enemy. I observed that he took a direction which would quickly bring him within range of my companion's rifle, but I was so amazed at the speed with which he ran that I could think of nothing else.

Every one knows that the ostrich has nothing worthy of the name of wings--merely a small tuft of feathers at each side, with which he cannot make even an attempt to fly; but every one does not know, probably, that with his stout and long legs he can pass over the ground nearly at the ordinary speed of a locomotive engine. I proved this to my own satisfaction by taking accurate observation. On first observing the tremendous speed at which he was going, I seized my note-book, and pulling out my watch, endeavoured to count the number of steps he took in a minute. This, however, I found was totally impossible; for his legs, big though they were, went so fast that I could no more count them than I could count the spokes of a carriage-wheel. I observed, however, that there were two bushes on the plain in the direction of his flight, which he would soon have to pass. I therefore laid down my note-book and rifle, and stood with my watch in hand, ready to note the precise instants at which he should pass the first and second. By afterwards counting the number of footsteps on the ground between the bushes, and comparing the result with the time occupied in passing between the two, I thus proposed to myself to ascertain his rate of speed.

Scarcely had I conceived this idea when the bird passed the first bush, and I glanced at my watch; then he passed the second, and I glanced again. Thus I noted that he took exactly ten seconds to pass from one bush to the other. While I was in the act of jotting this down I heard the report of Peterkin's rifle, and looking up hastily, saw the tail-feathers of the ostrich knocked into the air, but the bird itself passed on uninjured. I was deeply mortified at this failure, and all the more so that, from past experience, I had been led to believe that my friend never missed his mark. Hurrying up, I exclaimed--

"Why, my dear fellow, what can have come over you?"

Poor Peterkin seemed really quite distressed; he looked quite humbled at first.

"Ah!" said he, "it's all very well for you to say, `What has come over you?' but you ought to make allowance for a man who has carried a heavy load all the forenoon. Besides, he was almost beyond range. Moreover, although I have hunted a good deal, I really have not been in the habit of firing at animal locomotives under full steam. Did you ever see such a slapping pace and such an outrageous pair of legs, Ralph?"

"Never," said I. "But come with me to yonder bushes. I'm going to make a calculation."

"What's a calcoolashun?" inquired our guide, who came up at that moment, panting violently.

"It's a summation, case of counting up one, two, three, etcetera--and may be multiplying, subtracting, and dividing into the bargain."

"Ho! dat's what me been do at de missionary school."

"Exactly; but what sort of calculation Ralph means to undertake at present I know not. Perhaps he's going to try to find out whether, if we were to run at the rate of six miles an hour till doomsday, in the wrong direction, there would be any chance of our ever sticking that ostrich's tail again on his big body. But come along; we shall see."

On reaching the spot I could scarcely believe my eyes. Each step this bird had taken measured fourteen feet in length! I always carried a rolled-up yard-measure about with me, which I applied to the steps, so that I could make no mistake. There were exactly thirty of those gigantic paces between the two bushes. This multiplied by six gave 180 steps, or 2,520 feet in one minute, which resulted in 151,200 feet, or 50,400 yards, or very nearly thirty miles in the hour.

"No wonder I only knocked his tail off," said Peterkin.

"On the contrary," said I, "the wonder is that under the circumstances you hit the bird at all."

On further examination of the place where we had seen the ostrich before it was alarmed, we ascertained that his ordinary walking pace varied from twenty to twenty-six inches in length.

After this unsuccessful hunt we returned to our comrades, and proceeded to the rendezvous where we expected to find Jack; but as he was not there, we concluded that he must have wandered farther than he intended, so, throwing down our packs, we set about preparing the camp and a good supper against his return. Gradually the sun began to sink low on the horizon; then he dipped below it, and the short twilight of those latitudes was rapidly merging into night; but Jack did not return, and the uneasiness which we had all along felt in regard to him increased so much that we could not refrain from showing it.

"I'll tell you what it is, Ralph," cried Peterkin, starting up suddenly: "I'm not going to sit here wasting the time when Jack may be in some desperate fix. I'll go and hunt for him."

"Me tink you right," said our guide; "dere is ebery sort ob ting here-- beasties and mans. P'raps Massa Jack am be kill."

I could not help shuddering at the bare idea of such a thing, so I at once seconded my companion's proposal, and resolved to accompany him.

"Take your double-barrel, Ralph, and I'll lend our spare big gun to Mak."

"But how are we to proceed? which way are we to go? I have not the most distant idea as to what direction we ought to go in our search."

"Leave that to Mak. He knows the ways o' the country best, and the probable route that Jack has taken. Are you ready?"

"Yes. Shall we take some brandy?"

"Ay; well thought of. He'll perhaps be the better of something of that sort if anything has befallen him. Now, then, let's go."

Leaving our men in charge of the camp, with strict injunctions to keep good watch and not allow the fires to go down, lest they should be attacked by lions, we three set forth on our nocturnal search. From time to time we stood still and shouted in a manner that would let our lost friend know that we were in search of him, should he be within earshot, but no answering cry came back to us; and we were beginning to despair, when we came upon the footprints of a man in the soft soil of a swampy spot we had to cross. It was a clear moonlight night, so that we could distinguish them perfectly.

"Ho!" exclaimed our guide, as he stooped to examine the marks.

"Well, Mak, what do you make of it?" inquired Peterkin anxiously.

Mak made no reply for a few seconds; then he rose, and said earnestly,

"Dat am Massa Jack's foot."

I confess that I was somewhat surprised at the air of confidence with which our guide made this statement; for after a most careful examination of the prints, which were exceedingly indistinct, I could discern nothing to indicate that they had been made by Jack.

"Are you sure, Mak?" asked Peterkin.

"Sartin sure, massa."

"Then push on as fast as you can."

Presently we came to a spot where the ground was harder and the prints more distinct.

"Ha! you're wrong, Mak," cried Peterkin, in a voice of disappointment, as he stooped to examine the footsteps again. "Here we have the print of a naked foot; Jack wore shoes. And, what's this? blood!"

"Yis, massa, me know dat Massa Jack hab shoes. But dat be him's foot for all dat, and him's hurt somehow for certain."

The reader may imagine our state of mind on making this discovery. Without uttering another word, we quickened our pace into a smart run, keeping closely in the track of Jack's steps. Soon we observed that these deviated from side to side in an extraordinary manner, as if the person who made them had been unable to walk straight. In a few minutes more we came on the footprints of a rhinoceros--a sight which still further increased our alarm. On coming out from among a clump of low bushes that skirted the edge of a small plain, we observed a dark object lying on the ground about fifty yards distant from us. I almost sank down with an undefinable feeling of dread on beholding this.

We held our rifles in readiness as we approached it at a quick pace, for we knew not whether it was not a wild animal which might spring upon us the moment we came close enough. But a few seconds dispelled our dread of such an attack and confirmed our worst fears, for there, in a pool of blood, lay Jack's manly form. The face was upturned, and the moon, which shone full upon it, showed that it was pale as death and covered with blood. His clothes were rent and dishevelled and covered with dust, as if he had struggled hard with some powerful foe, and all round the spot were footprints of a rhinoceros, revealing too clearly the character of the terrible monster with which our friend had engaged in unequal conflict.

Peterkin darted forward, tore open Jack's shirt at the breast, and laid his hand upon his heart.

"Thank God," he muttered, in a low, subdued tone, "he's not dead! Quick, Ralph--the brandy-flask."

I instantly poured a little of the spirit into the silver cup attached to the flask, and handed it to Peterkin, who, after moistening Jack's lips, began assiduously to rub his chest and forehead with brandy. Kneeling down by his side I assisted him, while I applied some to his feet. While we were thus engaged we observed that our poor friend's arms and chest had received several severe bruises and some slight wounds, and we also discovered a terrible gash in his right thigh which had evidently been made by the formidable horn of the rhinoceros. This, and the other wounds which were still bleeding pretty freely, we stanched and bound up, and our exertions were at length rewarded by the sight of a faint tinge of colour returning to Jack's cheeks. Presently his eyes quivered, and heaving a short, broken sigh, he looked up.

"Where am I, eh? Why, what's wrong? what has happened?" he asked faintly, in a tone of surprise.

"All right, old boy. Here, take a swig of this, you abominable gorilla," said Peterkin, holding the brandy-flask to his mouth, while one or two tears of joy rolled down his cheeks.

Jack drank, and rallied a little.

"I've been ill, I see," he said gently. "Ah! I remember now. I've been hurt-- the rhinoceros; eh, have you killed it? I gave it a good shot. It must have been mortal, I think."

"Whether you've killed it or not I cannot tell," said I, taking off my coat and putting it under Jack's head for a pillow, "but it has pretty nearly killed you. Do you feel worse, Jack?"

I asked this in some alarm, observing that he had turned deadly pale again.

"He's fainted, man; out o' the way!" cried Peterkin, as he applied the brandy again to his lips and temples.

In a few seconds Jack again rallied.

"Now, Mak, bestir yourself," cried Peterkin, throwing off his coat. "Cut down two stout poles, and we'll make some sort of litter to carry him on."

"I say, Ralph," whispered Jack faintly, "do look to my wounds and see that they are all tightly bound up. I can't afford to lose another drop of blood. It's almost all drained away, I believe."

While I examined my friend's wounds and readjusted the bandages, my companions cut down two poles. These we laid on the ground parallel to each other and about two feet apart, and across them laid our three coats, which we fastened in a rough fashion by means of some strong cords which I fortunately happened to have with me. On this rude litter we laid our companion, and raised him on our shoulders. Peterkin and I walked in rear, each supporting one of the poles; while Makarooroo, being the stoutest of the three, supported the entire weight of the other ends on his broad shoulders. Jack bore the moving better than we had expected, so that we entertained sanguine hopes that no bones were broken, but that loss of blood was all he had to suffer from.

Thus slowly and with much difficulty we bore our wounded comrade to the camp.

CHAPTER NINE.

I DISCOVER A CURIOUS INSECT, AND PETERKIN TAKES A STRANGE FLIGHT.

It happened most fortunately at this time that we were within a short day's journey of a native village, to which, after mature consideration, we determined to convey Jack, and remain there until he should be sufficiently recovered to permit of our resuming our journey. Hitherto we had studiously avoided the villages that lay in our route, feeling indisposed to encounter unnecessarily the risk of being inhospitably received--perhaps even robbed of our goods, if nothing worse should befall us. There was, however, no other alternative now; for Jack's wounds were very severe, and the amount of blood lost by him was so great that he was as weak as a child. Happily, no bones were broken, so we felt sanguine that by careful nursing for a few weeks we should get him set firmly upon his legs again.

On the following morning we set forth on our journey, and towards evening reached the village, which was situated on the banks of a small stream, in the midst of a beautiful country composed of mingled plain and woodland.

It chanced that the chief of this village was connected by marriage with King Jambai--a most fortunate circumstance for us, as it ensured our being hospitably received. The chief came out to meet us riding on the shoulders of a slave, who, although a much smaller man than his master, seemed to support his load with much case. Probably habit had strengthened him for his special work. A large hut was set apart for our accommodation; a dish of yams, a roast monkey, and a couple of fowls were sent to us soon after our arrival, and, in short, we experienced the kindest possible reception.

None of the natives of this village had ever seen a white face in their lives, and, as may well be imagined, their curiosity and amazement were unbounded. The people came constantly crowding round our hut, remaining, however, at a respectful distance, and gazed at us until I began to fear they would never go away.

Here we remained for three weeks, during which time Jack's wounds healed up, and his strength returned rapidly. Peterkin and I employed ourselves in alternately tending our comrade, and in scouring the neighbouring woods and plains in search of wild animals.

As we were now approaching the country of the gorilla--although, indeed, it was still far distant--our minds began to run more upon that terrible creature than used to be the case; and our desire to fall in with it was increased by the strange accounts of its habits and its tremendous power that we received from the natives of this village, some of whom had crossed the desert and actually met with the gorilla face to face. More than once, while out hunting, I have been so taken up with this subject that I have been on the point of shooting a native who appeared unexpectedly before me, under the impression that he was a specimen of the animal on which my thoughts had been fixed.

One day about a week after our arrival, as I was sitting at the side of Jack's couch relating to him the incidents of a hunt after a buffalo that Makarooroo and I had had the day before, Peterkin entered with a swaggering gait, and setting his rifle down in a corner, flung himself on the pile of skins that formed his couch.

"I'll tell you what it is," said he, with the look and tone of a man who feels that he has been unwarrantably misled--"I don't believe there's such a beast as a gorilla at all; now, that's a fact."

There was something so confident and emphatic in my comrade's manner that, despite my well-grounded belief on that point, I felt a sinking at the heart. The bare possibility that, after all our trouble and toil and suffering in penetrating thus far towards the land which he is said to inhabit, we should find that there really existed no such creature as the gorilla was too terrible to think upon.

"Peterkin," said I anxiously, "what do you mean?"

"I mean," replied he slowly, "that Jack is the only living specimen of the gorilla in Africa."

"Come, now, I see you are jesting."

"Am I?" cried Peterkin savagely--"jesting, eh? That means expressing thoughts and opinions which are not to be understood literally. Oh, I would that I were sure that I am jesting! Ralph, it's my belief, I tell you, that the gorilla is a regular sell--a great, big, unnatural hairy do!"

"But I saw the skeleton of one in London."

"I don't care for that. You may have been deceived, humbugged. Perhaps it was a compound of the bones of a buffalo and a chimpanzee."

"Nay, that were impossible," said I quickly; "for no one pretending to have any knowledge of natural history and comparative anatomy could be so grossly deceived."

"What like was the skeleton, Ralph?" inquired Jack, who seemed to be rather amused by our conversation.

"It was nearly as tall as that of a medium-sized man--I should think about five feet seven or eight inches; but the amazing part about it was the immense size and thickness of its bones. Its shoulders were much broader than yours, Jack, and your chest is a mere child's compared with that of the specimen of the gorilla that I saw. Its legs were very short--much shorter than those of a man; but its arms were tremendous-- they were more than a foot longer than yours. In fact, if the brute's legs were in the same proportion to its body as are those of a man, it would be a giant of ten or eleven feet high. Or, to take another view of it, if you were to take a robust and properly proportioned giant of that height, and cut down his legs until he stood about the height of an ordinary man, that would be a gorilla."

"I don't believe it," cried Peterkin.

"Well, perhaps my simile is not quite so felicitous as--"

"I don't mean that," interrupted Peterkin; "I mean that I don't believe there's such a brute as a gorilla at all."

"Why, what has made you so sceptical?" inquired Jack.

"The nonsense that these niggers have been telling me, through the medium of Mak as an interpreter; that is what has made me sceptical. Only think, they say that a gorilla is so strong that he can lift a man by the nape of the neck clean off the ground with one of his hind feet! Yes, they say he is in the habit of sitting on the lower branches of trees in lonely dark parts of the wood watching for prey, and when a native chances to pass by close enough he puts down his hind foot, seizes the wretched man therewith, lifts him up into the tree, and quietly throttles him. They don't add whether or not he eats him afterwards, or whether he prefers him boiled or roasted. Now, I don't believe that."

"Neither do I," returned Jack; "nevertheless the fact that these fellows recount such wonderful stories at all, is, to some extent, evidence in favour of their existence: for in such a country as this, where so many wonderful and horrible animals exist, men are not naturally tempted to invent new creatures; it is sufficient to satisfy their craving for the marvellous that they should merely exaggerate what does already exist."

"Go to, you sophist! if what you say be true, and the gorilla turns out to be only an exaggerated chimpanzee or ring-tailed roarer, does not that come to the same thing as saying that there is no gorilla at all-- always, of course, excepting yourself?"

"Credit yourself with a punched head," said Jack, "and the account shall be balanced when I am sufficiently recovered to pay you off. Meanwhile, continue your account of what the niggers say about the gorilla."

Peterkin assumed a look of offended dignity as he replied--

"Without deigning any rejoinder to the utterly absurd and totally irrelevant matter contained in the preliminary sentences of your last remark, I pass on to observe that the natives of these wilds hold the opinion that there is one species of the gorilla which is the residence of the spirits of defunct niggers, and that these fellows are known by their unusual size and ferocity."

"Hold," cried I, "until I get out my note-book. Now, Peterkin, no fibs."

"Honour bright," said he, "I'll give it you just as I got it. These possessed brutes are never caught, and can't be killed. (I only hope I may get the chance to try whether that be true or not.) They often carry off natives into the woods, where they pull out their toe and finger nails by the roots and then let them go; and they are said to be uncommonly fond of sugar-cane, which they steal from the fields of the natives sometimes in a very daring manner."

"Is that all?" said I.

"All!" exclaimed my comrade. "How much more would you have? Do you suppose that the gorilla can do anything it likes--hang by its tail from the moon, or sit down on its nose and run round on its chin?"

"Massa Jack," said Makarooroo, entering the hut and interrupting our conversation at this point, "de chief hims tell to me for to tell to you dat w'en you's be fit for go-hid agin hims gib you cottle for sit upon."

"Cottle, Mak! what's cottle?" inquired Jack, with a puzzled look.

"Ho, massa, you know bery well; jist cottle--hoxes, you know."

"Indeed, I don't know," replied Jack, still more puzzled.

"I've no doubt," interposed Peterkin, "that he means cuttle, which is the short name for cuttle-fish, which, in such an inland place as this, must of course be hoaxes! But what do you mean, Mak? Describe the thing to us."

Mak scratched his woolly pate, as if he were quite unable to explain himself.

"O massas, you be most stoopid dis yer day. Cottle not a ting; hims am a beast, wid two horn an' one tail. Dere," said he, pointing with animation to a herd of cattle that grazed near our hut, "dat's cottle, or hoxes."

We all laughed at this proposal.

"What!" cried Jack, "does he mean us to ride upon `hoxes' as if they were horses?"

"Yis, massa, hims say dat. Hims hear long ago ob one missionary as hab do dat; so de chief he tink it bery good idea, an' hims try too, an' like it bery much; only hims fell off ebery tree steps an' a'most broke all de bones in him's body down to powder. But hims git up agin and fell hoff agin. Oh, hims like it bery much!"

"If we follow the chief's example," said I, laughing, "we shall scarcely be in a fit state to hunt gorillas at the end of our journey; but now I come to think of it, the plan seems to me not a bad one. You know a great part of our journey now lies over a comparatively desert country, where we shall be none the worse of a ride now and then on ox-back to relieve our limbs. I think the proposal merits consideration."

"Right, Ralph," said Jack.--"Go, Mak, and tell his majesty, or chieftainship, or his royal highness, with my compliments, that I am much obliged by the offer, and will consider it. Also give him this plug of tobacco; and see you don't curtail its dimensions before it leaves your hand, you rascal."

Our guide grinned as he left the hut to execute his mission, and we turned to converse on this new plan, which, the more we thought of it, seemed the more to grow in our estimation as most feasible.

"Now, lads, leave me," said Jack, with a sigh, after we had chatted for more than an hour. "If I am to go through all that our worthy host seems to have suffered, it behoves me to get my frame into a fit state to stand it. I shall therefore try to sleep."

So saying he turned round on his side, and we left him to his slumbers.

As it was still early in the afternoon, we two shouldered our rifles and strolled away into the woods, partly with the intention of taking a shot at anything that might chance to come in our way, but chiefly with the view of having a pleasant chat about our prospect of speedily reaching that goal of our ambition--the gorilla country.

"It seems to me," observed Peterkin, as we walked side by side over an open grassy and flower-speckled plain that lay about a couple of miles distant from the village--"it seems to me that we shall never reach this far-famed country."

"I have no doubt that we shall," said I; "but tell me, Peterkin, do you really doubt the existence of the gorilla?"

"Well, since you do put it to me so very seriously, I can scarce tell what I believe. The fact is, that I'm such a sceptical wretch by nature that I find it difficult to believe anything unless I see it."

I endeavoured to combat this very absurd state of mind in my companion by pointing out to him very clearly that if he were to act upon such a principle at all times, he would certainly disbelieve many of the commonest facts in nature, and give full credit, on the other hand, to the most outrageous absurdities.

"For instance," said I, "you would believe that every conjurer swallows fire, and smoke, and penknives, and rabbits, because you see him do it; and you would disbelieve the existence of the pyramids, because you don't happen to have seen them."

"Ralph," said my companion seriously, "don't go in too deep, else I shall be drowned!"

I was about to make some reply, when my attention was attracted by a very singular appearance of moisture at the foot of a fig-tree under which we were passing. Going up to it I found that there was a small puddle of clear water near the trunk. This occasioned me much surprise, for no rain had fallen in that district since our arrival, and probably there had been none for a long period before that. The ground everywhere, except in the large rivers and water-courses, was quite dry, insomuch that, as I have said, this little solitary pool (which was not much larger than my hand) occasioned us much surprise.

"How comes it there?" said I.

"That's more than I can tell," replied Peterkin. "Perhaps there's a small spring at the root of the tree."

"Perhaps there is," said I, searching carefully round the spot in all directions; but I found nothing to indicate the presence of a spring-- and, indeed, when I came to think of it, if there had been a spring there would also certainly have been a water-course leading from it. But such was not the case. Presently I observed a drop of water fall into the pool, and looking up, discovered that it fell from a cluster of insects that clung to a branch close over our heads.

I at once recognised this water-distilling insect as an old acquaintance. I had seen it before in England, although of a considerably smaller size than this African one. My companion also seemed to be acquainted with it, for he exclaimed--

"Ho! I know the fellow. He's what we used at home to call a `frog-hopper' after he got his wings, and a `cuckoo-spit' before that time; but these ones are six times the size of ours."

I was aware that there was some doubt among naturalists as to whence these insects procured the water they distilled. My own opinion, founded on observations made at this time, led me to think the greater part of the moisture is derived from the atmosphere, though, possibly, some of it may be procured by suction from the trees. I afterwards paid several visits to this tree, and found, by placing a vessel beneath them, that these insects distilled during a single night as much as three or four pints of water!

Turning from this interesting discovery, we were about to continue our walk, when we observed a buffalo bull feeding in the open plain, not more than five or six hundred yards off from us.

"Ha! Ralph, my boy," cried Peterkin enthusiastically, "here is metal more attractive! Follow me; we must make a detour in order to get to leeward of him."

We set off at a brisk pace, and I freely confess that, although the contemplation of the curious processes of the water-distilling insect afforded me deeper and more lasting enjoyment, the gush of excitement and eagerness that instantly followed the discovery of the wild buffalo bull enabled me thoroughly to understand the feeling that leads men-- especially the less contemplative among them--infinitely to prefer the pleasures of the chase to the calmer joys attendant upon the study of natural history.

At a later period that evening I had a discussion with my companions on that subject, when I stood up for the pursuit of scientific knowledge as being truly elevating and noble, while the pursuit of game was, to say the least of it, a species of pleasure more suited to the tastes and condition of the savage than of the civilised man.

To this Peterkin replied--having made a preliminary statement to the effect that I was a humbug--that a man's pluck was brought out and his nerves improved by the noble art of hunting, which was beautifully scientific in its details, and which had the effect of causing a man to act like a man and look like a man--not like a woman or a nincompoop, as was too often the case with scientific men.

Hereupon Jack announced it as his opinion that we were both wrong and both right; which elicited a cry of "Bravo!" from Peterkin. "For," said Jack, "what would the naturalist do without the hunter? His museums would be almost empty and his knowledge would be extremely limited. On the other hand, if there were no naturalists, the hunter--instead of being the hero who dares every imaginable species of danger, in order to procure specimens and furnish information that will add to the sum of human knowledge--would degenerate into the mere butcher, who supplies himself and his men with meat; or into the semi-murderer, who delights in shedding the blood of inferior animals. The fact is, that the naturalist and the hunter are indispensably necessary to each other--'both are best,' to use an old expression; and when both are combined in one, as in the case of the great American ornithologist Audubon, that is best of all."

"Betterer than both," suggested Peterkin.

But to return from this digression.

In less than quarter of an hour we gained a position well to leeward of the buffalo, which grazed quietly near the edge of the bushes, little dreaming of the enemies who were so cautiously approaching to work its destruction.

"Keep well in rear of me, Ralph," said Peterkin, as we halted behind a bush to examine our rifles. "I'll creep as near to him as I can, and if by any chance I should not kill him at the first shot, do you run up and hand me your gun."

Without waiting for a reply, my companion threw himself on his breast, and began to creep over the plain like a snake in the grass. He did this so well and so patiently that he reached to within forty yards of the bull without being discovered. Then he ceased to advance, and I saw his head and shoulders slowly emerge from among the grass, and presently his rifle appeared, and was slowly levelled. It was one of our large-bore single-barrelled rifles.

He lay in this position for at least two minutes, which seemed to me a quarter of an hour, so eager was I to see the creature fall. Suddenly I heard a sharp snap or crack. The bull heard it too, for it raised its huge head with a start. The cap of Peterkin's rifle had snapped, and I saw by his motions that he was endeavouring, with as little motion as possible, to replace it with another. But the bull caught sight of him, and uttering a terrific roar charged in an instant.

It is all very well for those who dwell at home in security to think they know what the charge of an infuriated buffalo bull is. Did they see it in reality, as I saw it at that time, tearing madly over the grass, foaming at the mouth, flashing at the eyes, tossing its tail, and bellowing hideously, they would have a very different idea from what they now have of the trials to which hunters' nerves are frequently exposed.

Peterkin had not time to cap. He leaped up, turned round, and ran for the woods at the top of his speed; but the bull was upon him in an instant.

Almost before I had time to realise what was occurring, I beheld my companion tossed high into the air. He turned a distinct somersault, and fell with a fearful crash into the centre of a small bush. I cannot recall my thoughts on witnessing this. I remember only experiencing a sharp pang of horror and feeling that Peterkin must certainly have been killed. But whatever my thoughts were they must have been rapid, for the time allowed me was short, as the bull turned sharp round after tossing Peterkin and rushed again towards the bush, evidently with the intention of completing the work of destruction.

Once again I experienced that strange and sudden change of feeling to which I have before referred. I felt a bounding sensation in my breast which tingled to my finger-ends. At the same time my head became clear and cool. I felt that Providence had placed the life of my friend in my hands. Darting forward in advance of the bush, I awaited the charge of the infuriated animal. On it came. I knew that I was not a sufficiently good shot to make sure of hitting it in the brain. I therefore allowed it to come within a yard of me, and then sprang lightly to one side. As it flew past, I never thought of taking aim or putting the piece to my shoulder, but I thrust the muzzle against its side and pulled both triggers at once.

From that moment consciousness forsook me, and I knew not what had occurred for some minutes after. The first object that met my confused vision when I again opened my eyes was Peterkin, who was seated close beside me on the body of the dead buffalo, examining some bloody scratches on the calf of his left leg. He had evidently been attempting to restore me to consciousness, for I observed that a wet handkerchief lay on my forehead. He muttered to himself as he examined his wounds--

"This comes of not looking to one's caps. Humph! I do believe that every bone in my body is--ah! here's another cut, two inches at least, and into the bone of course, to judge from the flow of blood. I wonder how much blood I can afford to lose without being floored altogether. Such a country! I wonder how high I went. I felt as if I'd got above the moon. Hollo, Ralph! better?"

I sat up as he said this, and looked at him earnestly.

"My dear Peterkin, then you're not killed after all."

"Not quite, but pretty near. If it had not been for that friendly bush I should have fared worse. It broke my fall completely, and I really believe that my worst hurts are a few scratches. But how are you, Ralph? Yours was a much more severe case than mine. You should hold your gun tighter, man, when you fire without putting it to your shoulder."

"How? why? what do you mean?"

"Simply this, that in consequence of your reckless manner of holding your rifle, it came back with such a slap on your chest that it floored you."

"This, then, accounts for the pain I feel in it. But come," said I, rising and shaking my limbs to make sure that no bones were broken; "we have reason to be very thankful we have escaped so easily. I made sure that you were killed when I saw you flying through the air."

"I always had a species of cat-luck about me," replied Peterkin, with a smile. "But now let us cut off a bit o' this fellow to take back with us for Jack's supper."

With some difficulty we succeeded in cutting out the buffalo's tongue by the root, and carried it back to the village, where, after displaying it as an evidence of our prowess, we had it cooked for supper.

The slight hurts that we had received at the time of this adventure were speedily cured, and about two weeks after that we were all well enough to resume our journey.

CHAPTER TEN.

WATER APPRECIATED--DESTRUCTIVE FILES, ETCETERA.

Our first start from the village where we had been entertained so hospitably and so long was productive of much amusement to ourselves and to the natives.

We had determined to accept of three oxen from the chief, and to ride these when we felt fatigued; but we thought it best to let our native porters carry our baggage on their shoulders, as they had hitherto done.

When the animals were led up to our hut, we could not refrain from laughing. They were three sturdy-looking dark-skinned oxen, with wicked-looking black eyes and very long horns.

"Now, Jack, do you get up first," said Peterkin, "and show us what we are to expect."

"Nay, lad; I am still entitled to be considered an invalid: so you must get up first, and not only so, but you must try them all, in order that I may be enabled to select the quietest."

"Upon my word, you are becoming despotic in your sickness, and you forget that it is but a short time since I came down from a journey to the sky, and that my poor bones are still tender. But here goes. I was born to be victimised, so I submit to the decrees of Fate."

Peterkin went up to one of the oxen and attempted to mount it; but the animal made a demonstration of an intention to gore him, and obstinately objected to this.

"Hold him tight, Mak," he cried, after several futile attempts to mount. "I was always good at leap-frog when a schoolboy; see if I don't bring my powers into play now."

So saying, he went behind the ox, took a short race and sprang with the agility of a monkey over its tail on to its back! The ox began to kick and sidle and plunge heavily on receiving this unexpected load; but its rider held on well, until it took it into its head to dart under a neighbouring tree, the lower branches of which swept him off and caused him to fall with a heavy plump to the ground.

"I told you so," he cried, rising with a rueful face, and rubbing himself as he limped forward. However, his pain was more than half affected, for the next minute he was on the back of another ox. This one also proved restive, but not so much so as the first. The third was a very quiet animal, so Jack appropriated it as his charger.

Having bade adieu to the chief and rubbed noses with him and with several of our friends in the village, we all three got upon our novel steeds and set forth. But we had not got away from the village more than a mile when the two restive oxen began to display a firm determination to get rid of their intolerable burden. Mine commenced to back and sidle, and Peterkin's made occasional darts forward, and then stopping suddenly, refused to budge a step. We lost all patience at last, and belaboured them soundly with twigs, the effect of which was to make them advance rather slowly, and evidently under protest.

"Look out for branches," cried Peterkin as we came up to a narrow belt of wood.

I had scarcely time to raise my head when I was swept off my seat and hurled to the ground by a large branch. Peterkin's attention was drawn to me, and his ox, as if aware of the fact, seized the opportunity to swerve violently to one side, thereby throwing its rider off. Both animals gave a bellow, as of triumph, erected their tails, and ran away. They were soon recaptured, however, by our negroes; and mounting once more, we belaboured them well and continued our journey. In course of time they became more reconciled to their duties; but I cannot say that I ever came to enjoy such riding, and all of us ultimately agreed that it was a most undesirable thing to journey on ox-back.

Thus we commenced our journey over this desert or plain of Africa, and at the end of many weeks found ourselves approaching that part of the country near the equator in which the gorilla is said to dwell. On the way we had many adventures, some of an amusing, some of a dangerous character, and I made many additions to my collection of animals, besides making a number of valuable and interesting notes in my journal; but all this I am constrained to pass over, in order to introduce my reader to those regions in which some of our most wonderful adventures occurred.

One or two things, however, I must not omit to mention.

In passing over the desert we suffered much from want of water. Frequently the poor oxen had to travel two or three days without tasting a drop, and their distress was so great that we more than once thought of turning them adrift at the first good watering-place we should come to, and proceed, as formerly, on foot; for we had all recovered our wonted vigour, and were quite capable of standing the fatigues of the journey as well as our men. But several times we had found the country destitute of game, and were reduced to the point of starvation; so we continued to keep the oxen, lest we should require them for food.

On one occasion we were wending our way slowly along the bed of what in the rainy season would become a large river, but which was now so thoroughly dry that we could not find even a small pool in which the oxen might slake their thirst. They had been several days absolutely without a drop of water, while we were reduced to a mouthful or two per man in the day. As we could not exist much longer without the life-giving fluid, Jack dismounted, and placing the load of one of the men on the ox's back, sent him off in advance to look for water. We had that morning seen the footprints of several animals which are so fond of water that they are never found at any great distance from some spot where it may be found. We therefore felt certain of falling in with it ere long.

About two hours afterwards our negro returned, saying that he had discovered a pool of rain-water, and showing the marks of mud on his knees in confirmation of the truth of what he said.

"Ask him if there's much of it, Mak," said Jack, as we crowded eagerly round the man.

"Hims say there be great plenty ob it--'nuff to tumble in."

Gladdened by this news we hastened forward. The oxen seemed to have scented the water from afar, for they gradually became more animated, and quickened their pace of their own accord, until they at last broke into a run. Peterkin and I soon outstripped our party, and quite enjoyed the gallop.

"There it is," cried my comrade joyfully, pointing to a gleaming pond in a hollow of the plain not two hundred yards off.

"Hurrah!" I shouted, unable to repress my delight at the sight.

The oxen rushed madly forward, and we found that they were away with us. No pulling at our rope-bridles had any effect on them. My companion, foreseeing what would happen, leaped nimbly off just as he reached the margin of the pond. I being unable to collect my thoughts for the emergency, held on. My steed rushed into the water up to the neck, and stumbling as he did so, threw me into the middle of the pond, out of which I scrambled amidst the laughter of the whole party, who came up almost as soon as the oxen, so eager were they to drink.

After appeasing our own thirst we stood looking at the oxen, and it really did our hearts good to see the poor thirsty creatures enjoy themselves so thoroughly. They stood sucking in the water as if they meant to drink up the whole pond, half shutting their eyes, which became mild and amiable in appearance under the influence of extreme satisfaction. Their sides, which had been for the last two days in a state of collapse, began to swell, and at last were distended to such an extent that they seemed as if ready to burst. In point of fact the creatures were actually as full as they could hold; and when at length they dragged themselves slowly, almost unwillingly, out of the pool, any sudden jerk or motion caused some of the water to run out of their mouths!

Some time after that we were compelled to part with our poor steeds, in consequence of their being bitten by an insect which caused their death.

This destructive fly, which is called tsetse, is a perfect scourge in some parts of Africa. Its bite is fatal to the horse, ox, and dog, yet, strange to say, it is not so to man or to wild animals. It is not much larger than the common house-fly, and sucks the blood in the same manner as the mosquito, by means of a proboscis with which it punctures the skin. When man is bitten by it, no more serious evil than slight itching of the part follows. When the ox is bitten no serious effect follows at first, but a few days afterwards a running takes place at the eyes and nose, swellings appear under the jaw and on other parts of the body, emaciation quickly follows, even although the animal may continue to graze, and after a long illness, sometimes of many weeks, it dies in a state of extreme exhaustion.

The tsetse inhabits certain localities in great numbers, while other places in the immediate neighbourhood are entirely free. Those natives, therefore, who have herds of cattle avoid the dangerous regions most carefully; yet, despite their utmost care, they sometimes come unexpectedly on the habitat of this poisonous fly, and lose the greater part of their cattle.

When our poor oxen were bitten and the fatal symptoms began to appear, we knew that their fate was sealed; so we conducted them into a pleasant valley on which we chanced to alight, where there was plenty of grass and water, and there we left them to die.

Another incident occurred to us in this part of our journey which is worthy of record.

One day Peterkin and I had started before our party with our rifles, and had gone a considerable distance in advance of them, when we unexpectedly came upon a band of natives who were travelling in an opposite direction. Before coming up with their main body, we met with one of their warriors, who came upon us suddenly in the midst of a wooded spot, and stood rooted to the earth with fear and amazement; at which, indeed, we were not much surprised, for as he had probably never seen white faces before, he must have naturally taken us for ghosts or phantoms of some sort.

He was armed with shield and spear, but his frame was paralysed with terror. He seemed to have no power to use his weapons. At first we also stood in silent wonder, and returned his stare with interest; but after a few seconds the comicality of the man's appearance tickled Peterkin so much that he burst into a fit of laughter, which had the effect of increasing the terror of the black warrior to such a degree that his teeth began to chatter in his head. He actually grew livid in the face. I never beheld a more ghastly countenance.

"I say, Ralph," observed my companion, after recovering his composure, "we must try to show this fellow that we don't mean him any harm, else he'll die of sheer fright."

Before I could reply, or any steps could be taken towards this end, his party came up, and we suddenly found ourselves face to face with at least a hundred men, all of whom were armed with spears or bows and arrows. Behind them came a large troop of women and children. They were all nearly naked, and I observed that they were blacker in the skin than most of the negroes we had yet met with.

"Here's a pretty mess," said Peterkin, looking at me.

"What is to be done?" said I.

"If we were to fire at them, I'd lay a bet they'd run away like the wind," replied my comrade; "but I can't bear to think of shedding human blood if it can possibly be avoided."

While we spoke, the negroes, who stood about fifty yards distant from us, were consulting with each other in eager voices, but never for a moment taking their eyes off us.

"What say you to fire over their heads?" I suggested.

"Ready, present, then," cried Peterkin, with a recklessness of manner that surprised me.

We threw forward our rifles, and discharged them simultaneously.

The effect was tremendous. The whole band--men, women, and children--uttered an overwhelming shriek, and turning round, fled in mad confusion from the spot. Some of the warriors turned, however, ere they had gone far, and sent a shower of spears at us, one of which went close past my cheek.

"We have acted rashly, I fear," said I, as we each sought shelter behind a tree.

No doubt the savages construed this act of ours into an admission that we did not consider ourselves invulnerable, and plucked up courage accordingly, for they began again to advance towards us, though with hesitation. I now saw that we should be compelled to fight for our lives, and deeply regretted my folly in advising Peterkin to fire over their heads; but happily, before blood was drawn on either side, Makarooroo and Jack came running towards us. The former shouted an explanation of who and what we were to our late enemies, and in less than ten minutes we were mingling together in the most amicable manner.

We found that these poor creatures were starving, having failed to procure any provisions for some time past, and they were then on their way to another region in search of game. We gave them as much of our provisions as we could spare, besides a little tobacco, which afforded them inexpressible delight. Then rubbing noses with the chief, we parted and went on our respective ways.

CHAPTER ELEVEN.

HOW WE MET WITH OUR FIRST GORILLA, AND HOW WE SERVED HIM.

"It never rains but it pours," is a true proverb. I have often noticed, in the course of my observations on sublunary affairs, that events seldom come singly. I have often gone out fishing for trout in the rivers of my native land, day after day, and caught nothing, while at other times I have, day after day, returned home with my basket full.

As it was in England, so I found it in Africa. For many days after our arrival in the gorilla country, we wandered about without seeing a single creature of any kind. Lions, we ascertained, were never found in those regions, and we were told that this was in consequence of their having been beaten off the field by gorillas. But at last, after we had all, severally and collectively, given way to despair, we came upon the tracks of a gorilla, and from that hour we were kept constantly on the qui vive, and in the course of the few weeks we spent in that part of the country, we "bagged," as Peterkin expressed it, "no end of gorillas"--great and small, young and old.

I will never forget the powerful sensations of excitement and anxiety that filled our breasts when we came on the first gorilla footprint. We felt as no doubt Robinson Crusoe did when he discovered the footprint of a savage in the sand. Here at last was the indubitable evidence of the existence and presence of the terrible animal we had come so far to see. Here was the footstep of that creature about which we had heard so many wonderful stories, whose existence the civilised world had, up to within a very short time back, doubted exceedingly, and in regard to which, even now, we knew comparatively very little.

Makarooroo assured us that he had hunted this animal some years ago, and had seen one or two at a distance, though he had never killed one, and stated most emphatically that the footprint before us, which happened to be in a soft sandy spot, was undoubtedly caused by the foot of a gorilla.

Being satisfied on this head, we four sat down in a circle round the footprint to examine it, while our men stood round about us, looking on with deep interest expressed in their dark faces.

"At last!" said I, carefully brushing away some twigs that partly covered the impression.

"Ay, at last!" echoed Jack, while his eyes sparkled with enthusiasm.

"Ay," observed Peterkin, "and a pretty big last he must require, too. I shouldn't like to be his shoemaker. What a thumb, or a toe. One doesn't know very well which to call it."

"I wonder if it's old?" said I.

"As old as the hills," replied Peterkin; "at least 50 I would judge from its size."

"You mistake me. I mean that I wonder whether the footprint is old, or if it has been made recently."

"Him's quite noo," interposed our guide.

"How d'ye know, Mak?"

"'Cause me see."

"Ay; but what do you see that enables you to form such an opinion?"

"O Ralph, how can you expect a nigger to understand such a sentence as that?" said Jack, as he turned to Mak and added, "What do you see?"

"Me see one leetle stick brok in middel. If you look to him you see him white and clean. If hims was old, hims would be mark wid rain and dirt."

"There!" cried Peterkin, giving me a poke in the side, "see what it is to be a minute student of the small things in nature. Make a note of it, Ralph."

I did make a note of it mentally on the spot, and then proposed that we should go in search of the gorilla without further delay.

We were in the midst of a dark gloomy wood in the neighbourhood of a range of mountains whose blue serrated peaks rose up into the clouds. Their sides were partly clothed with wood. We were travelling--not hunting--at the time we fell in with the track above referred to, so we immediately ordered the men to encamp where they were, while we should go after the gorilla, accompanied only by Mak, whose nerves we could depend on.

Shouldering our trusty rifles, and buckling tight the belts of our heavy hunting-knives, we sallied forth after the manner of American Indians, in single file, keeping, as may well be supposed, a sharp lookout as we went along. The fact was that long delay, frequent disappointment, and now the near prospect of success, conspired together to fill us with a species of nervous excitement that caused us to start at every sound.

The woods here were pretty thick, but they varied in their character so frequently that we were at one time pushing slowly among dense, almost impenetrable underwood, at another walking briskly over small plains which were covered in many places with large boulders. It was altogether a gloomy, savage-looking country, and seemed to me well suited to be the home of so dreadful an animal. There were few animals to be seen here. Even birds were scarce, and a few chattering monkeys were almost the only creatures that broke the monotonous silence and solitude around us.

"What a dismal place!" said Peterkin, in a low tone. "I feel as if we had got to the fag-end of the world, as if we were about plunging into ancient chaos."

"It is, indeed," I replied, "a most dreary region. I think that the gorillas will not be disturbed by many hunters with white faces."

"There's no saying," interposed Jack. "I should not wonder, now, if you, Ralph, were to go home and write a book detailing our adventures in these parts, that at least half the sportsmen of England would be in Africa next year, and the race of gorillas would probably become extinct."

"If the sportsmen don't come out until I write a book about them, I fear the gorillas will remain undisturbed for all time to come."

At that time, reader, I was not aware of the extreme difficulty that travellers experience in resisting the urgent entreaties of admiring and too partial friends!

Presently we came to a part of the forest where the underwood became so dense that we could scarcely make our way through it at all, and here we began for the first time to have some clearer conception of the immense power of the creature we were in pursuit of; for in order to clear its way it had torn down great branches of the trees, and in one or two places had seized young trees as thick as a man's arm, and snapped them in two as one would snap a walking-cane.

Following the track with the utmost care for several miles, we at length came to a place where several huge rocks lay among the trees. Here, while we were walking along in silence, Makarooroo made a peculiar noise with his tongue, which we knew meant that he had discovered something worthy of special attention, so we came to an abrupt pause and looked at him.

"What is it, Mak?" inquired Jack.

The guide put his finger on his mouth to impose silence, and stood in a listening attitude with his eyes cast upon the ground, his nostrils distended, and every muscle of his dusky frame rigid, as if he were a statue of black marble. We also listened attentively, and presently heard a sound as of the breaking of twigs and branches.

"Dat am be gorilla," said the guide, in a low whisper.

We exchanged looks of eager satisfaction.

"How shall we proceed, Mak?" inquired Jack.

"We mus' go bery slow, dis way," said the guide, imitating the process of walking with extreme caution. "No break leetle stick. If you break leetle stick hims go right away."

Promising Mak that we would attend to his injunctions most carefully, we desired him to lead the way, and in a few minutes after came so near to where the sound of breaking sticks was going on that we all halted, fearing that we should scare the animal away before we could get a sight of it amongst the dense underwood.

"What can he be doing?" said I to the guide, as we stood looking at each other for a few seconds uncertain how to act.

"Him's breakin' down branches for git at him's feed, s'pose."

"Do you see that?" whispered Peterkin, as he pointed to an open space among the bushes. "Isn't that a bit o' the hairy brute?"

"It looks like it," replied Jack eagerly.

"Cluck!" ejaculated Makarooroo, making a peculiar noise with his tongue. "Dat him. Blaze away!"

"But it may not be a mortal part," objected Peterkin. "He might escape if only wounded."

"Nebber fear. Hims come at us if hims be wound. Only we mus' be ready for him."

"All ready," said Jack, cocking both barrels of his rifle.--"Now, Peterkin, a good aim. If he comes here he shall get a quietus."

All this was said in the lowest possible whispers. Peterkin took a steady aim at the part of the creature that was visible, and fired.

I have gone through many wild adventures since then. I have heard the roar of the lion and the tiger in all circumstances, and the laugh of the hyena, besides many other hideous sounds, but I never in all my life listened to anything that in any degree approached in thundering ferocity the appalling roar that burst upon our ears immediately after that shot was fired. I can compare it to nothing, for nothing I ever heard was like it. If the reader can conceive a human fiend endued with a voice far louder than that of the lion, yet retaining a little of the intonation both of the man's voice and of what we should suppose a fiend's voice to be, he may form some slight idea of what that roar was. It is impossible to describe it. Perhaps Mak's expression in regard to it is the most emphatic and truthful: it was absolutely "horriboble!" Every one has heard a sturdy, well-grown little boy, when being thrashed, howling at the very top of his bent. If one can conceive of a full-grown male giant twenty feet high pouring forth his whole soul and voice with similarly unrestrained fervour, he may approximate to a notion of it.

And it was not uttered once or twice, but again and again, until the whole woods trembled with it, and we felt as if our ears could not endure more of it without the tympanums being burst.

For several moments we stood motionless with our guns ready, expecting an immediate attack, and gazing with awe, not unmingled--at least on my part--with fear, at the turmoil of leaves and twigs and broken branches that was going on round the spot where the monster had been wounded.

"Come," cried Jack at length, losing patience and springing forward; "if he won't attack us we must attack him."

We followed close on his heels, and next moment emerged upon a small and comparatively open space, in the midst of which we found the gorilla seated on the ground, tearing up the earth with its hands, grinning horribly and beating its chest, which sent forth a loud hollow sound as if it were a large drum. We saw at once that both its thighs had been broken by Peterkin's shot.

Of all the hideous creatures I had ever seen or heard of, none came up in the least degree to this. Apart altogether from its gigantic size, this monster was calculated to strike terror into the hearts of beholders simply by the expression of its visage, which was quite satanic. I could scarcely persuade myself that I was awake. It seemed as if I were gazing on one of those hideous creatures one beholds when oppressed with nightmare.

But we had little time to indulge in contemplation, for the instant the brute beheld us it renewed its terrible roar, and attempted to spring up; but both its legs at once gave way, and it fell with a passionate growl, biting the earth, and twisting and tearing bunches of twigs and leaves in its fury. Suddenly it rushed upon us rapidly by means of its fore legs or arms.

"Look out, Jack!" we cried in alarm.

Jack stood like a rock and deliberately levelled his rifle. Even at this moment of intense excitement I could not help marvelling at the diminutive appearance of my friend when contrasted with the gorilla. In height, indeed, he was of course superior, and would have been so had the gorilla been able to stand erect, but his breadth of shoulder and chest, and his length and size of arm, were strikingly inferior. Just as the monster approached to within three yards of him, Jack sent a ball into its chest, and the king of the African woods fell dead at our feet!

It is impossible to convey in words an idea of the gush of mingled feelings that filled our breasts as we stood beside and gazed at the huge carcass of our victim. Pity at first predominated in my heart, then I felt like an accomplice to a murder, and then an exulting sensation of joy at having obtained a specimen of one of the rarest animals in the world overwhelmed every other feeling.

The size of this animal--and we measured him very carefully--was as follows:--

Height, 5 feet 6 inches; girth of the chest, 4 feet 2 inches; spread of its arms, 7 feet 2 inches. Perhaps the most extraordinary measurement was that of the great thumb of its hind foot, which was 5 and a half inches in circumference. When I looked at this and at the great bunches of hard muscles which composed its brawny chest and arms, I could almost believe in the stories told by the natives of the tremendous feats of strength performed by the gorilla. The body of this brute was covered with grey hair, but the chest was bare and covered with tough skin, and its face was intensely black. I shuddered as I looked upon it, for there was something terribly human-like about it, despite the brutishness of its aspect.

"Now, I'll tell you what we shall do," said Jack, after we had completed our examination of the gorilla. "We will encamp where we are for the night, and send Makarooroo back to bring our fellows up with the packs, so that you, Ralph, will be able to begin the work of skinning and cleaning the bones at once. What say you?"

"Agreed, with all my heart," I replied.

"Well, then," observed Peterkin, "here goes for a fire, to begin with, and then for victuals to continue with. By the way, what say you to a gorilla steak? I'm told the niggers eat him.--Don't they, Mak?"

"Yis, massa, dey does. More dan dat, de niggers in dis part ob country eat mans."

"Eat mans!" echoed Peterkin in horror.

"Yis, eat mans, and womins, an' childerdens."

"Oh, the brutes! But I don't believe you, Mak. What are the villains called?"

"Well, it not be easy for say what dem be called. Miss'naries calls dem canibobbles."

"Ho!" shouted Peterkin, "canibobbles? eh! well done. Mak, I must get you to write a new dictionary; I think it would pay!"

"It won't pay to go on talking like this, though," observed Jack. "Come, hand me the axe. I'll fell this tree while you strike a light, Peterkin.--Be off with you, Mak.--As for Ralph, we must leave him to his note-book; I see there is no chance of getting him away from his beloved gorilla till he has torn its skin from its flesh, and its flesh from its bones."

Jack was right. I had now several long hours' work before me, which I knew could not be delayed, and to which I applied myself forthwith most eagerly, while my comrades lit the fire and prepared the camp, and Makarooroo set off on his return journey to bring up the remainder of our party.

That night, while I sat by the light of the camp-fire toiling at my task, long after the others had retired to rest, I observed the features of Jack and Peterkin working convulsively, and their hands clutching nervously as they slept, and I smiled to think of the battles with gorillas which I felt assured they must be fighting, and the enormous "bags" they would be certain to tell of on returning from the realms of dreamland to the regions of reality.

CHAPTER TWELVE.

PETERKIN'S SCHOOLDAY REMINISCENCES.

The day following that on which we shot our first gorilla was a great and memorable day in our hunting career in Africa, for on that day we saw no fewer than ten gorillas: two females, seven young ones--one of which was a mere baby gorilla in its mother's arms--and a huge lone male, or bachelor gorilla, as Peterkin called him. And of these we killed four--three young ones, and the old bachelor. I am happy to add that I saved the lives of the infant gorilla and its mother, as I shall presently relate.

The portion of country through which we travelled this day was not so thickly wooded as that through which we had passed the day before, so that we advanced more easily, and enjoyed ourselves much as we went along. About the middle of the day we came to a spot where there were a number of wild vines, the leaves of which are much liked by the gorilla, so we kept a sharp lookout for tracks.

Soon we came upon several, as well as broken branches and twigs, in which were observed the marks of teeth, showing that our game had been there. But we passed from the wood where these signs were discovered, out upon an open plain of considerable extent. Here we paused, undecided as to whether we should proceed onward or remain there to hunt.

"I vote for advancing," said Peterkin, "for I observe that on the other side of this plain the wood seems very dense, and it is probable that we may find Mister Gorilla there.--What think you, Mak?"

The guide nodded in reply.

"I move," said Jack, "that as the country just where we stand is well watered by this little brook, besides being picturesque and beautiful to look upon, we should encamp where we are, and leaving our men to guard the camp, cross this plain--we three take Mak along with us, and spend the remainder of the day in hunting."

"I vote for the amendment," said I.

"Then the amendment carries," cried Jack, "for in all civilised societies most votes always carry; and although we happen to be in an uncivilised region of the earth, we must not forget that we are civilised hunters. The vote of two hunters ought certainly to override that of one hunter."

Peterkin demurred to this at once, on the ground that it was unfair.

"How so?" said I.

"In the first place," replied he, looking uncommonly wise, and placing the point of his right finger in the palm of his left hand--"in the first place, I do not admit your premises, and therefore I object to your conclusion. I do not admit that in civilised societies most votes carry; on the contrary, it too frequently happens that, in civilised societies, motions are made, seconded, discussed, and carried without being put to the vote at all; often they are carried without being made, seconded, or discussed--as when a bottle-nosed old gentleman in office chooses to ignore the rights of men, and carry everything his own way. Neither do I admit that we three are civilised hunters; for although it is true that I am, it is well-known that you, Ralph, are a philosopher, and Jack is a gorilla. Therefore I object to your conclusion that your two votes should carry; for you cannot but admit that the vote of one hunter ought to override that of two such creatures, which would not be the case were there an equality existing between us."

"Peterkin," said I, "there is fallacy in your reasoning."

"Can you show it?" said he.

"No; the web is too much ravelled to disentangle."

"Not at all," cried Jack; "I can unravel it in a minute, and settle the whole question by proving that there does exist an equality between us; for it is well-known, and generally admitted by all his friends, and must be acknowledged by himself, that Peterkin is an ass."

"Even admitting that," rejoined Peterkin, "it still remains to be proved that a philosopher, a gorilla, and an ass are equal. Of course I believe the latter to be superior to both the former animals; but in consideration of the lateness of the hour, and the able manner in which you have discussed this subject, I beg to withdraw my motion, and to state that I am ready to accompany you over the plain as soon as you please."

At this point our conversation was interrupted by the shriek of a small monkey, which had been sitting all the time among the branches of the tree beneath which we stood.

"I declare it has been listening to us," cried Peterkin.

"Yes, and is shouting in triumph at your defeat," added Jack.

As he spoke, Makarooroo fired, and the monkey fell to the ground almost at our feet.

"Alas! it has paid a heavy price for its laugh," said Peterkin, in a tone of sadness.

The poor thing was mortally wounded; so much so that it could not even cry. It looked up with a very piteous expression in our faces. Placing its hand on its side, it coughed once or twice, then lying down on its back and stretching itself out quite straight, it closed its eyes and died.

I never could bear to shoot monkeys. There was something so terribly human-like in their sufferings, that I never could witness the death of one without feeling an almost irresistible inclination to weep. Sometimes, when short of provisions, I was compelled to shoot monkeys, but I did so as seldom as possible, and once I resolved to go supperless to bed rather than shoot one whose aspect was so sad and gentle that I had not the heart to kill it. My companions felt as I did in this matter, and we endeavoured to restrain Makarooroo as much as possible; but he could not understand our feelings, and when he got a chance of a shot, almost invariably forgot our injunctions to let monkeys alone unless we were absolutely ill off for food. To do him justice, however, I must add that we were at this particular time not overburdened with provisions, and the men were much pleased to have the prospect of a roast monkey for supper.

Having given our men a little tobacco, a gift which caused their black faces to beam with delight, we shouldered our rifles and set off across the plain towards the thick wood, which was not more than five miles distant, if so much.

It was a beautiful scene, this plain with its clumps of trees scattered over it like islands in a lake, and its profusion of wild flowers. The weather, too, was delightful--cooler than usual--and there was a freshness in the air which caused us to feel light of heart, while the comparative shortness of the grass enabled us to proceed on our way with light steps. As we walked along for some time in silence, I thought upon the goodness and the provident care of the Creator of our world; for during my brief sojourn in Africa I had observed many instances of the wonderful exactness with which things in nature were suited to the circumstances in which they were placed, and the bountiful provision that was made everywhere for man and beast. Yet I must confess I could not help wondering, and felt very much perplexed, when I thought of the beautiful scenes in the midst of which I moved being inhabited only by savage men, who seemed scarcely to appreciate the blessings by which they were surrounded, and who violated constantly all the laws of Him by whom they were created. My meditations were interrupted by Jack saying--

"I cannot help wondering why that poor monkey kept so still all the time we were talking. One would think that it should have been frightened away just as we came under the tree."

"I have no doubt," said I, "that although of course it could not understand what we said, yet it was listening to us."

"I'm not so certain that it did not understand," observed Peterkin. "You know that sailors believe that monkeys could speak if they chose, but they don't for fear that they should be made to work!"

"Well, whatever truth there may be in that, of this I am certain, they are the most deceptive creatures that exist."

"I don't agree with you," rejoined Peterkin. "It's my opinion that little boys are the greatest deceivers living."

"What! all little boys!" exclaimed Jack.

"No, not all. I have not so bad an opinion of the race as that. I've had a good deal to do with boys during my naval career, and among the middies of her Majesty's navy I have met with as fine little chaps as one would wish to see--regular bricks, afraid of nothing (except of doing anything that would be thought sneaking or shabby), ready to dare anything--to attack a seventy-four single-handed in a punt or a bumboat if need be; nevertheless, I've met boys, and a good many of them too, who would beat all the monkeys in Africa at sneaking and deceiving. I remember one rascal, who went to the same school with me, who was a wonderfully plausible deceiver. I can't help laughing yet when I think of the curious way he took to free himself of the restraint of school."

"How was it?" cried Jack; "tell us about it--do."

"Well, you must know," began Peterkin, "that this boy was what Jack tars would call a `great, stupid, lubberly fellow.' He was a very fair-haired, white eyelashed sort of chap, that seemed to grow at such a rate that he was always too big for his clothes, and showed an unusual amount of wrist and ankle even for a boy. Most people who met him thought him a very stupid boy at first; but those who came to know him well found that he was rather a sharp, clever fellow, but a remarkably shy dog. We called him Doddle.

"His mother was a widow, and he was an only son, and had been spoiled, of course, so that he was not put to school till he was nearly twelve years of age. He had been at several schools before coming to ours, but had been deemed by each successive schoolmaster a hopeless imbecile. And he was so mischievous that they advised his poor mother to take him away and try if she could not instil a little knowledge into him herself. The old lady was a meek, simple body, and quite as stupid as her hopeful son appeared to be. Hearing that our master was a sharp fellow, and somewhat noted as a good manager of obstreperous boys, she brought him to our school as a last resource, and having introduced him to the master, went her way.

"It was near the end of play-hour when she brought him, so he was turned out into the playground, and stood there looking like a mongrel cur turned unexpectedly into a kennel of pointers.

"'Well, Doddle,' said one of the sixth-form boys, going up to him and addressing him for the first time by the name which stuck to him ever after, 'where did you grow; and who cut you down and tossed you in here?'

"'Eh?' said Doddle, looking sheepish.

"'What's your name, man, and where did you come from, and how old are you, and how far can you jump without a race? and in fact I want to know all about you.'

"'My name's Tommy Thompson,' replied the boy, 'and I--'

"At that moment the bell rang, and the remainder of his sentence was drowned in the rush of the rest of us to the classroom.

"When all was quiet the master called Doddle up, and said, 'Well, Thompson, my boy, your mother tells me you have learned a little grammar and a little arithmetic. I hope that we shall instil into you a good deal of those branches of learning, and of many others besides, ere long. Let me hear what you can do.'

"'I can play hockey and dumps,' began Doddle, in a sing-song tone, and with the most uncommonly innocent expression of visage; 'an' I can--'

"'Stay, boy,' interrupted the master, smiling; 'I do not want to know what you can play at. Keep silence until I put a few questions to you. What is English grammar?'

"'Eh?'

"'Don't say "Eh!" When you fail to understand me, say "Sir?" interrogatively. What is English grammar?'

"'It's a book.'

"The master looked over the top of his spectacles at Doddle in surprise.

"'English grammar,' said he, slowly, and with a slight touch of sternness, `is indeed contained in a book; but I wish to know what it teaches.'

"'Eh?--a--I mean sir interrogatively.'

"'What does English grammar teach, boy?' cried the master angrily.

"Doddle laid hold of his chin with his right hand, and looked down at the floor with an air of profound thought, saying slowly, in an undertone to himself, `What--does--English--grammar--teach--teach-- grammar--teach? It--teaches--a--I don't know what it teaches. Perhaps you can tell me, sir?'

"He looked up, and uttered the last sentence with such an air of blank humility that we all had to cram our pocket handkerchiefs into our mouths to prevent a universal explosion. The master looked over his spectacles again at Doddle with an expression of unutterable amazement. We looked on with breathless interest, not unmingled with awe, for we expected some awful outbreak on the part of the master, who seemed quite unable to make up his mind what to do or say, but continued to stare for nearly a minute at the boy, who replied to the stare with a humble, idiotic smile.

"Suddenly the master said sharply, `How much are seven times nine?'

"`Five hundred and forty-two and a half,' answered Doddle, without a moment's hesitation.

"The master did not look surprised this time, but he took Doddle by the shoulder, and drawing him towards his chair, looked earnestly into his face. Then he said quietly, `That will do, Thompson; go to your seat.'

"This was all that occurred at that time. During a whole week the master tried by every means to get Doddle to learn something; but Doddle could learn nothing. Yet he seemed to try. He pored over his book, and muttered with his lips, and sometimes looked anxiously up at the ceiling, with an expression of agony on his face that seemed to indicate a tremendous mental effort. Every species of inducement was tried, and occasionally punishment was resorted to. He was kept in at play-hours, and put in a corner during school-hours; and once, the master having lost patience with him, he was flogged. But it was all one to Doddle. All the methods tried proved utterly unavailing. He could not be got to acquire a single lesson, and often gave such remarkable answers that we all believed him to be mad.

"On the Monday forenoon of his second week at the school, the master called him up again for examination.

"`Now, Thompson,' he began, `you have been a long time over that lesson; let us see how much of it you have learned. What is etymology?'

"`Etymology,' answered Doddle, `is--is--an irregular pronoun.'

"`Boy!' cried the master sternly.

"`Please, sir,' pleaded Doddle, with deprecatory air, `I--I suppose I was thinkin' o' one o' the other mologies, not the etty one.'

"`Ha!' ejaculated the master; `well, tell me, how many parts of speech are there?'

"`Nineteen,' answered the boy, quite confidently.

"`Oh!' exclaimed the master, with a good deal of sarcasm in his tone; `pray, name them.'

"In a very sing-song voice, and with an air of anxious simplicity, Doddle began, `Article, noun, adjective, pronoun, verb, adverb, preposition, conjunction, interjection, outerjection, beginning with ies in the plural--as, baby, babies; lady, ladies; hady, hadies. Please, sir, isn't that last one a bad word?'

"`The boy is a lunatic!' muttered the master.

"The boys in the class were far past laughing now; we were absolutely stunned. The master seemed perplexed, for Doddle was gazing at him with a look of mild self-satisfaction.

"`I say, Peterkin,' whispered the boy next to me, `as sure as you're alive that boy's shamming stupid.'

"Presently the master, who had been turning over the leaves of the grammar in a way that showed he was not conscious of what he was about, looked up, and said abruptly, `What is a proper noun?'

"`A well-behaved one,' replied Doddle.

"At this the whole school tittered violently.

"'Silence, boys,' cried the master, in a tone that produced the desired effect so thoroughly that you might have heard a pin drop. Then laying his hand on Doddle's shoulder, he looked him full in the face, and said solemnly, 'Thompson, I have found you out. Go, sir, to your seat, and remain behind when the other boys go to the playground.'

"We observed that Doddle grew very red in the face as he came back to his seat, and during the rest of the hour he never once looked up.

"During the whole of the play-hour the master and he remained shut up together in the schoolroom. We never discovered what took place there between them, for neither threats nor coaxing could induce Doddle afterwards to speak on the subject; but from that day forward he was a changed boy. He not only learned his lessons, but he learned them well, and in the course of time became one of the best scholars in the school; so that although he never would admit it, we all came to the conclusion he had been shamming stupid--attempting to deceive the master into the belief that he was incurable, and thus manage to get rid of lessons and school altogether."

"A most remarkable boy," observed Jack when Peterkin concluded. "Certainly he beat the monkeys hollow."

"I wonder," said I, "what the master said or did to him that wrought such a mighty change."

"Don't know," replied Peterkin; "I suppose he told him that now he had found him out, he would flay him alive if he didn't give in, or something of that sort."

We had now entered the dark forest that edged the plain over which we had been walking, and further conversation on this subject was stopped, and the subject itself banished utterly from our minds by the loud, startling cry of a gorilla at no great distance from us.

"Hist! that's him," whispered Peterkin.

Instantly throwing our rifles into a position of readiness we pushed rapidly through the underwood in the direction whence the cry had come.

CHAPTER THIRTEEN.

WE GET INTO "THE THICK OF IT"--GREAT SUCCESS.

In a few minutes we came upon a female gorilla, which, all unconscious of our approach, was sitting at the foot of a vine, eating the leaves. There were four young ones beside her, engaged in the same occupation. In order to approach within shot of these, we had to creep on all fours through the brushwood with the greatest caution; for gorillas are sharp-sighted, and they have a remarkably acute sense of hearing, so that sometimes the breaking of a dry twig under one's foot is sufficient to alarm them.

We did not venture to speak even in whispers as we advanced; but by a sign Jack told Peterkin to take the lead. Jack himself followed. Makarooroo went next, and I brought up the rear.

In all our hunting expeditions we usually maintained this arrangement, where it was necessary. Peterkin was assigned the post of honour, because he was the best shot; Jack, being next best, came second; and I came last, not because our guide was a better shot than I, but because he was apt to get excited and to act rashly, so that he required looking after. I was at all times ready to lay hold of him by the hair of his woolly head, which, as he was nearly naked, was the only part of him that one could grasp with any degree of firmness.

After creeping in this manner for some distance, we got within range. Peterkin and Jack took aim and fired together. The old gorilla and one of the young ones fell instantly, and from their not struggling it was evident that they were shot quite dead. The guide and I fired immediately after, but only the one that I fired at fell. The other two ran off as fast as they could. Sometimes they ran on all fours; and I observed that while running in this fashion the hind legs passed between the arms, or, as it were, overstepped them. Occasionally, however, they rose and ran on their hind legs, in a stooping position.

When they did this I was particularly struck with their grotesque yet strong resemblance to man, and I do not think that I could at that time have prevailed upon myself to fire at them. I should have felt like a murderer. In truth, my thoughts and sensations just then were anything but agreeable. Nevertheless I was so excited by the chase that I am quite certain no one, to look at me, could have guessed what was passing in my mind.

We ran as rapidly as was possible in such a tangled forest, but we had no chance with the young gorillas. Peterkin at last ran himself out of breath. Stopping suddenly, he said, pantingly--

"It's--o'--no use whatever. Ho! dear me, my bellows are about exploded."

"We've no chance in a race with these hairy men," responded Jack, as he wiped the perspiration from his forehead.--"Why did you miss, Mak?"

"'Cause me no could hit, s'pose, massa."

"Very justly and modestly said," remarked Peterkin, with an approving nod. "'Tis a pity that men are not more generally animated with your spirit, Mak. Most people, when they do wrong or make a mistake, are too apt to try to excuse themselves."

"Yes," I added, with a laugh; "particularly when they blow the tails out of ostriches."

Peterkin shook his head, and said solemnly, "Ralph, my boy, don't take to joking. It don't agree with your constitution. You'll get ill if you do; and we can't afford to have you laid up on our hands in these out-o'-the-way regions."

"Come, now, let us back to the gorillas and secure them, lest their comrades carry them away," said Jack, turning to retrace our steps.

I was anxious to shoot as many gorillas as possible, in order that I might study the peculiarities of, and differences existing between, the different species--if there should be such--and between various individuals of the same species in all stages of development. I had made an elaborate examination of our first gorilla, and had taken copious notes in regard to it. Being desirous of doing the same as far as possible with the female and the two young ones we had just killed, I hastened back with my companions, and we fastened them securely among the branches of a conspicuous tree, intending to send out some of our men for them on our return to camp.

After this we resumed our search for more, but wandered about for several hours without meeting with any, although we observed recently-made footprints in abundance. We went as nearly as possible in a direction parallel to our camp, so that although we walked far we did not increase our distance from it to any great extent.

Presently Makarooroo made a peculiar "cluck" with his tongue, and we all came to an abrupt stand.

"What is't, Mak?"

The negro did not speak, but pointed eagerly in front of him, while the whites of his eyes seemed to sparkle with animation, and raised his gun to shoot.

We came up at the moment, and through an opening in the bushes saw what he was about to fire at. It was a female gorilla, with a baby gorilla in her arms. Fierce and hairy though she was, there was a certain air of tenderness about this mother, as she stroked and pawed her little one, that went straight to my heart, and caused me almost involuntarily to raise my arm and strike up the muzzle of Makarooroo's gun, at the moment he pulled the trigger. The consequence of this act was that the ball passed close over their heads. The report of the piece was instantly followed by a roar of consternation, mingled with rage, from the mother, and a shriek of terror from the baby, which again was immediately followed by a burst of laughter from us, as we beheld the little baby clasp its arms tightly round its mother, while she scampered wildly away from us.

Mak looked at me in amazement.

"What for you be do dat, massa?"

"To prevent you from committing murder, you rascal," said I, laughing. "Have you no feelings of natural pity or tenderness, that you could coolly aim at such a loving pair as that?"

The guide seemed a little put out by this remark, and went on reloading his gun without making reply. He had received enough of moral education at the mission stations to appreciate to some extent the feelings by which I was actuated; yet he had been so long accustomed and so early inured to harsh, unfeeling deeds, that the only idea that probably occurred to him on seeing this mother and her baby was, how near he could get to them in order to make sure of his aim.

"Ah! Ralph," said Jack, as we resumed our march, "you're too tender-hearted, my boy, for a hunter in Africa. There you've lost a chance of getting a gorilla baby, which you have been desiring so much the last few days, and which you might have stuck in a bottle of spirits, and sent home to be held up to universal admiration in Piccadilly, who knows."

"Ay, who knows?" echoed Peterkin. "I think it more probable, however, that it would be held up to universal ridicule. Besides, you forget that we have no spirits to preserve it in, except our own, which I admit are pretty high--a good deal overproof, considering the circumstances in which we are placed, and the unheard-of trials we have to endure. I'm sure I don't know what ever induced me to come, as a Scotch cousin of mine once said, `so far frae my ain fireside' to endure trials. I do believe I've had more trials since I came to this outrageous land than all the criminals of the last century in England put together have had."

"Peterkin," said I seriously, "trials are a decided benefit and blessing to mankind--"

"Oh, of course," interrupted Peterkin; "but then, as you have often retorted upon me that I am of the monkey kind, I think that I could get on pretty well without them."

"My opinion is that they are good both for man and monkey," said Jack. "Just consider, now: it must have been a terrible trial for yon gorilla-mamma to hear a bullet pass within an inch of her head, and have her sweet little darling frightened almost out of its wits. Well, but just think of the state of satisfaction and rejoicing that she must be in now at having escaped. Had it not been for that trial she would now have been in her ordinary humdrum condition. I quite agree with Ralph that trials are really a blessing to us."

"I declare it is quite refreshing to hear that you `agree' with anybody, Jack," rejoined Peterkin, in a tone of sarcasm.--"Perhaps Mr Rover will kindly enlarge on this most interesting subject, and give us the benefit of his wisdom.--And, Mak, you lump of ebony, do you keep a sharp lookout for gorillas in the meantime."

The guide, whose appreciation of fun was very considerable, said, "Yis, massa," grinned from ear to ear, in doing which he displayed a double row of tremendous white teeth, and pretended to be gazing earnestly among the bushes on either side in search of game, as he followed us. The moment we began to talk, however, I observed that he came close up behind, and listened with all his ears. If eager expansion indicates anything, I may add that he listened with all his eyes too!

"I shall have much pleasure in obliging you, Peterkin," said I, with a smile. "And in the first place--"

"O Ralph, I entreat you," interrupted Peterkin, "do not begin with a `first place.' When men begin a discourse with that, however many intermediate places they may have to roam about in and enlarge on, they never have a place of any kind to terminate in, but go skimming along with a couple of dozen `lastlies,' like a stone thrown over the surface of a pond, which, after the first two or three big and promising bounds, spends itself in an endless succession of twittering ripples, and finally sinks, somehow or nohow, into oblivion."

"Ahem! Shakespeare?" said Jack.

"Not at all," retorted Peterkin. "If anybody gave utterance to the sentiment before, it was Shelley, and he must have been on the sea-shore at the time with a crotchet, if not a crab, inside of him.--But pray go on, Ralph."

"Well, then, in the first place," I repeated with emphasis, whereat Peterkin sighed, "trials, when endured in a proper spirit, improve our moral nature and strengthen our hearts; the result of which is, that we are incited to more vigorous mental, and, by consequence, physical exertion, so that our nervous system is strengthened and our muscular powers are increased."

"Very well put, indeed," cried Peterkin. "Now, Ralph, try to forget your `secondly,' omit your `thirdly,' throw your `fourthly' to the winds, and let your `first place' be your `last place,' and I'll give you credit for being a wise and effective speaker."

I gave in to my volatile friend at that time, as I saw that he would not allow me to go on, and, to say truth, I thought that I had exhausted my subject. But, after all, Peterkin did not require to be incited either to good thoughts or good actions. With all his exuberant fun and jocularity, he was at bottom one of the most earnest and attached friends I ever possessed. I have lived to know that his superficial lightness of character overlaid as deeply earnest and sympathetic a spirit as ever existed.

While we were thus conversing and wandering through the forest, we again came upon the fresh tracks of a gorilla, and from their great size we conjectured them to be those of a solitary male. It is a remarkable fact that among several of the lower animals we find specimens of that unnatural class of creatures which among men are termed old bachelors! Among the gorillas these solitaires are usually very large, remarkably fierce, uncommonly ugly, desperately vindictive, and peculiarly courageous; so much so that the natives hold them in special dread. It is of these wild men of the woods that their most remarkable and incredible stories are related.

"I don't think it's a gorilla at all," said Jack, stooping down to examine the footprints, which in that place were not very distinct; "I think an elephant or a rhinoceros must have passed this way."

"No, massa, them's not deep 'nuff for dat. Hims be a gorilla--a bery big one, too."

"Don't let us talk then, lest we should scare it," whispered Peterkin. "Lead the way, Mak; and mind, when we come close enough, move your great carcass out of the way and let me to the front."

"No, no, lad," said Jack. "Fair play. It's my turn now."

"So be it, my boy. But get on."

The tracks led us a considerable distance deeper into the wood, where the trees became so thick that only a species of twilight penetrated through them. To add to our discomfort, the light, we knew, would soon fail us altogether, as evening was drawing on apace, so we quickened our pace to a smart run.

We had not proceeded far when we were brought to a sudden standstill by one of those awfully loud and savage roars which we at once recognised as being that of a gorilla. It sounded like what we might term barking thunder, and from its intensity we were assured that our conjectures as to the creature being a solitary male gorilla were correct.

"Dat him, massas!" cried our guide quickly, at the same time cocking both barrels of his rifle. "Look hout! we no hab go after him no more. Him's come to fight us. Most always doos dot--de big ole gorilla."

We saw from the deeply earnest expression of the negro's countenance that he felt himself now to be in a very serious position, which would demand all his nerve and coolness.

Again the roar was repeated with terrible loudness and ferocity, and we heard something like the beating of a huge bass drum, mingled with the cracking of branches, as though some heavy creature were forcing its way through the underwood towards us.

We were all much impressed with this beating sound, and, as is often the case when men are startled by sounds which they cannot account for, we were more filled with the dread of this incomprehensible sound than of the gorilla which we knew was approaching us. We might, indeed, have asked an explanation from Makarooroo, but we were all too much excited and anxious just then to speak.

We drew together in a group.

Jack, who stood a little in front of us, having claimed the first shot, was whispering something about its being a pity there was so little light, when his voice was drowned by a repetition of the roar, so appalling that we each started, feeling as though it had been uttered close to our ears. Next instant the bushes in front of us were torn aside, and the most horrible monster I ever saw, or hope to set eyes on, stood before us.

He was evidently one of the largest-sized gorillas. In the gloom of the forest he appeared to us to be above six feet high. His jet-black visage was working with an expression of rage that was fearfully satanic. His eyes glared horribly. The tuft of hair on the top of his head rose and fell with the working of his low wrinkled forehead in a manner that peculiarly enhanced the ferocity of his expression. His great hairy body seemed much too large for his misshapen legs, and his enormous arms much too long for the body. It was with the fists at the ends of those muscular arms that he beat upon his bulky chest, and produced the unaccountable sounds above referred to. As he stood there uttering roar upon roar--apparently with the view of screwing up his courage to attack us--displaying his great canine teeth, and advancing slowly, step by step, I felt a mingling of powerful emotions such as I had never felt before in all my life, and such as cannot by any possibility be adequately described.

I felt quite self-possessed, however, and stood beside my comrades with my rifle ready and my finger on the trigger.

"Now!" whispered Peterkin. But Jack did not move.

"Now!" said he again, more anxiously, as the immense brute advanced, beating its chest and roaring, to within eight yards of us. Still Jack did not move, and I observed that it was as much as Peterkin could do to restrain himself.

As it took the next step, and appeared about to spring, Jack pulled the trigger. The cap alone exploded! Like a flash of light the other trigger was pulled; it also failed! some moisture must have got into the nipples in loading. Almost as quick as thought Jack hurled his piece at the brute with a force that seemed to me irresistible. The butt struck it full in the chest, but the rifle was instantly caught in its iron gripe. At that moment Peterkin fired, and the gorilla dropped like a stone, uttering a heavy groan as it fell prone with its face to the earth--not, however, before it had broken Jack's rifle across, and twisted the barrel as if it had been merely a piece of wire!

"That was a narrow escape, Jack," said I seriously, after we had recovered from the state of agitation into which this scene had thrown us.

"Indeed it was; and thanks to Peterkin's ever-ready rifle that it was an escape at all. What a monstrous brute!"

"Much bigger than the first one," said Peterkin.--"Where is your measure, Ralph? Out with it."

I pulled out my measure, and applying it to the prostrate carcass, found that the gorilla we had now shot was five feet eight inches in height, and proportionately large round the chest. It seemed to be a mass of sinews and hard muscles, and as I gazed at its massive limbs I could well imagine that it had strength sufficient to perform many, at least, if not all of the wonderful feats ascribed to it by the natives.

Shortly after the death of the gorilla, night settled down upon the scene, so we hurried back towards our camp, where we arrived much exhausted, yet greatly elated, by our successful day's sport.

I spent a great part of that night making entries in my note-book, by the light of our camp-fires, while my companions slept. And, truly, I enjoyed such quiet hours after days of so great mental and physical excitement. I observed, also, that the negroes enjoyed those seasons exceedingly. They sat round the blaze, talking and laughing, and recounting, I have no doubt, their feats of daring by flood and field; then, when they began to grow sleepy, they sat there swaying to and fro, making an occasional remark, until they became too sleepy even for that, when they began to nod and wink and start, and almost fell into the fire, so unwilling did they seem to tear themselves away from it, even for the distance of the few feet they required to draw back in order to enable them to lie down. At last nature could hold out no longer, and one by one they dropped back in their places.

I, too, began to nod at last, and to make entries in my note-book which were too disjointed at last to be comprehensible; so I finally resigned myself to repose, and to dream, as a matter of course.

CHAPTER FOURTEEN.

OUR PLANS ARE SUDDENLY ALTERED--WICKED DESIGNS DISCOVERED.

For several weeks after this we wandered about in the woods searching for gorillas. We were very successful, and shot so many that I had the satisfaction of making elaborate notes of specimens of nearly all ages and kinds.

But an event was looming in the future which we little thought of, and which ultimately compelled us to abandon the gorilla country and retrace our steps towards the southern part of the continent.

One day we set out, as was our wont, to hunt for gorillas, accompanied only by our faithful follower Makarooroo. It chanced to be a lovely day, and the country through which we were passing was exceedingly beautiful, so that we found more pleasure at that time in conversing together on the beauties of nature and on the wonderful works of nature's God than in contemplating our chances of falling in with game.

"It's a splendid country," said Jack, as we walked along under the shade of some magnificent ebony trees. "I wish that it were inhabited by a Christian people. Perhaps this may be the case one of these days, but I don't think we shall live to see it."

"There's no saying, Jack," observed Peterkin. "Does not the Bible speak of a `nation being born in a day?' Of course that must be figurative language; nevertheless it must mean something, and I incline to think that it means that there shall be a time when men shall flock rapidly, and in unusually great numbers, to the Saviour."

"It may be so," observed I, "but I have made up my mind on this point, that Christian people are not sufficiently awake to the terrible condition of the natives of countries such as this, or to the fact that they have much in their power to do for the amelioration of both their temporal and spiritual welfare. I, for one, will, if spared to return home, contribute more largely than I have been wont to do to the cause of missions."

"Talking of that," said Peterkin, "do you think it right to support the missions of other churches besides your own?"

"Do I think it right?" I exclaimed in surprise. "Of course I do. I think it one of the greatest evils that can befall a Christian, that he should become so narrow-minded as to give only to his own church, and think only of his own church's missions. Why, surely a soul saved, if a matter of rejoicing in heaven, ought to be a matter of joy on earth, without reference to the particular church which was the instrument used by the Holy Spirit for that end. I feel very strongly that all Christians who love our Saviour with deep sincerity must of necessity have a warm feeling towards His people in all churches. At any rate we ought to cultivate such a feeling."

"Who can these be?" cried Jack, stopping and pointing to some figures that appeared to be approaching us in the distance.

"They are negroes, at any rate," said I; "for they seem to be black, and are evidently naked."

"Warriors, too, if I mistake not. They have not yet observed us. Shall we hide and let them pass?"

Jack hesitated a moment, then leaping behind a bush, cried--

"Ay, 'tis well to be cautious when nothing is to be gained by daring. These fellows outnumber us, and war-parties are not to be trusted--at least not if these of Africa resemble those of North America."

"Hollo! there's a white man with them," cried Peterkin, as he peeped over the bushes behind which we were hid.

"You don't say so, eh? So there is. Come; we have nothing to fear from the party of a traveller.--What, Mak, you shake your head! What mean you?"

Makarooroo increased the shaking of his head, and said, "Me no know dat, massa. P'raps hab more to fear dan you tink."

"Oh, stuff! come along. Why, Mak, it seems as if gorilla-hunting had failed to improve your courage."

As Jack said this he stepped out from among the bushes and advanced to meet the strangers. Of course we all followed, and although we carried our rifles in a careless manner, as if we expected no evil, yet we held ourselves in readiness to take instant action if necessary.

The moment the negroes perceived us, they set up a great shout and brandished their spears and guns, but the voice of their leader was instantly heard commanding them to halt. They obeyed at once, and the European stranger advanced alone to meet us. As he drew near we observed that he was a splendid-looking man, nearly as large as Jack himself, with a handsome figure and a free, off-hand gait. But on coming closer we saw that his countenance, though handsome, wore a forbidding, stern expression.

"Dat am a slabe-dealer," whispered our guide, as the stranger came up and saluted us in French.

Jack replied in the same language; but on learning that we were

Englishmen, he began to talk in our own tongue, although he evidently understood very little of it.

"Do you travel alone with the natives?" inquired Jack, after a few preliminary remarks.

"Yaas, sair, I doos," replied the stranger, who was a Portuguese trader, according to his own account.

"You seem to carry little or no merchandise with you," said Jack, glancing towards the party of natives, who stood at some distance looking at us and conversing together eagerly.

"I has none wis me, true, bot I has moche not ver' far off. I bees go just now to seek for ivory, and ebony, and sl-a---w'at you call him? barwood."

The man corrected himself quickly, but the slip confirmed Makarooroo's remark and our own suspicions that he was a slave-dealer.

"De day is far gone," he continued, putting as amiable a smile on his countenance as possible; "perhaps you vill stop and we have dine togedder."

Although we did not much like the appearance of our new friend or his party, we felt that it would be uncourteous in so wild a country, where we had so few chances of meeting with white faces, to refuse, so we agreed. A camp-fire was speedily kindled, and the two parties mingled together, and sat down amicably to discuss roast monkey and venison steaks together.

During the course of the meal the Portuguese trader became so communicative and agreeable that we all began to think we had judged him harshly. We observed, too, that Makarooroo and the negroes had fraternised heartily, and our guide was singing and laughing, and making himself agreeable at a very uncommon rate, so much so as to call forth our surprise.

"Mak seems to be mad to-day," observed Peterkin, as one of our guide's jovial laughs rang through the wood and was echoed by his new acquaintances.

"Bees him not always so?" inquired the Portuguese.

"He's always hearty enough," replied Jack, "but I must confess I never saw him in such high spirits as he seems to be in just now. It must be the effect of meeting with new faces, I suppose."

"Ah! s'pose so," remarked the trader.

I was struck with the manner in which this was said. There was a tone of affected indifference, such as one assumes when making a passing remark, but at the same time a dark frown rested for one moment on his brow, and he cast a piercing vindictive glance at our guide. Next moment he was smiling blandly and making some humorous remark to Peterkin.

I looked at my companions, but they had evidently not observed this little piece of by-play. It seemed to me so unaccountable, considering that the two men had never met before, that I resolved to watch them. I soon observed that Makarooroo's mirth was forced, that he was in fact acting a part, and I noticed once or twice that he also cast an occasional stealthy and piercing glance at the Portuguese. It afterwards turned out that both men had been acting the same part, and that each had suspected what the other was doing.

When our meal was concluded we prepared to resume our separate routes.

"I goes to de west," observed the Portuguese, in a casual way, as he buckled on the belt that supported his hunting-knife.

"Indeed! I had understood you to say that you were going south."

"No; you not have onderstand me. I goes to de west, ver' long way."

"Then, sir, I wish you a safe and pleasant journey," said Jack, lifting his cap.

"De same to you, sairs, an' goot plenty of gorillas to you. Farder nord dey be more plenty. Adieu!"

We took off our caps to each other, and saying farewell, we turned away, and soon lost sight of the party.

"Ho! de yaller-faced villain," exclaimed Makarooroo between his clinched teeth, after we were out of earshot.

"Why, what's wrong, Mak?" inquired Peterkin, in great surprise.

"Ho! noting porteekler," replied the guide, with an air and tone of sarcasm that quite amused us. "Hims not go sout', ho no! hims go west, ho yis! Hims advise us to go nort', ho dear! dat bery clibber, bery mush clibber; but we is clibberer, we is, ho! ho! ho!"

Our worthy guide looked so terribly fierce as he uttered this fiendish laugh, that we all came to a stand and gazed at him in surprise; we fancied that something must have deranged his mind.

"Mak," said Peterkin, "you are mad. What mean you by such grimaces?"

Pursing his lips tightly, and looking at each of us for a few moments in silence, he finally crossed his arms on his chest, and turning eagerly to Jack, said with extreme volubility--

"Dat rascal! dat tief! Him's no trader, him's slabe-dealer; hims no go west, hims go south; an' w'at for hims go? W'at for hims carry guns so many, eh? Hims go" (here the guide dropped his voice into a whisper of intense bitterness)--"hims go for attack village an' take all peepils away for be slabes. No pay for 'em--tief!--take dem by force."

"Why, how did you come to know all this," said Jack, "or rather to suspect it? for you cannot be sure that you are right."

"W'at, no can be sure me right? ho, yis, me sartin sure. Me bery clibber. Stop, now. Did him--dat tief!--speak bery mush?"

"Certainly he did, a good deal."

"Yis, ho! An' did him make you speak bery mush?"

"I rather think he did," replied Peterkin, laughing at our guide's eagerness.

"Yis, ho! hims did. An' did him ax you plenty question, all 'bout where you go, an' where you come from, an' de way back to village where we be come from? An' did hims say, when him find you was come from sout, dat hims was go west, though before dat hims hab say dat hims be go sout, eh?"

"Certainly," said Jack, with a thoughtful look, "he did say all that, and a great deal more to that effect."

"Yis, ho! hims did. Me know bery well. Me see him. An' me also dood to de niggers what hims do to you. Me talk an' laugh an' sing, den me ax dem questions. But dey bery wise; dey no speak mush, but dey manage to speak 'nuff for me. Yis, me bam--bam--eh?"

"Boozle," suggested Peterkin.

"Vis, bamboozle dem altogidder, ho! ho!"

After a little further explanation we found that this Portuguese trader was a man-stealer, on his way to one of the smaller villages, with the intention of attacking it. Makarooroo ascertained that they meant to proceed direct to that of King Jambai, first, however, getting one of the neighbouring tribes to pick a quarrel with that monarch and go to war with him; and we now recollected, with deep regret, that in our ignorance of what the Portuguese was, we had given him a great deal of information regarding the village of our late hospitable entertainer which might prove very useful to him, and very hurtful to poor King Jambai, in the event of such a raid being carried out.

But, in addition to this, Makarooroo had ascertained that it was possible that, before going to King Jambai's village, they might perhaps make a descent on that of our friend Mbango, with whom we had left poor Okandaga. It was this that raised the wrath of our guide to such a pitch.

The instant we heard it Jack said--

"Then that settles the question of our future proceedings. We must bid adieu to the gorillas at once, and dog the steps of this marauding party, so as to prevent our good friends Mbango and Jambai being surprised and carried into slavery along with all their people. It seems to me that our path is clear in this matter. Even if we were not bound in honour to succour those who have treated us hospitably, we ought to do our best to undo the evil we have done in telling their enemies so much about them. Besides, we must save Okandaga, whatever happens. What say you, comrades?"

"Of course we must," said Peterkin. I also heartily concurred.

"You's a good man," said Makarooroo, his eyes glistening with emotion.

"If I did not stand by you at such a time as this," replied Jack, smiling, "I should certainly be a very bad man."

"But what are we to do about our goods?" inquired I, "We cannot hope to keep up with these robbers if we carry our goods with us; and yet it seems hard to leave them behind, for we should fare ill, I fear, in this country if we travel as beggars."

"We shall easily manage as to that," replied Jack. "I have observed that one of our niggers is a sensible, and, I am disposed to think, a trustworthy fellow--"

"D'you mean the man with the blind eye and the thumping big nose?" inquired Peterkin.

"The same. Well, I shall put him in charge, and tell him to follow us to Mbango's village; then we four shall start off light, and hunt our way south, travelling as fast as we can, and carrying as many strings of beads, by way of small change, as we can stuff into our pockets and fasten about our persons."

"The very thing," cried Peterkin. "So let's put it in practice at once."

"Ay, this very night," said Jack, as we hurried back to the spot where our goods had been left.

As we went along in silence I noticed that Peterkin sighed once or twice very heavily, and I asked him if he was quite well.

"Well? Ay, well enough in body, Ralph, but ill at ease in mind. How can it be otherwise when we are thus suddenly and unexpectedly about to take leave of our dear friends the gorillas? I declare my heart is fit to break."

"I sympathise with you, Peterkin," said I, "for I have not yet made nearly as many notes in regard to these monster-monkeys as I could have wished. However, I am thankful for what I have got, and perhaps we may come back here again one of these days."

"What bloodthirsty fellows!" cried Jack, laughing. "If you talk so, I fear that Mak and I shall have to cut your acquaintance; for, you see, he and I have got a little feeling left."

"Well, it's natural, I fancy," observed Peterkin, "that gorillas should feel for their kindred. However, I console myself with the thought that the country farther south is much better filled with other game, although the great puggy is not there. And then we shall come among lions again, which we can never find, I believe, in the gorilla country. I wonder if the gorilla has really driven them out of this part of Africa."

"Some think it probable," observed I, "but we cannot make sure of that point."

"Well, we can at all events make sure of this point," cried Peterkin, as we came in sight of our encampment, "that lions are thick enough in the country whither we are bound; so let's have a good supper, and hurrah for the south! It's a bright prospect before us. A fair lady to be saved; possibly a fight with the niggers, and lion, elephant, rhinoceros, alligator, hippopotamus, and buffalo shooting by way of relaxation in the intervals of the war!"

CHAPTER FIFTEEN.

AN UNEXPECTED MEETING--WE FLY, AND I MAKE A NARROW ESCAPE FROM AN APPALLING FATE.

During many days after the incidents narrated in the last chapter did Jack, and Peterkin, and Makarooroo, and I, push across the continent through bush and brake, over hill and dale, morass and plain, at our utmost possible speed. We did not, during the whole course of our journey, overtake the Portuguese slave-dealer; but we thought little of that, for it was not very probable that we should hit upon exactly the same route, and we entertained sanguine hopes that the energy and speed with which we kept steadily and undeviatingly on our way would enable us to reach the village of Mbango before the slave-dealer and his party.

When I look back upon that time now, and reflect calmly on the dangers we encountered and the hardships we endured, I confess that I am filled with amazement. I might easily fill several volumes such as this with anecdotes of our encounters with wild animals, and other adventures; but however interesting these might be in themselves, I must not forget that some of the main incidents of our sojourn in Africa have yet to be related, and that there is a limit to the patience of even youthful readers.

Our power of enduring fatigue and sustained active exertion, with comparatively short intervals of nightly repose, was much greater than I could have believed to be possible. I have no doubt that anxiety to save Okandaga from the terrible fate that hung over her enabled us to bear up under fatigues which would at other times have overcome us. I know not well how it was that I kept up with my strong and agile comrades. Oftentimes I felt ready to drop down as I walked, yet somehow I never thought of falling behind, but went doggedly on, and at nights found myself little worse in condition than they. Peterkin, although small, was tough and springy, and his spirits seemed rather to rise than otherwise as his strength abated. As for Jack, I never saw any one like him. He seemed like a lion roaming in his strength over his native deserts. So hardened had we all become during the course of our travels that we found ourselves not only equal to Makarooroo in pedestrian powers, but superior; for when occasion required we could almost knock him up, but I am free to admit that we never succeeded in doing this thoroughly. In short, we were all as nearly as possible equal to each other, with the exception of Jack, who seemed in every way invulnerable.

During this long and hurried but intensely interesting and delightful journey we came upon, at different times, almost every species of animal, plant, and tree peculiar to the African continent. Oftentimes we passed by droves and herds of elephants, deer, buffalo, giraffes, antelopes, and zebras; we saw rhinoceroses, alligators, leopards, lions, apes of several kinds, and smaller monkeys innumerable. We also saw great numbers of birds--some curious on account of their habits and form, others beautiful and bright as the rainbow.

Yet although, as I have said, this journey was very delightful, our feelings were at different times exceedingly varied, and not unfrequently pained; for while we saw around us much that was beautiful, innocent, and lovely, we also witnessed the conflicts of many wild creatures, and sometimes came across evidences of the savage and cruel dispositions of the human beings by whom the country was peopled. We always, however, carefully avoided native villages, being anxious not to be interrupted on our forced march. Neither did we turn aside to hunt, although we were much tempted so to do, but contented ourselves with killing such animals as we required for our daily subsistence; and of these we shot as many as we required without having to turn aside from our straight course.

Thus we went on day after day, and slept under the shade of the trees or under the wide canopy of heaven night after night, until we arrived one day at a beautiful valley, bordered by a plain, and traversed by a river, where Peterkin met with a sad accident, and our onward progress was for a short period arrested.

It happened thus:--The region through which we chanced to be passing was peopled by so many natives that we had the utmost difficulty in avoiding them, and more than once were compelled to halt during the daytime in some sequestered dell, and resume our journey during the night.

One day--it was, if I remember rightly, about two o'clock in the afternoon-- we came suddenly in sight of a native village on the banks of the river whose course we were at that time following, and made a wide detour in order to avoid it. We had passed it several miles, and were gradually bending into our course again, when we came unexpectedly upon a band of natives who had been out hunting and were returning to their village with the spoils of the chase on their shoulders. Both parties at once came to an abrupt halt, and we stood for several minutes looking at each other--the natives in speechless amazement, while we conversed in whispers, uncertain what to do.

We knew that if we made friendly advances we should no doubt be welcomed, but then we should certainly be compelled to go back with them to their village and spend at least a day or two with them, as we could not hope to give them a satisfactory reason for our going on at once. We also knew that to go on in spite of them would produce a quarrel, and, of course, a fight, which, as it would certainly result in bloodshed, was by all means to be avoided for we could not bear to think that a mere caprice of ours in visiting Africa should be the means of causing the death of a single human being, if we could prevent it.

"What is to be done?" said Peterkin, looking at Jack in despair.

"I don't know," replied Jack. "It's very awkward. It will never do to go all the way back to the village with these stupid fellows, and we cannot tell them our real reason for going on; for, in the first place, they would perhaps not believe us, or, in the second place, they might offer to join us."

"Fight," said Makarooroo in a low tone, grinding his teeth together and clutching his rifle.

I felt deep sympathy with the poor fellow, for I knew well that in disposition he was naturally the reverse of quarrelsome, and that his present state of mind was the consequence of anxiety for the deliverance of his faithful bride.

"No, no," replied Jack quickly; "we shall not fight."

"Suppose we bolt!" whispered Peterkin, brightening up as the idea occurred to him--"regularly run away!"

We seized at the idea instantly. We were all of us hard of muscle and strong of wind now, and we knew that we could outstrip the savages.

"We'll do it!" said Jack hastily. "Let us scatter, too, so as to perplex them at the outset."

"Capital! Then here goes. I'm off," cried Peterkin.

"Stay!" said Jack.

"Why?" demanded Peterkin.

"Because we must appoint a place of rendezvous if we would hope to meet again."

"True; I forgot that."

"D'you all see yonder blue mountain-peak?"

"Let us meet there. If we miss each other at the base, let us proceed to the summit and wait. Away!"

As Jack uttered the last word we all turned right about and fled like the wind. The savages instantly set up a hideous yell, and darted after us; but we made for the thick woods, and scattering in all directions, as had been previously arranged, speedily threw them off the scent, and finally made our escape.

For the first time since landing on the continent of Africa, I now found myself totally alone in the wild forest. After separating from my companions, I ran at my utmost speed in the direction of a dense jungle, where I purposed taking shelter until the natives should pass by, and then come out and pursue my way leisurely. But I was prevented from adopting this course in consequence of two very fleet negroes discovering my intention, and, by taking a short cut, frustrating it. I was compelled, therefore, to keep in the more open part of the forest, and trust simply to speed and endurance for escape.

I should think that I ran nearly two miles at full speed, and kept well ahead of my pursuers. Indeed, I had distanced them considerably; but feeling that I could not hold out long at such a killing pace, I pulled up a little, and allowed them to gain on me slightly. I was just about to resume my full speed, and, if possible, throw them at once far behind, when my foot was caught by a thorny shrub, and I fell headlong to the ground. I was completely stunned for a moment or two, and lay quite motionless. But my consciousness suddenly returned, accompanied by a feeling of imminent danger, which caused me to spring up and renew my headlong career. Glancing over my shoulder, I saw that the two natives had gained so much on me that had I lain a few seconds longer I must inevitably have been captured.

I exerted myself now beyond my powers. My head, too, from the shock I had received, became confused, and I scarce knew whither I was going. Presently a loud, dull roar, as if of distant thunder, struck upon my ear, and I beheld what appeared to me to be a vast white plain covered with mist before. Next moment I found myself on the brink of a precipice of a hundred feet deep, over which, a little to my left, a large river fell, and thundered down into a dark abyss, whence issued those clouds of spray which I had taken for a white plain in the confusion of my brain and vision.

I made a desperate effort to check myself, but it was too late. My heels broke off the earthy edge of the cliff, and I obtained just one awful glance of the horrid turmoil directly below me as I fell over with a mass of debris. I uttered an involuntary shriek of agony, and flung my arms wildly out. My hand clutched the branch of an overhanging bush. This, slight though it was, was the means, under God, of saving my life. The branch broke off, but it checked my fall, and at the same time swung me into the centre of a tree which projected out from the cliff almost horizontally. Through this tree I went crashing with fearful violence, until I was arrested by my chest striking against a stout branch. This I clutched with the tenacity of despair, and wriggling myself, as it were, along it, wound my arms and legs round it, and held on for some time with the utmost fervour of muscular energy.

My position now was beyond conception horrible. I shut my eyes and prayed earnestly for help. Presently I opened them, and in the position in which I then lay, the first thing I saw was the boiling water of the fall more than a hundred feet below me. My agony was such that large drops of perspiration broke out all over my forehead. It was many minutes before I could summon up courage to turn my head so as to look upward, for I had a vague feeling that if I were to move the branch on which I lay would break off. When I did so, I observed that the branches over my head completely screened the sky from me, so that I knew I had escaped one danger; for the natives, believing, no doubt, that I had fallen down into the river, would at once give up their hopeless pursuit. The branch on which I lay was so slender that it swayed about with every motion that I made, and the longer I remained there the more nervous did I become.

At last I bethought me that unless I made a manful effort I should certainly perish, so I looked about me until I became accustomed to the giddy position. Then I perceived that, by creeping along the branch until I gained the trunk of the tree, I could descend by means of it to the face of the precipice from which it projected, and thus gain a narrow ledge of rock that overhung the abyss. In any other circumstances I would as soon have ventured to cross the Falls of Niagara on a tight-rope; but I had no other alternative, so I crept along the branch slowly and nervously, clinging to it, at the same time, with terrible tenacity. At last I gained the trunk of the tree and breathed more freely, for it was much steadier than the branch.

The trunk projected, as I have said, almost horizontally from the precipice, so I had to draw myself carefully along it, not daring to get on my hands and knees, and finally reached the ledge above referred to. Compared with my former position, this was a place of temporary safety, for it was three feet wide, and having a good head, I had no fear of falling over. But on looking up my heart sank within me, for the bare cliff offered no foothold whatever. I do not believe that a monkey could have climbed it. To descend the precipice was equally impossible, for it was like a wall. My only hope, therefore, lay in the ledge on which I stood, and which, I observed, ran along to the right and turned round a projecting rock that hid the remainder of it from view.

Hasting along it, I found, to my inexpressible relief, that it communicated with the top of the precipice. The ascent was difficult and dangerous; but at last I succeeded in passing the most serious part, and soon gained the summit of the cliff in safety, where I immediately fell on my knees and returned thanks for my deliverance.

I had passed nearly an hour in the trying adventure which I have just related, and feeling that my companions would naturally begin soon to be anxious about me, I started for our rendezvous, which I reached in little more than an hour and a half. Here I found Jack seated alone beside a stream of water, from which he occasionally lifted a little in the hollow of his hand and drank greedily.

"Ah, Ralph, my boy!" he exclaimed joyfully as I came up, "I'm glad you've come. I had begun to fear that you must have been captured. Ay, drink, lad! You seem warm enough, though I scarcely think you can be much more so than I am. What a run we have had, to be sure! But, what, Ralph--your clothes are much torn, and your face and hands are scratched. Why, you must have got among thorns. Not badly hurt, I trust?"

"Oh no; nothing to speak of. I have, however, had a narrow escape. But before I speak of that, what of Peterkin?"

"I don't know," replied Jack, with an anxious expression; "and to say truth, I begin to feel uneasy about him, for he ought to have been here almost as soon as myself."

"How so? Did you, then, run together?"

"Latterly we did. At first we separated, and I knew not what had become either of him or you. The fact is, I had enough to do to look out for myself, for a dozen of rascally niggers kept close upon my heels and tried my powers of running somewhat; so I took to the thick wood and made a detour, to throw them off the scent. All at once I heard a smashing of the bushes right in front of me, and before I knew what I was about, Peterkin bounced through the underwood and almost plunged into my arms. We both gave an involuntary yell of alarm.

"`There's two of 'em right on my heels,' said he in a gasp, as he dashed off again. `Come along with me, Jack.'

"I followed as fast as I could, and we crossed an open plain together, when I looked over my shoulder, and saw that all the other fellows had given up the chase except the two mentioned by Peterkin. These kept on after us, and somehow or other we got separated again, just after re-entering the wood on the other side of the plain. Of course I ran on, expecting to see my companion every minute. Finally I came to the rendezvous, and here I found that the savages had given up all hope of overtaking me, for I could see nothing of them."

"How long ago is that?" I inquired quickly.

"About an hour."

"Then poor Peterkin must have been caught," said I, in a voice of despair.

"No, that is not likely," replied Jack; "for I climbed a high tree and saw the savages recrossing the plain alone. I think it probable he may have lost his way, and is afraid to climb trees or to fire off his gun to signal us, for fear of being heard or seen by the niggers. I have sent Mak, who came here soon after I did, to search for him."

"It may be as you say, Jack, but we must go at once to look for him."

"With all my heart, Ralph. I only waited until you had sufficiently rested."

"The body cannot rest when the mind is ill at ease. Come, let us start at once. I shall tell you of my little adventure as we go along."

We soon reached the edge of the plain where Jack had been separated from his companion, and here we proceeded to make a careful search. Being certain that the savages were now out of earshot, we began to halloo occasionally as we went along. But monkeys and parrots alone replied to us.

"This is the very spot where I last saw him," said Jack, leading me to a palm-tree which stood a little within the outer verge of the wood; "and here are his footsteps faintly indicated on the grass."

"Ah! then let us follow these up," said I eagerly.

"We might, if we were North American backwoodsmen or Red Indians; but I can scarcely follow. Stay, here they enter upon a piece of soft ground, and are more distinct. Now, then, we shall get on."

For nearly quarter of an hour we followed the footprints; then we came to dry ground again, and lost all traces of them. We wandered about perseveringly, nevertheless, and were rewarded by again discovering them about quarter of a mile farther on, leading down to the banks of the river on another part of which I had had such a narrow escape.

While we were advancing--I in front--I felt the ground beneath me suddenly begin to give way with a crackling sound. I instinctively threw up my arms and sprang back.

"Hollo, Ralph!" cried my companion, seizing me with one hand by the collar, and hauling, or rather lifting me back, as if I had been a poodle dog. "Why, you were as near as possible into a pitfall."

"Thanks to you, Jack, that I am not actually in," said I, putting my somewhat twisted costume to rights. "But, I say, does it not strike you that perhaps Peterkin has fallen into one of these?"

We both started and listened with breathless attention, for at that moment we heard a faint groan not far from us. It was repeated almost immediately, though so faintly that we could scarcely ascertain the direction whence it came. We advanced cautiously, however, a few paces, and discovered a hole in the ground, from which, at that very moment, the dishevelled head of poor Peterkin appeared, like Jack coming out of his box. His sudden appearance and serio-comic expression would have been at any other time sufficient to have set us off in fits of laughter; but joy at finding him, and anxiety lest he should prove to be seriously hurt, restrained us at that time effectually.

"My dear fellow!" cried Jack, hurrying forward.

"Keep back! avaunt ye. Oh dear me, Jack, my poor head!" said Peterkin with a sigh, pressing his hand to his forehead; "what an intolerable whack I have got on my miserable caput. There; don't come nearer, else you'll break through. Reach me your hand. That's it; thank'ee."

"There you are, all safe, my boy," cried Jack, as he drew Peterkin out of the hole.--"But hollo! I say, Ralph, run down for some water; I believe the poor fellow has fainted."

I sprang down the river-bank, and speedily returned with some water in the crown of my wide-awake. Peterkin had recovered before I came back, and a long draught quite restored him, so that in a few minutes he was able to relate how the accident had befallen him.

"You see," said he, in a jocular tone, for it was a most unusually severe accident indeed that could drive the fun out of our little friend--"you see, after I lost sight of Jack, I took a leaf out of the hare's book, and doubled on my course. This brought me, unhappily, to the banks of the river, where I came upon one of the pitfalls that are made by the niggers here to catch wild beasts, and in I went. I kept hold of the surface boughs, however, scrambled out again, and pushed on. But I had not gone ten yards when the ground began to crackle and sink. I made a desperate bound to clear it, but my foot caught in a branch, and down I went head foremost into the pit. And that's the whole of my story. How long I remained there I know not. If I had known what time it was when I dived in, and you were to tell me what o'clock it is now, we might arrive at a knowledge of the time I have spent at the bottom of that hole. All that I can positively affirm is, that I went in, and within in the last ten minutes I came out!"

We laughed at this free-and-easy manner of narrating the incident, and then prepared to return to our rendezvous; but on attempting to walk, Peterkin found that he had received a greater shake than at first he had imagined. Several times during our march he became giddy, and had to be supported; and after reaching our encampment, where we found Makarooroo waiting for us, he fainted. We were therefore obliged to make up our minds to encamp where we were for a few days.

CHAPTER SIXTEEN.

AN UNFORTUNATE DELAY, AND A TERRIBLE VISITOR.

Only those who have been forcibly held back when filled with the deepest anxiety to go forward, can form any thing like a conception of our state of mind during the few days that succeeded that on which Peterkin met with his accident.

We felt like chained hounds when the huntsmen pass by. We knew that every hour increased the distance between us and the slave-dealer's party, who, unless we succeeded in passing them and reaching the villages first, would infallibly succeed in their villainous design. But Peterkin was unable to proceed without great risk, as whenever he attempted to walk steadily for any distance his head became giddy, and we were compelled to halt, so that a day or two's rest was absolutely necessary. Poor Makarooroo was nearly beside himself with impatience; but to do him justice, he endeavoured to conceal the state of his feelings when in Peterkin's presence.

During this period of forced inaction, although of course I had nothing to do, I found it impossible to apply my mind closely to the study of any of the strange and beautiful objects by which I was surrounded. Anxiety banished from me almost entirely the love of study, as well as the power of observation. Nevertheless, one or two things that I saw were so curious that they could not but make a deep impression on my memory.

I discovered a spider of a very remarkable kind, which was such an ingenious creature as to be capable of making a door to the entrance of its house. I came upon the animal one day while taking a stroll a short distance from our camp. It was as large as a shilling, reddish in colour, and from the fierce, rapid way in which it ran about hither and thither as if in search of prey, it had an exceedingly horrible and voracious aspect. The hole of this creature is visible only when its owner is absent from home. It is quite evident either that there are no thieves among the lower animals there, or that there is nothing in the hole to steal, for when he goes out he leaves the door open behind him. When he returns he shuts the door, and the hole becomes invisible, in consequence of the door being coated with earth on the outside. Its inside is lined with a pure white silky substance, which at once attracted my attention as I passed. On trying to pick up the door, I found that it was attached by a hinge to the hole, and on being shut it fitted exactly.

Perhaps the most singular discovery I made was a tree, the stem of which had been so completely surrounded by spiders' webs that it could not be seen, and I had to cut through the network with my knife in order to get at the tree. The lines of those webs were as thick as coarse threads, and pretty strong, as I had reason to know; for when walking back to camp the same evening, meditating deeply on our unfortunate detention, I ran my head into the middle of a spider's web, and was completely enveloped in it, so much so that it was with considerable difficulty I succeeded in clearing it away. I was as regularly netted as if a gauze veil had been thrown over me.

On our third morning after the accident we set forth again, and continued our journey by forced marches as Peterkin could bear it. Although the two past days and nights had been absolutely lost, and could not now be recalled, yet the moment we set out and left our camp behind us, the load of anxiety was at once lifted off our minds, and we hurried forward with an elasticity of step and spirit that was quite delightful. We felt like prisoners set free, and kept up a continual flow of conversation, sometimes in reference to the scenery and objects around us, at other times in regard to our future plans or our past experiences.

"It seems to me," said Jack, breaking silence at the end of a long pause which had succeeded an animated discussion as to whether it were better to spend one's life in the civilised world or among the wilds of Africa, in which discussion Peterkin, who advocated the wild life, was utterly, though not admittedly, beaten--"it seems to me that, notwithstanding the short time we stayed in the gorilla country, we have been pretty successful. Haven't we bagged thirty-three altogether?"

"Thirty-six, if you count the babies in arms," responded Peterkin.

"Of course we are entitled to count these."

"I think you are both out in your reckoning," said I, drawing out my note-book; "the last baby that I shot was our thirty-seventh."

"What!" cried Peterkin, "the one with the desperately black face and the horrible squint, that nearly tore all the hair out of Jack's head before he managed to strangle him? That wasn't a baby; it was a big boy, and I have no doubt a big rascal besides."

"That may be so," I rejoined; "but whatever he was, I have him down as number thirty-seven in my list."

"Pity we didn't make up the forty," observed Jack.

"Ah! yes indeed," said Peterkin. "But let me see: could we not manage to make it up to that yet?"

"Impossible," said I. "We are far away from the gorilla land now, I know; for, in addition to the fact that we have seen no traces of gorillas for a long time, we have, within the last few days, seen several lions, which, you are well aware, do not exist in the gorilla country."

"True; but you mistake me," rejoined Peterkin. "I do not mean to make up the number to forty by killing three more, but by proving, almost to demonstration, that we have already been the death of that number, in addition to those noted down."

"You'll find that rather difficult," said Jack, laughing.

"Not at all," cried Peterkin. "Let me think a minute. You remember that enormously big, hairy fellow, that looked so like an ugly old man that Ralph refused point-blank to fire at him, whereupon you fired at him point-blank and wounded him in the shoulder as he was running away?"

"We treated several big fellows in that way," replied Jack; "which of them do you allude to?--the one that roared so loud and terrified you so much that you nearly ran away?"

"No, no; you know well enough which one I mean. The one that ran along the edge of the stagnant pool into which you tumbled as we were coming back."

"Oh yes! I remember," said Jack, laughing.

"Well, that fellow flew into such a horrible rage when he was wounded," continued Peterkin, "that I am perfectly certain he went straight home and murdered his wife in a passion; which brings up the number to thirty-eight.

Then there was that old woman-gorilla that I brought down when we were descending yon hill that was covered with such splendid vines. You remember? Well, I'm quite certain that the young man-gorilla beside her, who ran off and escaped, was her son, and that he went home straightway and died of grief. That makes thirty-nine. Then--"

"Oh, do be quiet, Peterkin, please," said I, with a shudder. "You put things in such a fearfully dark and murderous light that I feel quite as if I were a murderer. I feel quite uneasy, I assure you; and if it were not that we have killed all these creatures in the cause of science, I should be perfectly miserable."

"In the cause of science!" repeated Peterkin; "humph! I suspect that a good deal of wickedness is perpetrated under the wing of science."

"Come, come," said Jack; "don't you begin to grow sarcastic, Master Peterkin. I abominate sarcasm, and cannot tolerate sarcastic people. If you adopt that style, I shall revert to my natural habits as a gorilla, and tear you in pieces."

"There you exhibit your unnatural ignorance of your own natural habits," retorted Peterkin; "for you ought to know that gorillas never tear men in pieces--their usual mode being to knock you down with a blow of their huge paws."

"Well, I will knock you down if you prefer it."

"Thank you; I'd rather not. Besides, you have almost knocked me up already; so pray call a halt and let me rest a bit."

We were all very willing to agree to this request, having walked the last two or three miles at a very quick pace. Seating ourselves on the trunk of a fallen tree, we enjoyed the beautiful prospect before us. An open vista enabled us to see beyond the wood in which we were travelling into an extensive sweep of prairie-land on which the sinking sun was shedding a rich flood of light. It happened to be a deliciously cool evening, and the chattering of numerous parrots as well as the twittering songs of other birds--less gorgeous, perhaps, but more musical than they--refreshed our ears as the glories of the landscape did our eyes. While we were gazing dreamily before us in silent enjoyment, Jack suddenly interrupted our meditations by exclaiming--

"Hist! look yonder!"

He pointed as he spoke to a distant part of the plain on which the forest closely pressed.

"A zebra!" cried I, with delight; for besides the feeling of pleasure at seeing this splendid creature, I entertained a hope that we might shoot him and procure a steak for supper, of which at that time we stood much in need.

"I'm too tired to stalk it now," said Peterkin, with an air of chagrin.--"Are you up to it, Jack?"

"Quite; but I fear he's an animal that's very difficult to stalk in such an open country.--What say you, Mak?"

"Hims no be cotched dis yer night, massa; hims too far away an' too wide 'wake."

"What say you to a long shot, Peterkin? Your rifle is sighted for four hundred yards, and he seems to be little more than six hundred off."

"I'll try," said our friend, going down on one knee and adjusting the sight of his piece. Taking a long, steady aim, he fired, and in another instant the zebra lay dead on the plain. I need hardly add that our amazement was excessive. Even Peterkin himself could scarcely believe his eyes. Had his rifle been sighted for such a distance, the shot, although a splendid one, would not have amazed us so much, because we knew that our friend's aim was deadly; but as he had to elevate the muzzle above the object fired at and guess the amount of elevation, the shot was indeed wonderful. It was a long time before our guide could move, but when he did recover himself he danced and shouted like a madman with delight, and then, setting off with a bound, sped across the plain like a deer.

"Come along," cried Jack with a laugh--"let's follow; for Mak looked so rabid when he went off that I believe he'll eat the beast raw before we can claim our share, if we don't look sharp."

We all of us set off at a smart trot, and soon came to the spot where our prize lay. It was a splendid creature, and in prime condition. After examining it carefully, and descanting on the beauty of its striped skin, I sat down beside it and pulled out my note-book, while my comrades entered the forest to search for a suitable place on which to encamp, and to kindle a fire. A spot was quickly found, and I had scarcely finished making notes when they returned to carry the zebra into the encampment. We accomplished this with some difficulty, and laid it beside the fire. Then cutting four large steaks from its flanks we proceeded to sup, after which we made our arrangements for spending the night there. We little knew the startling surprise that was in store for us that night.

As the forest in that place happened to be swarming with wild animals of every kind, we deemed it prudent to set a watch as well as to keep up a blazing fire. Jack and I and the negro kept watch by turns; Peterkin, being still sufficiently an invalid to claim exemption from laborious duties, was permitted to rest undisturbed.

About midnight I aroused Jack, and having made him sit up, in order to show that he was thoroughly awake, I lay down and went to sleep.

How long I slept I cannot tell, but I was suddenly awakened by one of the most tremendous roars I ever heard. It was so chose to me that, in the confusion of my sleepy brain, it seemed to be far more terrible than that even of the gorilla. I was mistaken in this, however, and no doubt my semi-somnolent condition tended to increase its awfulness.

Springing into a sitting posture, and by an involuntary impulse reaching out my hand for my gun which lay close to me, I beheld a sight that was calculated to appal the stoutest heart. A lion of the largest size was in the very act of springing over the bushes and alighting on the zebra, which, as I have said, lay on the other side of the fire and not four yards off from us. As the light glared in the brute's eyes, and, as it were, sparkled in gleams on its shaggy mane, which streamed out under the force of its majestic bound, it seemed to my bewildered gaze as though the animal were in the air almost above my head, and that he must inevitably alight upon myself. This, at least, is the impression left upon my mind now that I look back upon that terrific scene. But there was no time for thought. The roar was uttered, the bound was made, and the lion alighted on the carcass of the zebra almost in one and the same moment. I freely confess that my heart quailed within me. Yet that did not prevent my snatching up my gun; but before I had time to cock it the crashing report of Jack's elephant rifle almost split the drum of my ear, and I beheld the lion drop as if it had been a stone.

It lay without motion, completely dead, and we found, on examination, that the ball had smashed in the centre of its forehead and completely penetrated its brain.

Some time elapsed before we could find words to express our feelings. Our guide, who had so completely enveloped his head and shoulders in grass when he lay down to sleep that he was the last to spring up, looked at the huge carcass of the lion with an expression of utter bewilderment.

"What a magnificent fellow! And what a splendid shot!" exclaimed Peterkin at last. "Why, Jack, I don't believe there's a finer lion in Africa. It's lucky, though, that you were on the qui vive."

"Yes," said I; "had it not been for you we might have been all killed by this time."

"No fear o' dat," chimed in our guide, as he sat down on the lion's shoulder, and began to stroke its mane; "hims was want him's supper off de zebra, ho! ho! Hims got him's supper off a bullet!"

"'Tis well that he has," observed Jack, as he reloaded his rifle. "To say truth, comrades, I scarcely deserve credit for being guardian of the camp, for I'm ashamed to say that I was sound asleep at the moment the lion roared. How I ever managed to take so quick and so good an aim is more than I can tell. Luckily my rifle was handy, and I had fallen asleep in a sitting posture. Had it been otherwise, I could scarcely have been in time to prevent the brute springing on us, had he felt so disposed."

Here was now another subject for my note-book, so I sat down, and began a minute inspection of the noble-looking animal, while my comrades, heaping fresh logs on the fire, sat down in front of it, and for upwards of an hour, "fought their battles o'er again."

It was a matter of deep regret to us all that we could not afford to carry away with us the skin of this lion as a memorial; but circumstanced as we then were, that was out of the question, so we contented ourselves with extracting his largest teeth and all his claws, which we still preserve in our museum as trophies of the adventure.

CHAPTER SEVENTEEN.

WE VISIT A NATURAL MENAGERIE, SEE WONDERFUL SIGHTS, AND MEET WITH STRANGE ADVENTURES.

We observed, on this journey, that the elephants which we met with in our farthest north point were considerably smaller than those farther to the south, yet though smaller animals, their tusks were much larger then those of the south. The weight of those tusks varied from twenty to fifty pounds, and I saw one that was actually upwards of one hundred pounds in weight-- equal, in fact, to the weight of a big boy or a little man. Such tusks, however, were rare.

At nights, when we encamped near to a river or pool of water, we saw immense numbers of elephants come down to drink and enjoy themselves. They seemed, in fact, to be intoxicated with delight, if not with water; for they screamed with joy, and filling their trunks with water, spurted it over themselves and each other in copious showers. Of course, we never disturbed them on such occasions, for we came to the conclusion that it would be the height of barbarity and selfishness to spoil the pleasure of so many creatures merely for the sake of a shot.

Frequently we were wont to go after our supper to one of those ponds, when we chanced to be in the immediate neighbourhood of one, and lying concealed among the bushes, watch by the light of the moon the strange habits and proceedings of the wild creatures that came there to drink. The hours thus passed were to me the most interesting by far that I spent in Africa. There was something so romantic in the kind of scenery, in the dim mysterious light, and in the grand troops of wild creatures that came there in all the pith and fire of untamed freedom to drink. It was like visiting a natural menagerie on the most magnificent scale; for in places where water is scarce any pool that may exist is the scene of constant and ever-changing visits during the entire night.

In fact, I used to find it almost impossible to tear myself away, although I knew that repose was absolutely needful, in order to enable me to continue the journey on the succeeding day, and I am quite certain that had not Peterkin and Jack often dragged me off in a jocular way by main force, I should have remained there all night, and have fallen asleep probably in my ambush.

One night of this kind that we passed I shall never forget. It was altogether a remarkable and tremendously exciting night; and as it is a good type of the style of night entertainment to be found in that wild country, I shall describe it.

It happened on a Saturday night. We were then travelling through a rather dry district, and had gone a whole day without tasting water. As evening approached we came, to our satisfaction, to a large pond of pretty good water, into which we ran knee-deep, and filling our caps with water, drank long and repeated draughts. Then we went into a piece of jungle about a quarter of a mile distant, and made our encampment, intending to rest there during the whole of the Sabbath.

I may mention here that it was our usual custom to rest on the Sabbath days. This we did because we thought it right, and we came ere long to know that it was absolutely needful; for on this journey southward we all agreed that as life and death might depend on the speed with which we travelled, we were quite justified in continuing our journey on the Sabbath. But we found ourselves at the end of the second week so terribly knocked up that we agreed to devote the whole of the next Sabbath to repose. This we did accordingly, and found the utmost benefit from it; and we could not avoid remarking, in reference to this on the care and tenderness of our heavenly Father, who has so arranged that obedience to His command should not only bring a peculiar blessing to our souls, but, so to speak, a natural and inevitable advantage to our bodies. These reflections seemed to me to throw some light on the passage, "The sabbath was made for man, and not man for the sabbath." But as this is not the place for theological disquisition, I shall not refer further to that subject.

Not having, then, to travel on the following day, we made up our minds to spend an hour or two in a place of concealment near the margin of this pond; and I secretly resolved that I would spend the whole night there with my note-book (for the moon, we knew, would be bright), and make a soft pillow of leaves on which I might drop and go to sleep when my eyes refused any longer to keep open.

The moon had just begun to rise when we finished our suppers and prepared to go to our post of observation. We took our rifles with us of course, for although we did not intend to shoot, having more than sufficient food already in camp, we could not tell but that at any moment those weapons might be required for the defence of our lives. Makarooroo had been too long accustomed to see wild animals to understand the pleasure we enjoyed in merely staring at them, so he was left in charge of our camp.

"Now, then," said Peterkin, as we left the encampment, "hurrah, for the menagerie!"

"You may well call it that," said Jack, "for there's no lack of variety."

"Are we to shoot?" inquired Peterkin.

"Better not, I think. We don't require meat, and there is no use in murdering the poor things. What a splendid scene!"

We halted to enjoy the view for a few seconds. The forest out of which we had emerged bordered an extensive plain, which was dotted here and there with scattered groups of trees, which gave to the country an exceedingly rich aspect. In the midst of these the pond lay glittering in the soft moonlight like a sheet of silver. It was surrounded on three sides by low bushes and a few trees. On the side next to us it was open and fully exposed to view. The moonlight was sufficiently bright to render every object distinctly visible, yet not so bright as to destroy the pleasant feeling of mysterious solemnity that pervaded the whole scene. It was wonderfully beautiful. I felt almost as if I had reached a new world.

Continuing our walk we quickly gained the bushes that fringed the margin of the pool, which was nowhere more than thirty yards broad, and on our arrival heard the hoofs of several animals that we had scared away clattering on the ground as they retreated.

"There they go already," cried Jack; "now let us look for a hillock of some kind on which to take up our position."

"We shall not have to look far," said I, "for here seems a suitable spot ready at our hand."

"Your eyes are sharp to-night, Ralph," observed Peterkin; "the place is splendid, so let's to work."

Laying down our rifles, we drew our hunting-knives, and began to cut down some of the underwood on the top of a small hillock that rose a little above the surrounding bushes, and commanded a clear view of the entire circumference of the pond. We selected this spot for the double reason that it was a good point of observation and a safe retreat, as animals coming to the pond to drink, from whatever quarter they might arrive, would never think of ascending a hillock covered with bushes, if they could pass round it.

Having cleared a space sufficiently large to hold us--leaving, however, a thin screen of shrubs in front through which we intended to peep--we strewed the ground with leaves, and lay down to watch with our loaded rifles close beside us. We felt certain of seeing a good many animals, for even during the process of preparing our unlace of retreat several arrived, and were scared away by the noise we made.

Presently we heard footsteps approaching.

"There's something," whispered Peterkin.

"Ay," returned Jack. "What I like about this sort o' thing is your uncertainty as to what may turn up. It's like deep-sea fishing. Hist! look out."

The steps were rapid. Sometimes they clattered over what appeared to be pebbly ground, then they became muffled as the animal crossed a grassy spot; at last it trotted out of the shade of the bushes directly opposite to us into the moonlight, and showed itself to be a beautiful little antelope of the long-horned kind, with a little fawn by its side. The two looked timidly round for a few seconds, and snuffed the air as if they feared concealed enemies, and then, trotting into the water, slaked their thirst together. I felt as great pleasure in seeing them take a long, satisfactory draught as if I had been swallowing it myself, and hoped they would continue there for some time; but they had barely finished when the rapid gallop of several animals was heard, and scared them away instantly.

The newcomers were evidently heavy brutes, for their tread was loud and quite distinct, as compared with the steps of the antelopes. A few seconds sufficed to disclose them to our expectant eyes. A large herd of giraffes trotted to the water's edge and began to drink. It was a splendid sight to behold these graceful creatures stooping to drink, and then raising their heads haughtily to a towering height as they looked about from side to side. In the course of a couple of hours we saw elands, springboks, gnus, leopards, and an immense variety of wild creatures, some of which fawned on and played with each other, while others fought and bellowed until the woods resounded with the din.

While we were silently enjoying the sight, and I attempting to make a few entries in my note-book, our attention was attracted to a cracking of the branches close to the right side of our hillock.

"Look out!" whispered Jack; but the warning was scarcely needed, for we instinctively seized our rifles. A moment after our hearts leaped violently as we heard a crashing step that betokened the approach of some huge creature.

"Are we safe here?" I whispered to Jack.

"Safe enough if we keep still. But we shall have to cut and run if an elephant chances to get sight of us."

I confess that at that moment I felt uneasy. The hillock on the summit of which we lay was only a place of comparative safety, because no animal was likely to ascend an elevated spot without an object in view, and as the purpose of all the nocturnal visitors to that pond was the procuring of water, we did not think it probable that any of them would approach unpleasantly near to our citadel; but if any wild beast should take a fancy to do so, there was nothing to prevent him, and the slight screen of bushes by which we were surrounded would certainly have been no obstacle in the way.

A hunter in the African wilds, however, has not much time to think. Danger is usually upon him in a moment. We had barely time to full-cock our rifles when the bushes near us were trodden down, and a huge black rhinoceros sauntered slowly up to us. So near was he that we could have sprung out from our hiding-place and have caught hold of him, had we chosen to do so.

This enormous unwieldy monster seemed to me so large that he resembled an elephant on short legs, and in the dim, mysterious moonlight I could almost fancy him to be one of those dreadful monsters of the antediluvian world of which we read so much in these days of geological research. I held my breath and glanced at my comrades. They lay perfectly motionless, with their eyes fixed on the animal, which hesitated on approaching our hillock. My blood almost stagnated in my veins. I thought that he must have observed us or smelt us, and was about to charge. He was only undecided as to which side of the hillock he should pass by on his way to the pond. Turning to the left, he went down to the water with a heavy, rolling gait, crushing the shrubs under his ponderous feet in a way that filled me with an exalted idea of his tremendous power.

I breathed freely again, and felt as if a mighty load had been lifted off me. From the suppressed sighs vented by my comrades, I judge that they also had experienced somewhat similar relief. We had not, however, had time to utter a whisper before our ears were assailed by the most tremendous noise that we had yet heard. It came from the opposite side of the pool, as if a great torrent were rushing towards us. Presently a black billow seemed to burst out of the jungle and roll down the sloping bank of the pond.

"Elephants!" exclaimed Jack.

"Impossible," said I; "they must be buffaloes."

At that instant they emerged into the full blaze of the moon, and showed themselves to be a herd of full-grown elephants, with a number of calves. There could not have been fewer than one hundred on the margin of the pond; but from the closeness of their ranks and their incessant movements I found it impossible to count their numbers accurately. This magnificent army began to drink and throw water about, waving their trunks and trumpeting shrilly at the same time with the utmost delight. The young ones especially seemed enjoy themselves immensely, and I observed that their mothers were very attentive to them, caressing them with their trunks and otherwise showing great fondness for their offspring.

"I say," whispered Peterkin, "what a regiment of cavalry these fellows would make, mounted by gorillas armed with scythe-blades for swords and Highland claymores for dirks!"

"Ay, and cannon-revolvers in their pockets!" added Jack. "But, look-- that hideous old rhinoceros. He has been standing there for the last two minutes like a rock, staring intently across the water at the elephants."

"Hush!" said I. "Whisper softly. He may hear us."

"There goes something else on our side," whispered Peterkin, pointing to the right of our hillock. "Don't you see it? There, against the--I do believe it's another giraffe!"

"So it is! Keep still. His ears are sharp," muttered Jack, examining the lock of his rifle.

"Come, come!" said I; "no shooting, Jack. You know we came to see, not to shoot."

"Very true; but it's not every day one gets such a close shot at a giraffe. I must procure a specimen for you, Ralph."

Jack smiled as he said this, and raised his rifle. Peterkin at the same moment quietly raised his, saying, "If that's your game, my boy, then here goes at the rhinoceros. Don't hurry your aim; we've lots of time."

As I waited for the reports with breathless attention, I was much struck at that moment by the singularity of the circumstances in which we were placed. On our left stood the rhinoceros, not fifteen yards off; on our right the giraffe raised his long neck above the bushes, about twenty yards distant, apparently uncertain whether it was safe to advance to the water; while in front lay the lake, reflecting the soft, clear moonlight, and beyond that the phalanx of elephants, enjoying themselves vastly. I had but two moments to take it all in at a glance, for Jack said "Now!" in a low tone, and instantly the loud report of the two rifles thundered out upon the night air.

Words cannot convey, and the reader certainly cannot conceive, any idea of the trumpeting, roaring, crashing, shrieking, and general hubbub that succeeded to the noise of our firearms. It seemed as if the wild beasts of twenty menageries had simultaneously commenced to smash the woodwork of their cages, and to dash out upon each other in mingled fury and terror; for not only was the crashing of boughs and bushes and smaller trees quite terrific, but the thunderous tread of the large animals was absolutely awful.

We were thoroughly scared, for, in addition to all this, from the midst of the horrid turmoil there came forth a royal roar close behind us that told of a lion having been secretly engaged in watching our proceedings; and we shuddered to think that, but for our firing, he might have sprung upon us as we lay there, little dreaming of his presence.

Since our last adventure with the king of beasts, Makarooroo had entertained us with many anecdotes of the daring of lions, especially of those monsters that are termed man-eaters; so that when we heard the roar above referred to, we all three sprang to our feet and faced about with the utmost alacrity. So intent were we on looking out for this dreadful foe--for we had made up our minds that it must be a man-eating lion--that we were utterly indifferent to the other animals. But they were not indifferent to us; for the wounded rhinoceros, catching sight of us as we stood with our backs towards him, charged at once up the hillock.

To utter three simultaneous yet fearfully distinct yells of terror, spring over the low parapet of bushes, and fly like the wind in three different directions, was the work of a moment. In dashing madly down the slope my foot caught in a creeping shrub, and I fell heavily to the earth.

The fall probably saved my life, for before I could rise the rhinoceros sprang completely over me in its headlong charge. So narrow was my escape that the edge of one of its ponderous feet alighted on the first joint of the little finger of my left hand, and crushed it severely. Indeed, had the ground not been very soft, it must infallibly have bruised it off altogether. The moment it had passed I jumped up, and turning round, ran in the opposite direction. I had scarcely gone ten paces when a furious growl behind me, and the grappling sound as of two animals in deadly conflict, followed by a fierce howl, led me to conclude that the lion and the rhinoceros had unexpectedly met each other, and that in their brief conflict the former had come off second best.

But I gave little heed to that. My principal thought at that moment was my personal safety; so I ran on as fast as I could in the direction of our encampment, for which point, I had no doubt, my companions would also make.

I had not run far when the growl of a lion, apparently in front, caused me to stop abruptly. Uncertain of the exact position of the brute, I turned off to one side, and retreated cautiously and with as little noise as possible, yet with a feeling of anxiety lest he should spring upon me unawares. But my next step showed me that the lion was otherwise engaged. Pushing aside a few leaves that obstructed my vision, I suddenly beheld a lion in the midst of an open space, crouched as if for a spring. Instinctively I threw forward the muzzle of my rifle; but a single glance showed me that his tail, not his head, was towards me. On looking beyond, I observed the head and shoulders of Jack, who, like the lion, was also in a crouching position, staring fixedly in the face of his foe. They were both perfectly motionless, and there could not have been more than fifteen or twenty yards between them.

The true position of affairs at once flashed across me. Jack in his flight had unwittingly run almost into the jaws of the lion; and I now felt convinced that this must be a second lion, for it could not have been the one that was disturbed by the rhinoceros, as I had been running directly away from the spot where these two brutes had met. Jack had crouched at once. We had often talked, over our camp-fire, of such an event as unexpectedly meeting a lion face to face; and Peterkin, who knew a good deal about such matters, had said that in such a case a man's only chance was to crouch and stare the lion out of countenance. We laughed at this; but he assured us positively that he had himself seen it done to tigers in India, and added that if a man turned and ran his destruction would be certain. To fire straight in the face of a lion in such a position would be excessively dangerous; for while the bullet might kill, it was more than probable it would glance off the bone of the forehead, which would be presented at an angle to the hunter. The best thing to do, he said, was to stare steadily at the creature until it began to wince, which, if not a wounded beast, it would certainly do; and then, when it turned slowly round, to slink away, take aim at its heart, and fire instantly.

The moon was shining full in Jack's face, which wore an expression of intense ferocity I had never before witnessed, and had not believed it possible that such a look could have been called up by him. The lower part of his face, being shrouded in his black beard, was undiscernible; but his cheeks and forehead were like cold marble. His dark brows were compressed so tightly that they seemed knotted, and beneath them his eyes glittered with an intensity that seemed to me supernatural. Not a muscle moved; his gaze was fixed; and it was not difficult to fancy that he was actually, instead of apparently, petrified.

I could not, of course, observe the visage of the lion, and, to say truth, I had no curiosity on that point; for just then it occurred to me that I was directly in the line of fire, and that if my friend missed the lion there was every probability of his killing me. I was now in an agony of uncertainty. I knew not what to do. If I were to endeavour to get out of the way, I might perhaps cause Jack to glance aside, and so induce the lion to spring. If, on the other hand, I should remain where I was, I might be shot. In this dilemma it occurred to me that, as Jack was a good shot and the lion was very close, it was extremely unlikely that I should be hit; so I resolved to bide my chance, and offering up a silent prayer, awaited the issue.

It was not long of coming. The fixed gaze of a bold human eye cowed at last even the king of the woods. The lion slowly and almost imperceptibly rose, and sidled gently round, with the intention, doubtless, of bounding into the jungle. I saw that if it did so it would pass very close to me so I cocked both barrels and held my piece in readiness.

The click of my locks attracted the lion's attention; its head turned slightly round. At that instant Jack's rifle sprang to his shoulder, and the loud crack of its report was mingled with and drowned by the roar of the lion, as he sprang with a terrible bound, not past me, but straight towards me. I had no time to aim, but throwing the gun quickly to my shoulder, drew both triggers at once.

I had forgotten, in my perturbation, that I carried Peterkin's heavy elephant rifle, charged with an immense quantity of powder and a couple of six-ounce balls. My shoulder was almost dislocated by the recoil, and I was fairly knocked head over heels. A confused sound of yells and roars filled my ear for a moment. I struggled to collect my faculties.

"Hollo! Jack!--Ralph! where are you?" shouted a voice that I well knew to be that of Peterkin. "Hurrah I'm coming. Don't give in! I've killed him! The rhinoceros is dead as a door-nail! Where have you--"

I heard no more, having swooned away.

CHAPTER EIGHTEEN.

STRANGE AND TERRIBLE DISCOVERIES--JACK IS MADE COMMANDER-IN-CHIEF OF AN ARMY.

When my consciousness returned, I found myself lying on my back beside our camp-fire, with my head resting on Peterkin's knee; and the first sound I heard was his pleasant voice, as he said--

"All right, Jack; he's coming round. I'm quite certain that no serious damage is done. I know well what sort o' rap he must have got. It'll bother him a little at first, but it won't last long."

Comforted not a little by this assurance, I opened my eyes and looked up.

"What has happened?" I inquired faintly.

"Ah! that's right, Ralph. I'm glad to hear your voice again. D'you know, I thought at first it was all over with you?"

"Over with him!" echoed Peterkin; "it's only begun with him. Ralph's days of valorous deeds are but commencing.--Here, my boy; put this flask to your mouth. It's lucky I fetched it with us. Here, drink."

"No, not until you tell me what has occurred," said I, for I still felt confused in my brain.

"Then I won't tell you a word until you drink," repeated my friend, as he looked anxiously in my face and held the flask to my lips.

I sipped a mouthful, and felt much revived.

"Now," continued Peterkin, "I'll tell you what has happened. We've floored a rhinoceros and a giraffe and a lion, which, to my thinking, is a pretty fair bag to make after dusk of a Saturday night! And my big rifle has floored you, which is the least satisfactory part of the night's entertainment, but which wouldn't have occurred had you remembered my instructions, which you never do."

"Oh, I recollect now," said I, as the spirits revived me. "I'm all right.--But, Jack, I trust that you have not received damage?"

"Not a scratch, I'm thankful to say; though I must confess I was near catching an ugly wound."

"How so?" I inquired quickly, observing a peculiar smile on Jack's face as he spoke.

"Oh, make your mind easy," put in Peterkin; "it was just a small bit of an escape he made. When you let drive at the lion so effectively, one of the balls went in at his mouth and smashed its way out at the back of his skull. The other ball shaved his cheek, and lodged in a tree not two inches from Jack's nose."

"You don't mean it!" cried I, starting up, regardless of the pain occasioned to my injured shoulder by the movement, and gazing intently in Jack's face.

"Come, come," said he, smiling; "you must not be so reckless, Ralph. Lie down again, sir."

"Peterkin, you should not talk lightly of so narrow an escape," said I reproachfully. "The fact that such a terrible catastrophe has nearly occurred ought to solemnise one."

"Granted, my dear boy; but the fact that such a catastrophe did not occur, ought, I hold, to make us jolly. There's no managing a fellow like you, Ralph. I knew that if I told you of this gravely, you would get into such a state of consternational self-reproachativeness, so to speak, that you would infallibly make yourself worse. And now that I tell it to you `lightly,' as you call it, you take to blowing me up."

I smiled as my friend said this, and held out my hand, which he grasped and squeezed. Feeling at the moment overcome with drowsiness, I unconsciously retained it in my grasp, and thus fell sound asleep.

Three days after this misadventure I was nearly as well as ever, and we were once more journeying by forced marches towards the south. Two days more, we calculated, would bring us to Mbango's village. As the end of our journey approached, we grew more desperately anxious to push forward, lest we should be too late to give them timely warning of the slave-dealer's approach. We also became more taciturn, and I could see plainly that the irrepressible forebodings that filled my own heart, were shared by my companions. Poor Makarooroo never spoke, save in reply to questions addressed pointedly to himself; and seeing the state of his mind, we forbore to trouble him with conversation.

Yet, even while in this anxious state, I could not avoid noticing the singular variety and beauty of both the animal and the vegetable kingdom in the regions through which we passed.

In one part of our journey we had to cross a portion of what is called desert country, but which, notwithstanding its name, was covered with grass, and in many places with bushes, and even trees. Its vegetation, however, as compared with other parts of the country, was light; and it was almost entirely destitute of water, there being no rivers or springs; only a few pools of rain-water were to be found in the hard beds of ancient river-courses. This desert land was inhabited by numbers of bushmen and other natives, as well as by large quantities of game of various kinds. But what struck me as being most singular was the great variety of tuberous roots with which the region was supplied, and which were evidently designed by our beneficent Creator to make up to the inhabitants in a great degree for the want of a full supply of water.

I also observed, with much interest, a species of plant which, like man, is capable of being, as it were, acclimatised. It is not by nature a tuber-bearing plant; yet here it had become so, in order to be able to retain a sufficiency of moisture during the dry season. Makarooroo also dug up for us several tuber-roots, which were the size of a large turnip, and filled with a most delicious juice, which, as we were much oppressed with thirst at the time, appeared to us like nectar. Besides these, we also procured water-melons in abundance at certain spots, which were a great treat, not only to us, but also to elephants, rhinoceroses, antelopes, and many other animals, whose footprints we found in great numbers, and whose depredations among the water-melons were very evident.

During the whole of this journey we made a point, as I have already remarked, of avoiding man; not that we were indifferent to him, but anxious not to be detained at that particular time. We were very fortunate in this matter, for we succeeded in eluding the observation of the natives of many villages that we passed, in escaping others by flight, and in conciliating those who caught us by making them liberal gifts of beads.

One day we came to a halt under the most magnificent tree I ever saw. It was a mowano tree, whose trunk consisted of six stems united in one. The circumference a yard or so from the ground was eighty-four feet-- upwards of nine yards in diameter.

"What a tree for a nobleman's park!" said Jack, as we gazed at it, lost in admiration.

"Ay; and behold a gentleman worthy to take up his residence under it," said Peterkin, pointing as he spoke to a living creature that sat among the grass near its roots.

"What can it be?" I exclaimed.

"The original father of all frogs!" replied Peterkin, as he darted forward and killed the thing with a stick.

"I believe it is a frog," said Jack.

We all burst into a fit of laughter, for undoubtedly it was a frog, but certainly the largest by far that any of us had ever seen. It was quite as large as a chicken!

"What a shame to have killed it!" said I. "Why did you do it?"

"Shame! It was no shame. In the first place, I killed it because I wish you to make scientific inspection of it; and in the second place, I wanted to eat it. Why should not we as well as Frenchmen eat frogs? By the way, that reminds me that we might introduce this giant species into France, and thereby make our fortunes."

"You greedy fellow," cried Jack, who was busying himself in lighting the fire, "your fortune is made already. How many would you have?"

"D'ye know, Jack, I have been in possession of my fortune, as you call it, so short a time that I cannot realise the fact that I have it.-- Hollo! Mak, what's wrong with you?"

Peterkin thus addressed our guide because he came into the camp at that moment with a very anxious expression of countenance.

"Dere hab bin fight go on here," said he, showing several broken arrows, stained with blood, which he had picked up near our encampment.

"Ha! so there has, unless these have been shot at wild beasts," said Jack, examining the weapons carefully.

"No, massa; no shot at wild beast. De wild beast hab bin here too, but dey come for to eat mans after he dead."

"Come, let us see the spot," said Jack.

Makarooroo at once led the way, and we all followed him to a place not a hundred yards distant, where there were evident traces of a fight having taken place. Jack seemed to be much distressed at the sight.

"There can be no question as to the fact," he remarked as we returned to our fire; "and at any other time or in any other place I would have thought nothing of it, for we know well enough that the natives here often go to war with each other; but just at this time, and so near to our friend Mbango--I fear, I fear much that that villain has been before us."

"No been long, massa," said Makarooroo earnestly. "If we go quick we ketch 'im."

"We shall go quick, Mak. But in order to do that, we must eat well, and sleep at least an hour or so. If we push on just now, after a hard day's journey, without food or rest, we shall make but slow progress; and even if we did come up with the slave-dealer, we should not be in a very fit state for a battle."

This was so obvious that we all felt the wisdom of Jack's remarks; so we ate a hearty supper, and then lay down to rest. Peterkin declared the frog to be excellent, but I could not at that time make up my mind to try it.

An hour and a half after lying down, our guide awakened us, and we set forth again with recruited energies.

That night the lions and hyenas roared around us more than was their wont, as if they were aware of our anxious condition, and were desirous of increasing our discomforts. We had to keep a sharp lookout, and once or twice discharged our rifles in the direction of the nearest sounds, not in the expectation of hitting any of the animals, but for the purpose of scaring them away.

Towards morning we came out upon an open plain, and left these evil prowlers of the night behind us.

About daybreak we came within sight of Mbango's village, but the light was not sufficient to enable us to distinguish any object clearly. Here again we came upon traces of war, in the shape of broken arrows and daggers, and human bones; for the poor wretches who had been slain had been at once devoured by wild beasts.

Hurrying forward with intense anxiety, we reached the outskirts of the village; and here a scene presented itself that was well calculated to fill our breasts with horror and with the deepest anxiety. Many of the houses had been set on fire, and were reduced to ashes. The mangled corpses of human beings were seen lying here and there amongst the embers--some partially devoured by wild beasts, others reduced to simple skeletons, and their bones left to whiten on the ruins of their old homes. In one place the form of a woman tied to a tree, and dreadfully mangled, showed that torture had been added to the other horrors of the attack.

With feelings of mingled rage, pity, and anxiety, we hastened towards the hut that had been the residence of Mbango, the chief. We found it, like the rest, in ruins, and among them discovered the remains of a child. Recollecting the little son of our friend Njamie, Okandaga's guardian, I turned the body over in some anxiety; but the features were too much mutilated to be recognisable.

"Alas! alas!" I exclaimed, as we collected in a group round this remnant of a little child, "what a dreadful sight! What an unhappy race of beings! Without doubt our friends have been slain, or carried into captivity."

Poor Makarooroo, who had been from the first going about among the ruins like a maniac, with a bewildered air of utter despair on his sable countenance, looked at me as if he hoped for a slight word that might reanimate hope in his bosom. But I could give him none, for I myself felt hopeless.

Not so, Jack. With that buoyancy of spirit that was peculiar to him, he suggested many ideas that consoled our guide not a little.

"You see," said he, "the rascally Portuguese trafficker in human flesh would naturally try to effect his object with as little bloodshed as possible. He would just fight until he had conquered, not longer; and then he would try to take as many prisoners as he could, in order to carry them away into slavery. Now, I cannot conceive it possible that he could catch the whole tribe."

"Of course not," interrupted Peterkin; "he had a comparatively small party. To take a whole tribe prisoners with such a band were impossible."

"Ay, but you forget," said I, "that he might easily prevail on some other tribe to go to war along with him, and thus capture nearly the whole. Yet some must have escaped into the woods, and it is probable that among these may have been the chief and his household. Okandaga may be safe, and not far off, for all we know."

The guide shook his head.

"At any rate," observed Jack, "if caught they would certainly be guarded with care from injury; so that if we could only find out which way they have gone, we might pursue and attack them."

"Four men attack forty or fifty!" said I despondingly.

"Ay, Ralph. Why not?" asked Peterkin.

"Oh, I doubt not our pluck to do it," I replied; "but I doubt very much our chances of success."

While we were yet speaking our attention was attracted by a low wail, and the appearance of some living object creeping amongst the ruins not far from us. At first we thought it must be a beast of prey lurking in the neighbourhood of the dead, and impatient at our having interrupted its hideous banquet; but presently the object sat up and proved to be a woman. Yet she was so covered with blood and dust, and so awfully haggard in appearance, that we could with difficulty believe her to be a human being.

At first she appeared to be in ignorance of our presence. And indeed so she actually was; for her whole soul was absorbed in the contemplation of the dead and mangled body of an infant which lay in her arms, and which she pressed ever and anon with frantic energy to her breast, uttering occasionally a wail of such heart-broken sadness that the tears sprang irresistibly into my eyes while I gazed upon her. There needed no explanation of her tale of woe. The poor mother had crept back to her hut after the fierce din of battle was over to search for her child, and she had found it; but ah, who can conceive the unutterable anguish of heart that its finding had occasioned!

"Speak to her, Mak," said Peterkin, in a husky voice; "she will be less afraid of you, no doubt, than of us."

Our guide advanced. The slight noise he made in doing so attracted the poor woman's attention, and caused her to look up with a wild, quick glance. The instant she saw us she leaped up with the agility of a leopard, clasped her dead child tightly to her breast, and uttering shriek upon shriek, rushed headlong into the jungle.

"After her!" cried Jack, bounding forward in pursuit. "She's our only chance of gaining information."

We all felt the truth of this, and joined in the chase at top speed. But although we ran fast and well, the affrighted creature at first outstripped us. Then, as we tired her out and drew near, she doubled on her track, and dived hither and thither among the thick underwood in a way that rendered it exceedingly difficult to catch her.

Peterkin was the first to come up with her. He gradually but perseveringly ran her down. When he came within a few yards of her, the poor creature sank with a low wail to the ground, and turning half round, glanced at her pursuer with a timid, imploring, yet despairing expression. Alas! despair mingled with it, because she knew too well the terrible cruelty of savage men when their blood is up, and she knew nothing yet of the hearts of Christians.

Peterkin, whose susceptible nature was ever easily touched, felt a thrill of self-reproach as the thought suddenly occurred that, however good his intentions might be, he was in reality running a helpless woman down like a bloodhound. He stopped short instantly, and acting, as on most occasions he did, impulsively, he threw his rifle away from him, unclasped his belt, and throwing it, with his hunting-knife, also away, sat down on the ground and held out both his hands.

There was something almost ludicrous in the act, but it had the effect of, to some extent, relieving the poor woman's fears. Seeing this, as we successively came up we all laid down our rifles, and stood before the crouching creature with our empty hands extended towards her, to show that we meant her no harm. Still, although she seemed less terrified, she trembled violently, and panted from her recent exertion, but never for a moment relaxed her hold of the dead child.

"Speak to her, Mak," said Jack, as the guide came up. "Tell her who and what we are at once, to relieve her feelings; and let her know especially that we are the bitter enemies of the villain who has done this deed."

While Makarooroo explained, the woman's countenance seemed to brighten up, and in a few minutes she began to tell with great volubility the events of the attack. The trader, she said, had come suddenly on them in the dead of night with a large band, and had at once routed the warriors of the village, who were completely taken by surprise. A few had escaped; but Mbango, with Okandaga and his household, had been taken prisoners, and carried away with many others.

"How long is it since this happened?" inquired Jack.

"She say two days, massa. Den dey go off to 'tack King Jambai."

"Ah! then it is too late to save him," returned Jack, in a tone of sadness.

Our hearts sank on learning this; but on questioning the woman further, we found that the marauding party, deeming themselves too weak to attack so large a village as that of King Jambai, had talked of turning aside to secure the assistance of another tribe not far distant, who, they knew, would be too glad to pick a quarrel with that chief.

"Then we shall do it yet!" cried Jack, springing up energetically. "We shall be in time to warn Jambai and to save Okandaga and her friends. Come, Mak, cheer up; things begin to look better."

The cheerful, confident voice in which our friend said this raised my hopes wonderfully, even although, on consideration, I could not see that our chances of success were very great. Our guide was visibly comforted, and we stepped aside to pick up our rifles with considerable alacrity.

During the brief period in which we were thus employed, the poor woman managed to creep away, and when we again looked round she was gone. Our first impulse was to give chase again, but the thought of the needless terror which that would occasion her deterred us, and before we could make up our minds what to do she was almost beyond our reach, and would certainly have cost us an hour of search, if not longer, to find her. Time pressed. To reach the village of King Jambai with the utmost possible speed was essential to the safety of the tribe, so we resolved to leave her, feeling as we did so that the poor creature could sustain herself on roots and berries without much difficulty or suffering until she reached the village of some neighbouring tribe.

We now pushed on again by forced marches, travelling by night and by day, shooting just enough game as we required for food, and taking no more rest than was absolutely necessary to enable us to hold on our way. In a short time we reached the village, which, to our great joy, we found in much the same state as it was when we left it.

King Jambai received us with great delight, and his people went into a state of immense rejoicing--firing guns, and shouting, and beating kettles and drums, in honour of the arrival of the "white faces;" which name was certainly a misnomer, seeing that our faces had by that time become the very reverse of white--indeed they were little lighter than the countenances of the good people by whom we were surrounded.

But the king's consternation was very great when we told him the reason of our unexpected visit, and related to him the details of the terrible calamity that had befallen poor Mbango and his people. He appeared sincerely grateful for the effort we had made to warn him of the impending attack, and seemed unable to express his thanks when we offered to aid him in the defence of his village.

We now deemed this a fitting moment to tell the king boldly of our having assisted in the escape of Okandaga from his village, and beg his forgiveness. He granted this at once, but strongly advised us to keep our secret quiet, and leave it to him to account to his warriors for the reappearance of the runaway maiden when retaken. Of course we could make no objection to this, so after thanking him we entered upon a discussion of the best method of frustrating the slave-dealer's designs.

"Tell the king," said Jack, addressing himself to our guide, "that if he will make me commander-in-chief of his forces, I will show him how white warriors manage to circumvent their enemies."

"I would like much," said Peterkin, laughing, "to know how Mak will translate the word `circumvent.' Your style is rather flowery, Jack, for such an interpreter; and upon my word, now I think of it, your presumption is considerable. How do you know that I do not wish to be commander-in-chief myself?"

"I shall make over the command to you with all my heart, if you wish it," said Jack, smiling blandly.

"Nay, I'll none of it. However suited I may be to the work, the work is not suited to me, so I resign in your favour."

"Well, then," said Jack, "since you decline to accept the chief command, I'll make you my second. Mak shall be my aide-de-camp; you and Ralph shall be generals of divisions."

"I thank you much, my honoured and honourable generalissimo; but perhaps before being thus liberal of your favours, it were well to ascertain that your own services are accepted."

"That is soon done.--What says the king, Mak?"

"Hims say that him's delighted to git you, an' you may doos how you like."

"That's plain and explicit. You see, Peterkin, that I'm fairly installed; so you and I will take a short walk together, and hold a consultation as to our plans in the approaching campaign, while Ralph arranges our hut and makes things comfortable."

"A glorious campaign, truly, to serve in an army of baboons, led by a white gorilla! I would deem it almost comical, did I not see too sure a probability of bloodshed before its conclusion," remarked Peterkin.

"That you shall not see, if I can prevent it; and it is for the purpose of consulting you on that point, and claiming your services in an old and appropriate character, that I drag you along with me now," said Jack, as he rose, and, making a bow to the king, left the hut.

CHAPTER NINETEEN.

PREPARATIONS FOR WAR, AND PECULIAR DRILL.

The plan which Jack and Peterkin concocted, while I was engaged in making the interior of our old residence as comfortable as possible, was as follows:--

Scouts were, in the first place, to be sent out that night all over the country, to ascertain the whereabouts of the enemy. Then, when the enemy should be discovered, they were to send back one of their number to report; while the remainder should remain to dog their steps, if need be, in order to ascertain whether Mbango and Okandaga were in their possession, and if so, where they were kept--whether in the midst of the warriors or in their rear.

This settled, the remainder of the warriors of the village were to be collected together, and a speech to be made to them by Jack, who should explain to them that they were to be divided into two bands: all who carried guns to be under the immediate charge of Jack himself; the others, carrying bows and spears, to be placed under me. Peterkin was to act a peculiar part, which will appear in the course of narration.

Having partaken of a hearty supper, we assembled the scouts, and having, through Makarooroo, given them their instructions, sent them away just as the shades of night began to fall. We next caused a huge bonfire to be kindled, and round this all the men of the village assembled, to the extent of several hundreds. The king soon appeared, and mounting the trunk of a fallen tree, made a long speech to his warriors, telling them of the danger that threatened them, in such vivid and lively terms that the greater part of them began to exhibit expressions of considerable uneasiness on their countenances. He then told them of the trouble that we had taken, in order to give them timely warning--whereat they cast upon us looks of gratitude; and after that introduced Jack to them as their commander-in-chief, saying, that as a white man led the enemy, nothing could be better than that a white man should lead them to meet the enemy--whereat the sable warriors gave a shout of satisfaction and approval.

Having been thus introduced, Jack mounted the trunk of the fallen tree, and Makarooroo got up beside him to interpret. He began, like a wise diplomatist, by complimenting King Jambai, and spoke at some length on courage in general, and on the bravery of King Jambai's warriors in particular; which, of course, he took for granted. Then he came to particulars, and explained as much of his intended movements as he deemed it good for them to know; and wound up by saying that he had three words of command to teach them, which they must learn to understand and act upon that very night. They were, "Forward!" "Halt!" and "Fire!" By saying the first of these words very slow and in a drawling voice, thus, "Forw-a-a-a-a-a-rd!" and the second in a quick, sharp tone, and the third in a ferocious yell that caused the whole band to start, he actually got them to understand and distinguish the difference between the commands, and to act upon them in the course of half an hour.

The drill of his army being thus completed, Jack dismissed them with a caution to hold themselves in readiness to answer promptly the first call to arms; and the king enforced the caution by quietly assuring them that the man who did not attend to this order, and otherwise respect and obey Jack as if he were the king, should have his heart, eyes, and liver torn out, and the rest of his carcass cast to the dogs--a threat which seemed to us very horrible and uncalled for, but which, nevertheless, was received by the black warriors with perfect indifference.

"Now, Mak," said Jack, as he descended to the ground, "do you come with me, and help me to place sentries."

"W'at be dat, massa?"

"Men who are placed to guard the village from surprise during the night," explained Jack.

"Ho! dat be de ting; me know someting 'bout dat."

"No doubt you do, but I daresay you don't know the best way to place them; and perhaps you are not aware that the pretty little threat uttered by the king shall be almost carried out in the case of every man who shall be found asleep at his post or who shall desert it."

The guide grinned and followed his commander in silence, while I returned to our hut and busied myself in cleaning the rifles and making other preparations for the expected fight.

At an early hour on the following morning we were awakened by the arrival of one of the scouts, who reported that the Portuguese trader, with a strong and well-armed force, was encamped on the margin of a small pond about fifteen miles distant from the village. The scout had gone straight to the spot on being sent out, knowing that it was a likely place for them to encamp, if they should encamp at all. And here he found them making active preparations for an attack on the village. Creeping like a serpent through the grass, the scout approached near enough to overhear their arrangements, which were to the elect that the attack should take place at midnight of the following day. He observed that there were many prisoners in the camp--men, women, and children-- and these were to be left behind, in charge of a small party of armed men; while the main body, under the immediate command of the Portuguese trader, should proceed to the attack of the village.

From the scout's description of the prisoners, we became convinced that they were none other than our friends Mbango and his people, and one woman answering to the description of Okandaga was among them.

"So, Mak, we shall save her yet," cried Jack heartily, slapping the shoulder of the guide, whose honest visage beamed with returning hope.

"Yis, massa. S'pose we go off dis hour and fight 'em?"

"Nay; that were somewhat too hasty a movement. `Slow but sure' must be our motto until night. Then we shall pounce upon our foes like a leopard on his prey. But ask the scout if that is all he has got to tell us."

"Hims say, massa, dat hims find one leetle chile--one boy--when hims go away from de camp to come back to here."

"A boy!" repeated Jack; "where--how?"

"In de woods, where hims was trow'd to die; so de scout take him up and bring him to here."

"Ah, poor child!" said I; "no doubt it must have been sick, and being a burden, has been left behind. But stay. How could that be possible if it was found between the camp and this village?"

On further inquiry, we ascertained that the scout, after hearing what he thought enough of their arrangements, had travelled some distance beyond the encampment, in order to make sure that there were no other bands connected with the one he had left, and it was while thus engaged that he stumbled on the child, which seemed to be in a dying condition.

"Hims say, too," continued Makarooroo, after interpreting the above information, "that there be one poor woman in awfable sorrow, screechin' and hollerowin' like one lion."

"Eh?" exclaimed Peterkin. "Describe her to us."

The scout did so as well as he could.

"As sure as we live," cried Peterkin, "it is our friend Njamie, and the child must be her boy! Come, show us the little fellow."

We all ran out and followed the scout to his hut, where we found his wives--for he had three of them--nursing the child as tenderly as if it had been their own. It was very much wasted, evidently through want of food and over-fatigue; but we instantly recognised the once sturdy little son of Njamie in the faded little being before us. He, too, recognised us, for his bright spectral eyes opened wide when he saw us.

"I knew it," said I.

"I told you so," cried Peterkin.--"Now, Mak, pump him, and let's hear what he knows."

The poor child was far too much exhausted to undergo the pumping process referred to. He could merely answer that Njamie and Okandaga and Mbango were prisoners in the camp, and then turned languidly away, as if he desired rest.

"Poor boy!" said Peterkin tenderly, as he laid his hand gently on the child's woolly pate.--"Tell them, Mak, to look well after him here, and they shall be paid handsomely for--nay" (here he interrupted himself), "don't say that. 'Tis a bad thing to offer to pay for that which people are willing to do for love."

"Right, lad," said Jack: "we can easily make these poor folk happy by giving them something afterwards, without saying that it is bestowed because of their kindness to the boy. The proper reward of diligent successful labour is a prize, but the best reward of love and kindness is a warm, hearty recognition of their existence.--Just tell them, Mak, that we are glad to see them so good and attentive to the little chap.-- And now, my generals, if it is consistent with your other engagements, I would be glad to have a little private consultation with you."

"Ready and willing, my lord," said Peterkin, as we followed Jack towards the king's palace. "But," he added seriously, "I don't like to be a general of division at all."

"Why not, Peterkin?"

"Why, you see, when I was at school I found division so uncommonly difficult, and suffered so much, mentally and physically, in the learning of it, that I have a species of morbid antipathy to the very name. I even intend to refuse a seat in parliament, when offered to me, because of the divisions that are constantly going on there. If you could only make me a general of subtraction now, or--"

"That," interrupted Jack, "were easily done, by deducting you from the force altogether, and commanding you to remain at home."

"In which case," rejoined Peterkin, "I should have to become general of addition, by revolunteering my services, in order to prevent the whole expedition from resolving itself into General Muddle, whose name and services are well-known in all branches of military and civil service."

"So that," added Jack, "it all comes to this, that you and Ralph and I must carry on the war by rule of three, each taking his just and appropriate proportion of the work to be done. Now, to change the subject, there's the sun getting up, and so is the king, if I may judge from the stir in his majesty's household."

Having begged the king to assemble his warriors together, Jack now proceeded to divide them into four companies, or bands, over which he appointed respective leaders. All the men who possessed guns were assembled together in one band, numbering about one hundred and fifty men. These Jack subdivided into two companies, one including a hundred, the other fifty men. The remainder, constituting the main army, were armed with bows and arrows, spears and knives. Of these a large force was told off to remain behind and guard the village.

This home-guard was placed under command of the king in person. The hundred musketeers were placed under Peterkin's command. The other fifty were given to me, along with a hundred spear and bow men. Jack himself took command of the main body of spearmen. As Peterkin had to act a special and independent part, besides commanding his hundred musketeers, Makarooroo was made over to him, to act as lieutenant.

All these arrangements and appointments were made in a cool, quiet, and arbitrary manner by Jack, to whom the natives, including the king, looked up with a species of awe amounting almost to veneration.

"Now," said our commander-in-chief to Lieutenant Mak, "tell the niggers I am going to make them a speech," (this was received with a grunt of satisfaction), "and that if they wish to have the smallest chance of overcoming their enemies, they had better give their closest attention to what I have to say."

Another grunt of acquiescence followed this announcement.

"Say that I am going to speak to them of things so mysterious that they shall not by any conceivable or possible effort understand them."

This being quite in accordance with the superstitions and tastes of the negroes, was received with eager acclamations of delight.

"Tell them," continued Jack, in a deep, solemn tone, and frowning darkly, "that we shall gain the victory only through obedience. Each man must keep his ears open and his eye on his leader, and must obey orders at once. If the order `Halt' should be given, and any man should have his mouth open at the time, he must keep his mouth open, and shut it after he has halted."

Here Jack took occasion to revert to the three orders, "Forward," "Halt," and "Fire," and repeated the lesson several times, until his men were quite perfect. Then he put the various bodies under their respective commanders, and telling the musketeers to make believe to fire (but making sure that they should not really do it, by taking their guns from them), he made each of us give the various words separately, so that our men should become familiar with our voices.

This done, he called the generals of divisions to him, and said--

"Now, gentlemen, I am going to review my troops, and to give them their final lesson in military tactics, with the double view of seeing that they know what they have got to do, and of impressing them with a due sense of the great advantage of even a slight knowledge of drill."

He then directed us to take command of our several companies (Makarooroo being placed on this occasion over the king's band), and pointed out the separate directions in which we were ultimately to post our troops, so as to advance upon the spot on which the king stood when the signal should be given. We had already taught the men the necessity of attacking in a compact single line, and of forming up into this position from what is termed Indian file, with which latter they were already acquainted. Of course we could not hope to teach them the principles of wheeling in the short time at our command. To overcome this difficulty, we told each band to follow its leader, who should walk in front; to advance when he advanced, to retire when he retired, and to turn this way or that way, according to his movements.

At a signal we gave the word "Forward!" and the whole band defiled into the woods before the king, and disappeared like a vision, to the unutterable amazement of his majesty, who stood perfectly motionless, with eyes and mouth open to their fullest extent.

Having marched together for some distance, each leader detached his men and led them, as it were, to opposite directions of the compass, three of the bands making a considerable detour, in order to get the spot where the king stood in the centre of us. Then we halted and awaited the next signal. In about ten minutes it was given--a loud whistle--and we gave the word "Forward" again. I say "we," because the result proved that we had done so. Being out of sight of the other bands, of course I could not see how they acted.

On I rushed over brake and bush and morass, my men following me in a very good line, considering the nature of the ground. I had divided them into four lines, with an interval of about six yards between each. And it was really wonderful how well they kept in that position. The other companies had been ordered to act in the same way.

On bursting out of the woods I saw that we had outstripped the other companies, so I held my men in check by running somewhat slower; and they had been so deeply impressed with the fatal consequences of not doing exactly as I did, that they stared at me with all their eyes, to the no small risk of their lives; for one or two dashed against trees, and others tumbled head over heels into holes, in their anxiety to keep their eyes upon me.

In a few seconds I observed Peterkin spring out of the woods, followed by his men, so I went on again at full speed. As we entered the village, our ranks were sadly broken and confused by the huts; but on gaining the open space where Jack stood, I was pleased to observe that the negroes tried, of their own accord, to regain their original formation, and succeeded so well that we came on in four tolerably straight and compact lines. Each commander having been forewarned to hold his men in check, or to push forward, so as to arrive at the central point at the same moment, Jack, Peterkin, Makarooroo, and I ran in upon the king together, and unitedly gave the word "Halt!" whereupon we found ourselves in the centre of a solid square.

So deeply had the men been impressed with the necessity of obedience that they had scarcely observed each other's approach. They now stood rooted to the ground in every possible attitude of suddenly-arrested motion, and all with their eyes and mouths wide open. In another moment the result of their combined movement became evident to them, and they uttered a yell of delighted surprise.

"Very good, very good indeed," said Jack; "and that concluding yell was very effective--quite magnificent.--But you see," he added, turning to me, "although such a yell is sufficiently appalling to us, it will no doubt be a mere trifle to men who are used to it. What say you to teaching them a British cheer?"

"Absurd," said I; "they will never learn to give it properly."

"I don't know that," rejoined Jack, in a doubtful manner.

"Try," said Peterkin.

"So I will.--Mak, tell them now that I'm going to continue the speech which this little review interrupted."

"They's all ready for more, massa."

This was patent to the meanest capacity; for the negroes stood gazing at their commander-in-chief with eyes and mouths and ears open, and nostrils expanded, as if anxious to gulp in and swallow down his words through every organ.

"There is a cry," said Jack, "which the white man gives when he enters into battle--a terrible cry, which is quite different from that of the black man, and which is so awful that it strikes terror into the heart of the white man's enemies, and has even been known to make a whole army fly almost without a shot being fired. We shall let you hear it."

Thereupon Jack and I and Peterkin gave utterance to a cheer of the most vociferous description, which evidently filled the minds of the natives with admiration.

"Now," resumed Jack, "I wish my black warriors to try that cheer--"

Some of the black warriors, supposing that the expression of this wish was a direct invitation to them to begin, gave utterance to a terrific howl.

"Stay! stop!" cried Jack, holding up his hand.

Every mouth was closed instantly.

"You must cheer by command. I will say `Hip, hip, hip!' three times; as soon as I say the third `hip,' out with the cry. Now then. Hip, hip--"

"'Popotamus," whispered Peterkin.

"Hip, hurrah!" shouted Jack.

"Hurl! ho! sh! kee! how!" yelled the savages, each man giving his own idea of our terror-inspiring British cheer.

"That will do," said Jack quietly; "it is quite evident that the war-cry of the white man is not suited to the throat of the black. You will utter your usual shout, my friends, when the signal is given; but remember, not before that.

"And now I come to the greatest mystery of all." (Every ear was eagerly attentive.) "The shot and bits of metal and little stones with which King Jambai's warriors are accustomed to kill will not do on this great and peculiar occasion. They will not answer the purpose--my purpose; therefore I have provided a kind of bullet which every one must use instead of his usual shot. No warriors ever used such bullets in the fight before. They are very precious, because I have only enough of them to give one to each man. But that will do. If the enemy does not fly at the first discharge, then you may load with your own shot."

So saying, Jack, with the utmost gravity, took from the pouch that hung at his side a handful of little balls of paper about the size of a musket bullet, which he began to distribute among the savages. We had observed Jack making several hundreds of these, the night previous to this memorable day, out of one or two newspapers we had carried along with us for wadding; but he would not at that time tell us what he was going to do with them. The negroes received this novel species of ammunition with deep interest and surprise. Never having seen printed paper before, or, in all probability, paper of any kind, they were much taken up with the mysterious characters imprinted thereon, and no doubt regarded these as the cause of the supernatural power which the bullets were supposed to possess.

"Remember," said Jack, "when these are discharged at the enemy, I do not say that they will kill, but I do say that they will cause the enemy to fly. Only, be assured that everything depends on your obedience. And if one single stone, or nail, or hard substance is put in along with these bullets, the chief part of my plans will be frustrated."

It was quite evident, from the expression of their sable countenances, that the idea of the bullets not killing was anything but agreeable. They were too deeply impressed, however, with Jack's power, and too far committed in the enterprise, and generally too much overwhelmed with mingled surprise and perplexity, to offer any objection.

"Now," said Jack in conclusion, "you may go and eat well. To-night, when it grows dark, hold yourselves in readiness to go forth in dead silence. Mind that: not a sound to be uttered until the signal, `Hip, hip, hip!' is given."

"And," added Peterkin, in an undertone to Makarooroo, "tell them that King Jambai expects that every man will do his duty."

This remark was received with a shout and a frightful display of white teeth, accompanied by a tremendous flourish of guns, bows, and spears.

There was something quite awful, not to say picturesque, in this displaying of teeth, which took place many times during the course of the above proceedings. You looked upon a sea of black ebony balls, each having two white dots with black centres near the top of it. Suddenly the ebony balls were gashed across, and a sort of storm, as it were, of deep red mingled with pure white swept over the dark cloud of heads before you, and vanished as quickly as it had appeared, only to reappear, however, at the next stroke of humour, or at some "touch of that nature" which is said on very high authority, to "make the whole world kin."

The proceedings eventually closed with a brief speech from the king, who referred to Peterkin's remark about each man doing his duty, and said that, "if each man did not do his duty--" Here his majesty paused for a minute, and wrought his countenance into horrible contortions, indicative of the most excruciating agony, and wound up with an emphatic repetition of that dire threat about the unnatural treatment of eyes, heart, liver, and carcass, which had on the previous evening sounded so awful in our ears, and had been treated with such profound indifference by those whom it was specially designed to affect.

"I didn't know, Jack," observed Peterkin gravely, as we returned to our hut, "that you were such an out-and-out humbug."

"You are severe, Peterkin. I scarcely deserve to be called a humbug for acting to the best of my judgment in peculiar circumstances."

"Peculiar circumstances!" responded Peterkin. "Truly they have received peculiar treatment!"

"That is as it should be," rejoined Jack; "at any rate, be they peculiar or be they otherwise, our plans are settled and our mode of action fixed, so we must e'en abide the issue."

CHAPTER TWENTY.

A WARLIKE EXPEDITION AND A VICTORY.

It was excessively dark that night when we set forth on our expedition.

The scout from whom we had already ascertained so much about the intended movements of the enemy also told us that they meant to set out at a little before midnight and march on the village by a certain route. Indeed, it was very unlikely that they would approach by any other, as the jungle elsewhere was so thick as to render marching, especially at night, very difficult.

Jack therefore resolved to place the greater proportion of his troops in ambush at the mouth of a small gully or dell a few miles from the enemy's camp, where they were almost certain to pass. But with a degree of caution that I thought highly creditable in so young and inexperienced a general, he sent out a considerable number of the most trustworthy men in advance, with instructions to proceed with the stealth of leopards, and to bring back instant information of any change of route on the part of the foe.

The troops placed in ambush at the dell above referred to were Peterkin's hundred musketeers, supported by Jack's spear and bow men. I was ordered to advance by a circuitous route on the camp itself with my fifty musketeers, followed by my small company of spearmen. My instructions were, to conceal my men as near to the camp as possible, and there await the first discharge of firearms from the dell, when I was to rise, advance upon the camp, utter a terrific shout when within fifty yards, rush forward to within twenty-five yards, halt, pour in one withering volley of blank cartridge, and charge without giving my men time to load.

Of course I could not speak to my men; but this was a matter of little consequence, as they were now well acquainted with our three words of command, "Forward," "Halt," and "Fire," and fully understood that they must under all circumstances follow their leader. I knew well enough that there must be no little danger in this arrangement, because the leader would necessarily be always in front of the muzzles of the loaded guns. But there was no help for it, so I resolved to act upon my usual principle--namely, that when a thing is inevitable, the best thing to do is to treat it as being unavoidable.

Having conducted my men stealthily and successfully to the vicinity of the enemy's camp, though with some difficulty, owing to the almost impenetrable nature of the jungle through which we had to pass in making the detour necessary to avoid falling in with the attacking force, we proceeded to advance to within as short a distance of it as possible without running the risk of being discovered. This was not difficult, for the men left to guard the camp, supposing, no doubt, that their presence in that part of the country was not suspected, had taken no precautions in the way of placing sentries; so we quickly arrived at the foot of a small mound about sixty yards or so from the encampment. At the foot of this mound I caused my men to lie down, giving them to understand, by signs, that they were on no account to move until I should return. Then I crept alone to the brow of the mound, and obtained a clear view of the camp.

The men who should have guarded it were, I found, busily employed in cooking their supper. There were, perhaps, upwards of a hundred of them. To my great satisfaction, I observed the captives sitting near to the fire; and although at so considerable a distance from them, I felt certain that I recognised the figures of Mbango and Okandaga. Hastening back to my men, I endeavoured to give them as much information as possible by means of signs, and then lay down beside them to await the signal from Jack's party.

Although the attack of both our parties was to be simultaneous, the first shot was to be fired by our troops in the dell. I will therefore describe their part of the engagement first. Jack described it to me minutely after all was over.

On reaching the dell Jack disposed his forces so as to command the only approach to it. The hundred musketeers he placed in a double row directly across the deepest and darkest part. The spearmen he divided into two bodies, which he posted on the flanks of the musketeers among the bushes. He then showed the rear rank of the latter how to point their pieces over the shoulders of the men in the front rank at a given signal, but carefully reiterated the order not to touch a trigger until the word "Fire" should be given.

"Now, Peterkin," said Jack, when these dispositions had been made, "it is time for you to get ready. Makarooroo and I can manage these fellows, so you have my permission to go and play your own independent part. Only let me warn you to remember your last exploit in this way, and see that you don't do yourself a damage."

"Thanks, noble general, for the permission," answered Peterkin, "of which I shall avail myself. In reference to your advice, I may remark that it is exceedingly valuable--so much so, indeed, that I would advise you not to part with it until asked for."

With that Peterkin ran into the jungle, and was soon lost to view.

On gaining a sufficient distance from the men, he took off the greater part of his clothes, and wound round his person several pieces of light-coloured cotton that he chanced to have with him, and some pieces of old newspaper. Then he decked his head with leaves and ragged branches, as he had done before in the haunted cave, making himself, in short, as wild and fantastic a looking creature as possible--the only difference between his getting-up on this and the former occasion being that he was white instead of black. For he wisely judged that a white demon must naturally appear infinitely more appalling and horrible to a negro than one of his own colour.

The two cones of moistened powder, however, which he had prepared for this occasion, were very much larger than the former, and had been fitted into two wooden handles, or cups, for safety. With these in his hands, he crept to the top of a steep, sloping mound or hill near the entrance to the dell, and considerably in advance of the troops. Here he sat down to await the approach of the enemy.

There is something very eerie and awe-inspiring in a solitary night-watch, especially if it be kept in a wild, lonesome place. Peterkin afterwards told me that, while sitting that night on the top of the mound, looking out upon a plain, over which the enemy were expected to approach, on the one hand, and down into the dark dell where our troops were posted, on the other hand, his heart more than once misgave him; and he could not help asking himself the questions, "What if our plans miscarry? What if our united volley and cheer, and my demoniac display, should fail to intimidate the negroes?" Such questions he did not like to dwell upon, for he knew that in the event of failure a regular pitched battle would be fought, and much blood would certainly flow.

While indulging in such thoughts, he observed a dark form glide past the foot of the mound on which he lay, and vanish in the obscurity of the dell, which was so surrounded by crags and rocky places covered with underwood that no light could penetrate into it. At first he was startled, and thought of giving the alarm to his comrades; but on second thoughts he concluded the person must have been one of his own scouts returned with news; at all events, he felt that one man could do no harm worth speaking of to so large a party.

Presently he observed a large band of men coming over the plain towards the entrance of the dell. These, he felt assured, must be the enemy; and he was right. They came on in a large, compact body, and were well-armed; yet, from the quick and unguarded manner of their approach, he could perceive that they suspected no ambush.

They entered the dell in a confused though solid and silent body; and Peterkin could observe, by the dim light, that they were led by one man, who walked in advance, whom he rightly judged to be the Portuguese slave-dealer.

The time for action had now come. He examined the points of his powder-cones, to ascertain that they were dry, then held a match in readiness, and listened intently to the footsteps of the foe.

I have already explained that Jack had drawn his musketeers across the dell, and placed the spearmen in the jungle on both flanks. They were arranged in such a way as to form three sides of a square, into which the unsuspecting enemy now marched. Jack allowed them to approach to within thirty paces of his musketeers, and then gave, in a loud, deep, sonorous tone, the word--"Hip! hip! hip!"

The compound cheer and yell that instantly followed the last hip was so tremendous, coming, as it did, from all sides except the rear, that the enemy were absolutely paralysed. They stood rooted to the earth, as motionless as if they had been transformed into stone.

Jack raised his hand, in which he held a bunch of white grass that could be distinctly seen in the dark.

Every muzzle was pointed on the instant, but not a sound was heard save the click of a hundred locks.

The sound was familiar to the enemy, although never before heard at one moment in such numbers. They started; but before a step could be taken, the word "Fire" was given.

Instantly a sheet of flame swept across the entire dell, and the united crash of a hundred guns seemed to rend the very earth. The surrounding cliffs reverberated and multiplied the horrid din, while, led by Jack, cheer followed cheer, or rather howls and yells filled the air, and kept awake the echoes of the place.

The enemy turned and fled, and the shrieks to which they gave utterance as they ran betokened the extremity of their terror. It wanted but one touch to complete their consternation, and that touch was given when Peterkin, lighting his powder-cones, showed himself on the mound, dancing in a blaze of fire, and shrieking furiously as the horrified tide of men swept by.

In the midst of his wild orgies, Peterkin acted an impromptu and unintentional part by tripping over the brow of the hill, and rolling down the steep declivity like a fire-wheel into the very midst of the flying crew. Jumping hastily up, he charged through the ranks of the foe, flung the two hissing cones high into the air, and darting into the jungle, hid himself effectually from view.

Meanwhile Jack still held the bunch of white straw aloft. Every eye was fixed on it, but not a man moved, because it remained stationary. This absence of pursuit in the midst of such appalling sights and sounds must, undoubtedly, have added to the mystery and therefore to the terrors of the scene.

Suddenly the white bunch was seen to dart forward. Jack, who now considered the enemy almost beyond the chance of being overtaken, gave the word, "Forward!" in the voice of a Stentor, following it up with "Hip, hip, hurrah!" and the whole host, musketeers and spearmen in a mingled mass, rushed yelling out upon the plain, and gave chase to the foe.

"Not so badly done," said Jack, with a quiet laugh, as he laid his hand on Peterkin's shoulder.

"Why, Jack, how did you find me out?"

"Easily enough, when it is considered that I saw you go in. The flame of your wild-fire indicated your movements pretty plainly to me, although terror and amazement no doubt blinded the eyes of every one else. Even Mak's teeth began to chatter when he saw you perform that singular descent of the hill, and no wonder. I hope no bones have been broken?"

"No; all right as far as that goes," replied Peterkin within a laugh; "but I've lost a good deal of skin. However, it'll grow again. I'm glad it's no worse. But I say, Jack, do you think our fellows won't overtake these rascals?"

"No fear of that. I took care to give them a good start, and if there be any truth in the generally received idea that terror lends wings, I'm pretty sure that each man in the enemy's ranks must have obtained the loan of several pairs to-night. But have you heard the sound of Ralph's guns?"

"No; the din here was enough to drown anything so distant."

"Well, we must away to him as fast as we can. I expect that poor Mak is off before us."

"But you'll wait until I put on my clothes?" said Peterkin, hasting back towards the place where he had undressed.

"Certainly, lad; only look alive."

Soon afterwards they left the place together.

While this was going on at the dell, I, on hearing the first shot, gave the word "Forward!" in a low tone. My men instantly rose and followed me, and I could not, even at that anxious moment, help admiring the serpent-like facility with which they glided from bush to bush, without the slightest noise. We descended a hill, crossed a small brook, and approached to within thirty yards of the camp without being discovered.

Suddenly I leaped on the top of a hillock, and shouted at the utmost pitch of my voice the single word "Halt!"

On hearing it all the men in the camp sprang to their arms, and stood gazing round them with looks of consternation.

My next word was, "Fire!"

A firm, tremendous crash burst from among the bushes, and my single person, enveloped in smoke and flame, was, I believe, the only object visible to those in the camp.

"Hip, hip, hip, hurrah! forward!" I shouted; and with a ferocious yell we poured like a whirlwind upon the foe.

The same result that had occurred at the dell took place here. The enemy never awaited our charge. They fled instantly, and so great was their terror that they actually threw down their arms, in order to facilitate their flight.

On gaining the camp, however, I found, to my sorrow, that we had done the thing only too vigorously; for we had not only put the enemy to flight, but we had also frightened away those whom we had come to deliver!

At this point in the engagement I came to learn how incompetent I was to command men in cases of emergency, for here my presence of mind utterly forsook me. In my anxiety to capture Mbango and his friends I ordered an immediate pursuit. Then it occurred to me that, in the event of my men being successful in overtaking the fugitives, they would instantly murder them all, so I tried to call them back; but, alas! they did not understand my words, and they were by this time so excited as to be beyond all restraint. In a few minutes I found myself left alone in the enemy's camp, and heard the shouts of pursued and pursuers growing gradually fainter and more distant, as they scattered themselves through the jungle.

Seating myself by the fire in a state of mind bordering on despair, I buried my face in my hands, and endeavoured to collect myself, and consider what, under the circumstances, should be now done.

CHAPTER TWENTY

ONE.

ARRANGEMENTS FOR PURSUING THE ENEMY, AND SUDDEN CHANGE OF PLANS.

"You seem to be taking it easy, old boy," said a voice close to my elbow.

I started, and looked up hastily.

"Ah! Peterkin. You there?"

"Ay; and may I not reply, with some surprise, you here?"

"Truly you may,--but what could I do? The men ran away from me, whether I would or no; and you are aware I could not make myself understood, not being able to--But where is Jack?"

I asked this abruptly, because it occurred to me at that moment that he and Peterkin should have been together.

"Where is Jack?" echoed Peterkin; "I may ask that of you, for I am ignorant on the point. He and I got separated in endeavouring to escape from the scrimmage caused by your valiant attack. You seem to have scattered the whole force to the winds. Oh, here he is, and Mak along with him."

Jack and our guide came running into the camp at that moment.

"Well, Ralph, what of Okandaga?"

"Ah! what of her indeed?" said Peterkin. "I forgot her. You don't moan to say she was not in the camp?"

"Indeed she was," said I, "and so were Mbango, and his wife Njamie, and one or two others whom I did not know; but my men went at them with such ferocity that they fled along with our enemies."

"Fled!" cried Jack.

"Ay; and I fear much that it will fare ill with them if they are overtaken, for the men were wild with excitement and passion."

"Come, this must be looked to," cried Jack, seizing his rifle and tightening his belt; "we must follow, for if they escape our hands they will certainly be retaken by their former captors."

We followed our comrade, without further remark, in the direction of the fugitives; but although we ran fast and long, we failed to come up with them. For two hours did we dash through bush and brake, jungle and morass, led by Makarooroo, and lighted by the pale beams of the moon. Then we came to a halt, and sat down to consult.

"Dem be gone," said our wretched guide, whose cup of happiness was thus dashed from his hand just as he was about to raise it to his lips.

"Now, don't look so dismal, Mak," cried Peterkin, slapping the man on the shoulder. "You may depend upon it, we will hunt her up somehow or other. Only let us keep stout hearts, and we can do anything."

"Very easily said, Master Peterkin," observed Jack; "but what course do you propose we should follow just now?"

"Collect our scattered men; go back to the village; have a palaver with

King Jambai and his chiefs; get up a pursuit, and run the foxes to earth."

"And suppose," said Jack, "that you don't know in which direction they have fled, how can we pursue them?"

"It is very easy to suppose all manner of difficulties," retorted Peterkin. "If you have a better plan, out with it."

"I have no better plan, but I have a slight addition to make to yours, which is, that when we collect a few of our men, I shall send them out to every point of the compass, to make tracks like the spokes of a wheel, of which the village shall be the centre; and by that means we shall be pretty certain to get information ere long as to the whereabouts of our fugitives. So now let us be up and doing; time is precious to-night."

In accordance with this plan, we rapidly retraced our steps to the dell, which had been appointed as our place of rendezvous. Here we found the greater part of our men assembled; and so well-timed had Jack's movements been, that not one of them all had been able to overtake or slay a single enemy. Thus, by able generalship, had Jack gained a complete and bloodless victory.

Having detached and sent off our scouts--who, besides being picked men, travelled without any other encumbrance than their arms--we resumed our journey homeward, and reached the village not long after sunrise, to the immense surprise of Jambai, who could scarcely believe that we had routed the enemy so completely, and whose scepticism was further increased by the total, and to him unaccountable, absence of prisoners, or of any other trophies of our success in the fight. But Jack made a public speech, of such an elaborate, deeply mysterious, and totally incomprehensible character, that even Makarooroo, who translated, listened and spoke with the deepest reverence and wonder; and when he had concluded, there was evidently a firm impression on the minds of the natives that this victory was--by some means or in some way or other quite inexplicable but highly satisfactory--the greatest they had ever achieved.

The king at once agreed to Jack's proposal that a grand pursuit should take place, to commence the instant news should be brought in by the scouts. But the news, when it did come, had the effect of totally altering our plans.

The first scout who returned told us that he had fallen in with a large body of the enemy encamped on the margin of a small pond. Creeping like a snake through the grass, he succeeded in getting near enough to overhear the conversation, from which he gathered two important pieces of information--namely, that they meant to return to their own lands in a north-easterly direction, and that their prisoners had escaped by means of a canoe which they found on the banks of the river that flowed past King Jambai's village.

The first piece of information decided the king to assemble his followers, and go off in pursuit of them at once; the second piece of news determined us to obtain a canoe and follow Mbango and his companions to the sea-coast, whither, from all that we heard, we concluded they must certainly have gone. As this, however, was a journey of many weeks, we had to take the matter into serious consideration.

"It is quite evident," said Jack, as we sat over our supper on the night after receiving the above news--"it is quite evident that they mean to go to the coast, for Mbango had often expressed to Mak a wish to go there; and the mere fact of their having been seen to escape and take down stream, is in itself pretty strong evidence that they did not mean to return to their now desolated village, seeing that the country behind them is swarming with enemies; and of course they cannot know that we have conquered the main body of these rascals. I therefore propose that we should procure a canoe and follow them: first, because we must at all hazards get hold of poor Okandaga, and relieve the anxiety of our faithful guide Makarooroo; and second, because it is just as well to go in that direction as in any other, in order to meet with wild animals, and see the wonders of this land."

"But what if King Jambai takes it into his black woolly head to decline to let us go?" said Peterkin.

"In that case we must take French leave of him."

"In which case," said I, in some alarm, "all my specimens of natural history will be lost."

Jack received this remark with a shake of his head and a look of great perplexity; and Peterkin said, "Ah, Ralph, I fear there's no help for it. You must make up your mind to say good-bye to your mummies--big puggies and all."

"But you do not know," said I energetically, "that Jambai will detain us against our will."

"Certainly not," replied Jack; "and for your sake I hope that he will not. At any rate I will go to see him about this point after supper. It's of no use presenting a petition either to king, lord, or common while his stomach is empty. But there is another thing that perplexes me: that poor sick child, Njamie's son, must not be left behind. The poor distracted mother has no doubt given him up for lost. It will be like getting him back from the grave."

"True," said I; "we must take him with us. Yet I fear he is too ill to travel, and we cannot await his recovery."

"He is not so ill as he seemed," observed Peterkin. "I went to see him only half an hour ago, and the little chap was quite hearty, and glad to see me. The fact is, he has been ill-used and ill-fed. The rest and good treatment he has received have, even in the short time he has been here, quite revived him."

"Good," said Jack; "then he shall go with us. I'll engage to take him on my back when he knocks up on the march--for we have a march before us, as I shall presently explain--and when we get into a canoe he will be able to rest."

"But what march do you refer to?" I asked.

"Simply this. Mak, with whom I have had a good deal of conversation on the subject, tells me that the river makes a considerable bend below this village, and that by taking a short cut of a day's journey or so over land we can save time, and will reach a small hamlet where canoes are to be had. The way, to be sure, is through rather a wild country; but that to us is an advantage, as we shall be the more likely to meet with game. I find, also, that the king has determined to follow the same route with his warriors in pursuit of the enemy, so that thus far we may travel together. At the hamlet we will diverge to the north-east, while we, if all goes well, embarking in our canoe, will proceed toward the west coast, where, if we do not overtake them on the way, we shall be certain to find them on our arrival. Okandaga has often longed to go to the mission station there, and as she knows it is in vain to urge Mbango to return to his destroyed village, she will doubtless advise him to go to the coast."

"What you say seems highly probable," said I; "and I think the best thing you can do is to go to the king at once and talk him over."

"Trust Jack for that," added Peterkin, who was at that moment deeply engaged with what he called the drumstick of a roast monkey. "Jack would talk over any creature with life, so persuasive is his eloquence. I say, Ralph," he added, holding the half-picked drumstick at arm's length, and regarding it with a critical gaze, "I wonder, now, how the drumstick of an ostrich would taste. Good, I have no doubt, though rather large for one man's dinner."

"It would be almost equal to gorilla ham, I should fancy," said Jack, as he left the hut on his errand to the king.

"O you cannibal, to think of such a thing!" cried Peterkin, throwing the bone of his drumstick after our retreating comrade.--"But 'tis always thus," he added, with a sigh: "man preys upon man, monkey upon monkey. Yet I had hoped better things of Jack. I had believed him to be at least a refined species of gorilla. I say, Ralph, what makes you look so lugubrious?"

"The difficulties, I suppose, that beset our path," said I sadly; for, to say truth, I did not feel in a jesting humour just then. I was forced, however, in spite of myself, to laugh at the expression of mingled disgust and surprise that overspread the mobile countenance of my friend on hearing my reply.

"`The difficulties,'" echoed he, "`that beset our path!' Really, Ralph, life will become insupportable to me if you and Jack go on in this fashion. A man of nerve and sanguine temperament might stand it, but to one like me, of a naturally timid and leaning nature, with the addition of low spirits, it is really crushing--quite crushing."

I laughed, and replied that he must just submit to be crushed, as it was impossible for Jack and me to change our dispositions to suit his convenience; whereupon he sighed, lighted his pipe, and began to smoke vehemently.

In the course of little more than an hour Jack returned, accompanied by Makarooroo, and from the satisfied expression of their faces I judged that they had been successful.

"Ah! I see; it's all right," said Peterkin, raising himself on one elbow as they entered the hut and seated themselves beside the fire. "Old Jambai has been `talked over.'"

"Right; but he needed a deal of talk--he was horribly obstinate," said Jack.

"Ho, yis; ho! ho! horribubly obsterlate," added Makarooroo in corroboration, rubbing his hands and holding his nose slyly over the bowl of Peterkin's pipe, in order to enjoy, as it were, a second-hand whiff.

"Here, there's a bit for yourself, old boy. Sit down and enjoy yourself while Jack tells us all about his interview with royalty," said Peterkin, handing a lump of tobacco to our guide, whose eyes glistened and white teeth gleamed as he received the much-prized gift.

Jack now explained to us that he had found the king in a happy state of satiety, smoking in his very curious and uneasy-looking easy-chair; that he had at first begged and entreated him (Jack) to stay and take command of his warriors, and had followed up his entreaties with a hint that it was just possible he might adopt stronger measures if entreaty failed.

To this Jack replied in a long speech, in which he pointed out the impossibility of our complying with the king's request under present circumstances, and the absolute necessity of our returning at some period or other to our native land to tell our people of the wonders we had seen in the great country of King Jambai. Observing that his arguments did not make much impression on the king, he brought up his reserve force to the attack, and offered all the remainder of our goods as a free gift to his majesty, stipulating only that he (the king) should, in consideration thereof, carefully send our boxes of specimens down to the coast, where the messengers, on arriving, should be handsomely paid if everything should arrive safely and in good order.

These liberal offers had a visible influence on the sable monarch, whose pipe indicated the state of his mind pretty clearly--thin wreaths of smoke issuing therefrom when he did not sympathise with Jack's reasoning, and thick voluminous clouds revolving about his woolly head, and involving him, as it were, in a veil of gauze, when he became pleasantly impressed. When Jack made mention of the valuable gifts above referred to, his head and shoulders were indistinctly visible amid the white cloudlets; and when he further offered to supply him with a few hundreds of the magical paper balls that had so effectually defeated his enemies the day before, the upper part of his person was obliterated altogether in smoke.

This last offer of Jack's we deemed a great stroke of politic wisdom, for thereby he secured that the pending war should be marked by the shedding of less blood than is normal in such cases. He endeavoured further to secure this end by assuring the king that the balls would be useless for the purpose for which they were made if any other substance should be put into the gun along with them, and that they would only accomplish the great end of putting the enemy to flight if fired at them in one tremendous volley at a time when the foe had no idea of the presence of an enemy.

All things being thus amicably arranged, we retired to rest, and slept soundly until daybreak, when we were awakened by the busy sounds of preparation in the village for the intended pursuit.

We, too, made active arrangements for a start, and soon after were trooping over the plains and through the jungle in the rear of King Jambai's army, laden with such things as we required for our journey to the coast, and Jack, besides his proportion of our food, bedding, cooking utensils, etcetera, carrying Njamie's little sick boy on his broad shoulders.

CHAPTER TWENTY

TWO.

WE MEET WITH A LUDICROUSLY AWFUL ADVENTURE.

The day following that on which we set out from King Jambai's village, as narrated in the last chapter, Jack, Peterkin, Makarooroo, Njamie's little boy, and I embarked in a small canoe, and bidding adieu to our hospitable friends, set out on our return journey to the coast.

We determined to proceed thither by another branch of the river which would take us through a totally new, and in some respects different, country from that in which we had already travelled, and which, in the course of a few weeks, would carry us again into the neighbourhood of the gorilla country.

One beautiful afternoon, about a week after parting from our friends, we met with an adventure in which the serious and the comic were strangely mingled. Feeling somewhat fatigued after a long spell at our paddles, and being anxious to procure a monkey or a deer, as we had run short of food, we put ashore, and made our encampment on the banks of the river. This done, we each sallied out in different directions, leaving Makarooroo in charge of the camp.

For some time I wandered about the woods in quest of game, but although I fired at many animals that were good for food, I missed them all, and was unwillingly compelled to return empty-handed. On my way back, and while yet several miles distant from the camp, I met Jack, who had several fat birds of the grouse species hanging at his girdle.

"I am glad to see that you have been more successful than I, Jack," said I, as we met.

"Yet I have not much to boast of," he replied. "It is to be hoped that Peterkin has had better luck. Have you seen him?"

"No; I have not even heard him fire a shot."

"Well, let us go on. Doubtless he will make his appearance in good time. What say you to following the course of this brook? I have no doubt it will guide us to the vicinity of our camp, and the ground immediately to the left of it seems pretty clear of jungle."

"Agreed," said I; and for the next ten minutes or so we walked beside each other in silence. Suddenly our footsteps were arrested by a low peculiar noise.

"Hark! is that a human voice?" whispered Jack, as he cocked his rifle.

"It sounds like it," said I.

At the same moment we heard some branches in an opposite direction crack, as if they had been broken by a heavy tread. Immediately after, the first sound became louder and more distinct. Jack looked at me in surprise, and gradually a peculiar smile overspread his face.

"It's Peterkin," said I, in a low whisper.

My companion nodded, and half-cocking our pieces, we advanced with slow and cautious steps towards the spot whence the sound had come. The gurgling noise of the brook prevented us from hearing as well as usual, so it was not until we were close upon the bushes that fringed the banks of the streamlet that we clearly discerned the tones of Peterkin's voice in conversation with some one, who, however, seemed to make no reply to his remarks. At first I thought he must be talking to himself, but in this I was mistaken.

"Let's listen for a minute or two," whispered my companion, with a broad grin.

I nodded assent, and advancing cautiously, we peeped over the bushes. The sight that met our eyes was so irresistibly comic that we could scarcely restrain our laughter.

On a soft grassy spot, close to the warbling stream, lay our friend Peterkin, on his breast, resting on his elbows, and the forefinger of his right hand raised. Before him, not more than six inches from his nose, sat the most gigantic frog I ever beheld, looking inordinately fat and intensely stupid. My memory instantly flew back to the scene on the coral island where Jack and I had caught our friend holding a quiet conversation with the old cat, and I laughed internally as I thought on the proverb, "The boy is the father of the man."

"Frog," said Peterkin, in a low, earnest voice, at the same time shaking his finger slowly and fixing his eyes on the plethoric creature before him--"frog, you may believe it or not as you please, but I do solemnly assure you that I never did behold such a great, big, fat monster as you are in all--my--life! What do you mean by it?"

As the frog made no reply to this question, but merely kept up an incessant puffing motion in its throat, Peterkin continued--

"Now, frog, answer me this one question--and mind that you don't tell lies-- you may not be aware of it, but you can't plead ignorance, for I now tell you that it is exceedingly wicked to tell lies, whether you be a frog or only a boy. Now, tell me, did you ever read `Aesop's Fables?'"

The frog continued to puff, but otherwise took no notice of its questioner. I could not help fancying that it was beginning to look sulky at being thus catechised.

"What, you won't speak! Well, I'll answer for you: you have not read `Aesop's Fables;' if you had you would not go on blowing yourself up in that way. I'm only a little man, it's true--more's the pity--but if you imagine that by blowing and puffing like that you can ever come to blow up as big as me, you'll find yourself mistaken. You can't do it, so you needn't try. You'll only give yourself rheumatism. Now, will you stop? If you won't stop you'll burst--there."

Peterkin paused here, and for some time continued to gaze intently in the face of his new friend. Presently he began again--

"Frog, what are you thinking of? Do you ever think? I don't believe you do. Tightened up as you seem to be with wind or fat or conceit, if you were to attempt to think the effort would crack your skin, so you'd better not try. But, after all, you've some good points about you. If it were not that you would become vain I would tell you that you've got a very good pair of bright eyes, and a pretty mottled skin, and that you're at least the size of a big chicken--not a plucked but a full-fledged chicken. But, O frog, you've got a horribly ugly big mouth, and you're too fat--a great deal too fat for elegance; though I have no doubt it's comfortable. Most fat people are comfortable. Oh! you would, would you?"

This last exclamation was caused by the frog making a lazy leap to one side, tumbling heavily over on its back, and rolling clumsily on to its legs again, as if it wished to escape from its tormentor, but had scarcely vigour enough to make the effort. Peterkin quietly lifted it up and placed it deliberately before him again in the same attitude as before.

"Don't try that again, old boy," said he, shaking his finger threateningly and frowning severely, "else I'll be obliged to give you a poke in the nose. I wonder, now, Frog, if you ever had a mother, or if you only grew out of the earth like a plant. Tell me, were you ever dandled in a mother's arms? Do you know anything of maternal affection, eh? Humph! I suspect not. You would not look so besottedly stupid if you did. I tell you what it is, old fellow: you're uncommonly bad company, and I've a good mind to ram my knife through you, and carry you into camp to my friend Ralph Rover, who'll skin and stuff you to such an extent that your own mother wouldn't know you, and carry you to England, and place you in a museum under a glass case, to be gazed at by nurses, and stared at by children, and philosophised about by learned professors. Hollo! none o' that now. Come, poor beast; I didn't mean to frighten you. There, sit still, and don't oblige me to stick you up again, and I'll not take you to Ralph."

The poor frog, which had made another attempt to escape, gazed vacantly at Peterkin again without moving, except in regard to the puffing before referred to.

"Now, frog, I'll have to bid you good afternoon. I'm sorry that time and circumstance necessitate our separation, but I'm glad that I have had the pleasure of meeting with you. Glad and sorry, frog, in the same breath! Did you ever philosophise on that point, eh? Is it possible, think you, to be glad and sorry at one and the same moment? No doubt a creature like you, with such a very small intellect, if indeed you have any at all, will say that it is not possible. But I know better. Why, what do you call hysterics? Ain't that laughing and crying at once-- sorrow and joy mixed? I don't believe you understand a word that I say. You great puffing blockhead, what are you staring at?"

The frog, as before, refused to make any reply; so our friend lay for some time chuckling and making faces at it. While thus engaged he happened to look up, and to our surprise as well as alarm we observed that he suddenly turned as pale as death.

To cock our rifles, and take a step forward so as to obtain a view in the direction in which he was gazing with a fixed and horrified stare, was our immediate impulse. The object that met our eyes on clearing the bushes was indeed well calculated to strike terror into the stoutest heart; for there, not three yards distant from the spot on which our friend lay, and partially concealed by foliage, stood a large black rhinoceros. It seemed to have just approached at that moment, and had been suddenly arrested, if not surprised, by the vision of Peterkin and the frog. There was something inexpressibly horrible in the sight of the great block of a head, with its mischievous-looking eyes, ungainly snout, and ponderous horn, in such close proximity to our friend. How it had got so near without its heavy tread being heard I cannot tell, unless it were that the noise of the turbulent brook had drowned the sound.

But we had no time either for speculation or contemplation. Both Jack and I instantly took aim--he at the shoulder, as he afterwards told me; I at the monster's eye, into which, with, I am bound to confess, my usual precipitancy, I discharged both barrels.

The report seemed to have the effect of arousing Peterkin out of his state of fascination, for he sprang up and darted towards us. At the same instant the wounded rhinoceros crossed the spot which he had left with a terrific rush, and bursting through the bushes as if it had been a great rock falling from a mountain cliff, went headlong into the rivulet.

Without moving from the spot on which we stood, we recharged our pieces with a degree of celerity that, I am persuaded, we never before equalled. Peterkin at the same time caught up his rifle, which leaned against a tree hard by, and only a few seconds elapsed after the fall of the monster into the river ere we were upon its banks ready for another shot.

The portion of the bank of the stream at this spot happened to be rather steep, so that the rhinoceros, on regaining his feet, experienced considerable difficulty in the attempts to clamber out, which he made repeatedly and violently on seeing us emerge from among the bushes.

"Let us separate," said Jack; "it will distract his attention."

"Stay; you have blown out his eye, Ralph, I do believe," said Peterkin.

On drawing near to the struggling monster we observed that this was really the case. Blood streamed from the eye into which I had fired, and poured down his hideous jaws, dyeing the water in which he floundered.

"Look out!" cried Jack, springing to the right, in order to get on the animal's blind side as it succeeded in effecting a landing.

Peterkin instantly sprang in the same direction, while I bounded to the opposite side. I have never been able satisfactorily to decide in my own mind whether this act on my part was performed in consequence of a sudden, almost involuntary, idea that by so doing I should help to distract the creature's attention, or was the result merely of an accidental impulse. But whatever the cause, the effect was most fortunate; for the rhinoceros at once turned towards me, and thus, being blind in the other eye, lost sight of Jack and Peterkin, who with the rapidity almost of thought leaped close up to its side, and took close aim at the most vulnerable parts of its body. As they were directly opposite to me, I felt that I ran some risk of receiving their fire. But before I had time either to reflect that they could not possibly miss so large an object at so short a distance, or to get out of the way, the report of both their heavy rifles rang through the forest, and the rhinoceros fell dead almost at my feet.

"Hurrah!" shouted Peterkin, throwing his cap into the air at this happy consummation, and sitting down on the haunch of our victim.

"Shame on you, Peterkin," said I, as I reloaded his rifle for him--"shame on you to crow thus over a fallen foe!"

"Ha, boy! it's all very well for you to say that now, but you know well enough that you would rather have lost your ears than have missed such a chance as this. But, I say, it'll puzzle you to stuff that fellow, won't it?"

"No doubt of it," answered Jack, as he drew a percussion cap from his pouch, and placed it carefully on the nipple of his rifle. "Ralph will not find it easy; and it's a pity, too, not to take it home with us, for under a glass case it would make such a pretty and appropriate pendant, in his museum, to that interesting frog with which you--"

"Oh, you sneaking eavesdropper!" cried Peterkin, laughing. "It is really too bad that a fellow can't have a little tete-a-tete with a friend but you and Ralph must be thrusting your impertinent noses in the way."

"Not to mention the rhinoceros," observed Jack.

"Ah! to be sure--the rhinoceros; yes, I might have expected to find you in such low company, for `birds of a feather,' you know, are said to `flock together.'"

"If there be any truth in that," said I, "you are bound, on the same ground, to identify yourself with the frog."

"By the way," cried Peterkin, starting up and looking around the spot on which his interesting tete-a-tete had taken place, "where is the frog? It was just here that--Ah!--oh!--oh! poor, poor frog!

"`Your course is run, your days are o'er; We'll never have a chat no more,'

"As Shakespeare has it. Well, well, who would have thought that so conversable and intelligent a creature should have come to such a melancholy end?"

The poor frog had indeed come to a sad and sudden end, and I felt quite sorry for it, although I could not help smiling at my companion's quaint manner of announcing the fact.

Not being gifted with the activity of Peterkin, it had stood its ground when the rhinoceros charged, and had received an accidental kick from the great foot of that animal which had broken its back and killed it outright.

"There's one comfort, however," observed Jack, as we stood over the frog's body: "you have been saved the disagreeable necessity of killing it yourself, Ralph."

This was true, and I was not sorry that the rhinoceros had done me this service; for, to say truth, I have ever felt the necessity of killing animals in cold blood to be one of the few disagreeable points in the otherwise delightful life of a naturalist. To shoot animals in the heat and excitement of the chase I have never felt to be particularly repulsive or difficult; but the spearing of an insect, or the deliberate killing of an unresisting frog, are duties which I have ever performed with a feeling of deep self-abhorrence.

Carefully packing my frog in leaves, and placing it in my pouch, I turned with my companions to quit the scene of our late encounter and return to our camp, on arriving at which we purposed sending back Makarooroo to cut off the horn of the rhinoceros; for we agreed that, as it was impossible to carry away the entire carcass, we ought at least to secure the horn as a memorial of our adventure.

CHAPTER TWENTY

THREE.

WE SEE STRANGE THINGS, AND GIVE OUR NEGRO FRIENDS THE SLIP.

During the two following days we passed through a country that was more thickly covered with the indiarubber vine than any place we had before met with in our African travels. I could not help feeling regret that such a splendid region should be almost, if not altogether, unknown and useless to civilised man. There seemed to be an unlimited supply of caoutchouc; but the natives practised a method of gathering it which had the effect of destroying the vine.

One day, some weeks after this, we came upon the habitation of a most remarkable species of monkey, named the Nshiego Mbouve, which we had often heard of, but had not up to that time been so fortunate as to see. Being exceedingly anxious to observe how this remarkable creature made use of its singular house, Peterkin and I lay down near the place, and secreting ourselves in the bushes, patiently awaited the arrival of the monkey, while Jack went off in another direction to procure something for supper.

"I don't believe he'll come home to-night," said Peterkin, after we had lain down. "People never do come in when any one chances to be waiting for them. The human race seems to be born to disappointment. Did you never notice, Ralph, how obstinately contrary and cross-grained things go when you want them to go otherwise?"

"I don't quite understand you," said I.

"Of course you don't. Yours seems to be a mind that can never take anything in unless it is hammered in by repetition."

"Come now, Peterkin, don't become, yourself, an illustration of your own remark in reference to cross-grained things."

"Well, I won't. But seriously, Ralph, have you not observed, in the course of your observant life, that when you have particular business with a man, and go to his house or office, you are certain to find him out, to use the common phrase? It would be more correct, however, to say `you are certain not to find him in.'"

"You are uncommonly particular, Peterkin."

"Truly I had need to be so, with such an uncommonly stupid audience."

"Thank you. Well?"

"Well, have you never observed that if you have occasion to call at a house where you have never been before, the number of that particular house is not in its usual place, and you find it after a search quite away from where it ought to be? Has it never struck you that when you take out your umbrella, the day is certain to become hot and sunny; while, if you omit to carry it with you, it is sure to rain?"

"From all of which you conclude," said I, "that the Nshiego will not come home to-night?"

"Exactly so; that is my meaning precisely."

After Peterkin said this, we relapsed into silence; and it was well that we did so, for had we continued our conversation even in the whispering tones in which it had up to that time been conducted, we should have frightened away the ape which now came, as it were, to rebuke Peterkin for his unbelief.

Coming quickly forward, the Nshiego Mbouve chambered quickly up the tree where its nest was built. This nest was not a structure into which it clambered, but a shelter or canopy formed of boughs with their leaves, somewhat in shape like an umbrella, under which it sat. The construction of this shelter exhibited a good deal of intelligent ingenuity on the part of the ape; for it was tied to the tree by means of wild vines and creepers, and formed a neat, comfortable roof, that was quite capable of shedding the night dews or heavy rains, and thus protecting its occupant.

We were greatly amused by the manner in which the creature proceeded to make itself comfortable. Just below the canopy was a small branch which jutted out horizontally from the stem of the tree. On this branch the ape seated itself, its feet and haunches resting thereon. Then it threw one arm round the tree, and hugging that lovingly to its side, gave what appeared to me to be a small sigh of satisfaction, and prepared to go to sleep.

At this Peterkin chuckled audibly. The Nshiego's eyes opened at once. I cocked my gun and took aim. The desire to procure a specimen was very strong within me, but an unconquerable aversion to kill an animal in such cozy circumstances restrained me. The Nshiego got up in alarm. I pointed the gun, but could not fire. It began to descend. I pulled the trigger, and, I am happy to add, missed my aim altogether, to the intense delight of Peterkin, who filled the woods with laughter, while the Nshiego Mbouve, dropping to the ground, ran shrieking from the spot.

My forbearance at this time was afterwards repaid by my obtaining two much finer specimens of this shelter-building ape, both of which were killed by Peterkin.

On quitting this place we had a narrow escape, the recollection of which still fills me with horror. We were walking rapidly back towards our encampment, chatting as we went, when Peterkin suddenly put his foot on what appeared to be the dead branch of a tree. No sooner had he done so than the curling folds of a black snake fully ten feet long scattered the dry leaves into the air, and caused us both to dart aside with a yell of terror.

I have thought that in the complicated and wonderful mechanism of man there lies a species of almost involuntary muscular power which enables him to act in all cases of sudden danger with a degree of prompt celerity that he could not possibly call forth by a direct act of volition. At all events, on the present emergency, without in the least degree knowing what I was about, I brought my gun from my shoulder into a horizontal position, and blew the snake's head off almost in an instant.

I have pondered this subject, and from the fact that while at one time a man may be prompt and courageous in case of sudden danger, at another time the same man may become panic-stricken and helpless, I have come to the conclusion that the all-wise Creator would teach us--even the bravest among us--the lesson of our dependence upon each other, as well as our dependence upon Himself, and would have us know that while at one time we may prove a tower of strength and protection to our friends, at another time our friends may have to afford succour and protection to us.

I have often wondered, in reference to this, that many men seem to take pride in bold independence, when it is an obvious fact that every man is dependent on his fellow, and that this mutual dependence is one of the chief sources of human happiness.

The black snake which I had killed turned out to be one of a very venomous kind, whose bite is said to be fatal, so that we had good cause to be thankful, and to congratulate ourselves on our escape.

In this region of Africa we were particularly fortunate in what we saw and encountered, as the narrative of our experiences on the day following the above incidents will show.

We had scarcely advanced a few miles on our journey on the morning of that day, when we came upon a part of the country where the natives had constructed a curious sort of trap for catching wild animals; and it happened that a large band of natives were on the point of setting out for a grand hunt at that time.

We were greeted with immense delight on our arrival, for those natives, we soon discovered, had already heard of our exploits in the lands of the gorilla, and regarded us as the greatest hunters that had ever been born. After a short conversation with the chief, through the medium of Makarooroo, we arranged to rest there a day, and accompany them on their hunting expedition; and the better to secure their good will, we presented some of the head men with a few of the beads which we still possessed. Then hauling our canoe out of the water, we prepared ourselves for the chase.

After a long and tedious march through somewhat dense jungle, we came upon the ground, which was partly open, partly clothed with trees and shrubs. Here the natives, who numbered several hundreds, spread themselves out in a long semicircular line, in order to drive the game into the trap.

As we followed them, or rather formed part of the line, I overheard the following conversation between Peterkin and Makarooroo, who chanced to be together.

"Now, Mak," said the former, examining the caps of his rifle, "explain to me what sort of trap this is that we're coming to, and what sort of brutes we may expect to find in it."

"De trap, massa," replied our faithful follower, drawing the back of his hand across his mouth--"de trap am be call hopo--"

"Called what-o?" inquired Peterkin.

"Hopo."

"Oh! go on."

"An' hims be made ob great number oh sticks tumble down--an' hole at de end ob dat; an' de beasties dat goes in be zebros, elosphants, eelands, buff'los, gaffs, nocrices, noos, an' great more noders ob which me forgit de names."

"Oh! you forgit de names, do you?"

"Yis, massa."

"Ah! it wouldn't be a great loss, Mak, if you were to forget the names of those you remember."

The conversation was interrupted at this point by the appearance of a buffalo, which showed that we were drawing near to the scene of action. But as Makarooroo's description is not remarkable for lucidity, I may explain here that the hopo, or trap, consists of two parts; one part may be termed the conducting hedges, the other the pit at their termination, and into which the game is driven. The conducting hedges are formed in the shape of the letter V. At the narrow extremity there is a narrow lane, at the end of which is the terminating pit. This pit is about eight feet deep and fifteen feet broad, and its edges are made to overlap in such a way that once the animals are in it, they have no chance whatever of getting out again. The surface of the pit is concealed by a thin crust of green rushes, and the hedges are sometimes a mile long, and nearly the same width apart at the outer extremities.

We were still a considerable distance from the outer ends of the hedges, when the natives spread out as above described, and I am convinced that our line extended over at least four miles of ground. The circle, of course, narrowed as they advanced, shouting wildly, in order to drive the game into the enclosure.

That the country was teeming with game soon became apparent, for ever and anon as we advanced a herd of gnus or buffaloes or hartbeests would dart affrighted from their cover, and sweep over the open ground into another place of shelter, out of which they were again driven as the line advanced. In the course of half an hour we drove out hartbeests, zebras, gnus, buffaloes, giraffes, rhinoceroses, and many other kinds of smaller game, either singly or in herds.

"Now, lads," said Jack, approaching Peterkin and me as we walked together, "it is quite evident that if we wish to see this sport in perfection we must get outside the hedge, and run along towards the pit; for there, in the natural course of things, we may expect the grand climax. What say you? Shall we go?"

"Agreed," said I.

"Ditto," cried Peterkin.

So without more words we turned aside, followed by Makarooroo, leaped the hedge, and running down along it soon reached the edge of the pit.

Here we found a number of the natives assembled with spears, looking eagerly through the interstices of the hedges in expectation of the advancing herds. We took up our stand on a convenient spot, and prepared to wait patiently. But our patience was not severely tried. We had not been more than five minutes stationed when the noise of the closing line was heard, and a herd of buffaloes dashed wildly out from a small piece of jungle in which they had sought shelter, and galloped over the plain towards us. Suddenly they halted, and stood for a moment snuffing the air, as if uncertain what to do; while we could see, even at that distance, that every muscle of their bodies trembled with mingled rage and terror. Before they could decide, a herd of gnus burst from the same place; and presently a dozen zebras galloped out, tossing up their heels and heads in magnificent indignation. These last scattered, and approached the hedges; which caused several natives to dart into the enclosure, who from beneath the shelter of oval shields as large as themselves, threw their spears with unerring certainty into the sides of the terrified creatures.

At this moment there was a general rush from the scattered groups of trees and clumps of jungle, for the animals were now maddened with terror, not only at the shouts of their human persecutors, but at their own wild cries and the increasing thunder of their tread.

The shouting and tumult now became excessive. It was almost bewildering. I looked round upon the faces of the negroes nearest to me. They seemed to be almost insane with suppressed excitement, and their dark faces worked in a manner that was quite awful to witness.

Presently there was a general and indiscriminate rush of all kinds of wild animals towards the narrow end of the hopo. The natives pressed in upon them with wild cries. Spears flew in all directions. Ere long the plain was covered with wounded animals struggling and bellowing in their death-agonies. As the rushing multitude drew nearer to the fatal pit, they became crowded together, and now the men near us began to play their part.

"Look out, Jack!" I cried, as a buffalo bull with glaring eyes and foaming jaws made a desperate effort to leap over the barrier in our very faces.

Jack raised his rifle and fired; at the same instant a spear was sent into the buffalo's breast, and it fell back to form a stumbling-block in the way of the rushing mass.

The report of the rifle caused the whole herd to swerve from our side so violently that they bore down the other side, until I began to fear the hedge would give way altogether; but they were met by the spears and the furious yells of the natives there, and again swept on towards the narrow lane.

And now the head of the bellowing mass came to the edge of the pit. Those in front seemed to suspect danger, for they halted suddenly; but the rush of those behind forced them on. In another moment the thin covering gave way, and a literal cataract of huge living creatures went surging down into the abyss.

The scene that followed was terrible to witness; and I could not regard it with other than feelings of intense horror, despite my knowledge of the fact that a large tribe of natives depended on the game then slain for their necessary food. The maddened animals attempted to leap out of the pit, but the overlapping edges already referred to effectually prevented this until the falling torrent filled it up; then some of them succeeded in leaping out from off the backs of their smothered comrades. These, however, were quickly met and speared by the natives, while ever and anon the great mass was upheaved by the frantic struggles of some gigantic creature that was being smothered at the bottom.

While this scene of wholesale destruction was going on, Makarooroo came up to me and begged me, with mysterious looks, to follow him out of the crowd.

I obeyed, and when we had got away from the immediate neighbourhood of the turmoil, I said,--"Well, Mak, what's wrong?"

"De chief, massa, hims tell me few moments ago dat canoe wid Mbango and oomans hab pass dis way to-morrow."

"To-morrow!" I exclaimed.

"No, me forgit; hab pass yistumday."

"Indeed!"

"Yis, an' de chief hims say hims want us to stop wid him and go hunt for week or two. P'raps he no let us go 'way."

"That's just possible, Mak. Have you told Jack?"

"No, massa."

"Then go bring him and Peterkin hither at once."

In a few minutes my companions were with me, and we held a brief earnest consultation as to what we should do.

"I think we should tell the chief we are anxious to be off at once, and leave him on good terms," said I.

Peterkin objected to this. "No," said he; "we cannot easily explain why we are anxious to be off so hastily. I counsel flight. They won't find out that we are gone until it is too late to follow."

Jack agreed with this view, so of course I gave in, though I could not in my heart approve of such a method of sneaking away. But our guide seemed also to be exceedingly anxious to be off, so we decided; and slipping quietly away under the shelter of the hedge, while the natives were still busy with their bloody work, we soon gained the forest. Here we had no difficulty in retracing our steps to the village, where, having picked up our little companion, Njamie's son, who had been left to play with the little boys of the place, we embarked, swept down the stream, and were soon far beyond the chance of pursuit.

CHAPTER TWENTY

FOUR.

A LONG CHASE, AND A HAPPY TERMINATION THEREOF.

Knowing that unless we advanced with more than ordinary speed we could not hope to overtake our friends for several days--a stern chase being proverbially a long one--we travelled a great part of the night as well as all day; and on our third day after quitting the scene of the curious hunt described in the last chapter, we descried the fugitives descending the river about a quarter of a mile ahead of us.

Unhappily we made a stupid mistake at this time. Instead of waiting until we were near enough to be recognised, we shouted to our friends the moment we saw their canoe. I cannot say that we knew them to be our friends, but we had every reason to suppose so. The result of our shout was that they supposed us to be enemies, and paddled away as if for their lives. It was in vain that we tried to show by signs that we were not enemies.

"Yell!" cried Peterkin, turning to Makarooroo, who sat close behind him.

Our guide opened his huge mouth, and gave utterance to a yell that might well have struck terror into the heart of Mars himself.

"Stop! stay!" cried Peterkin hastily. "I didn't mean a war-yell; I meant a yell of--of peace."

"Me no hab a yell ob peace," said Makarooroo, with a look of perplexity.

"I should not suppose you had," observed Jack, with a quiet laugh, as he dipped his paddle more energetically than ever into the stream.--"The fact is, Peterkin, that we shall have to go in for a long chase. There is no doubt about it. I see that there are at least four men in their canoe, and if one of them is Mbango, as we have reason to believe, a stout and expert arm guides them. But ho! give way! `never venture, never win.'"

With that we all plied our paddles with our utmost might. The chase soon became very exciting. Ere long it became evident that the crews of the two canoes were pretty equally matched, for we did not, apparently, diminish the distance between us by a single inch during the next half-hour.

"What if it turns out not to be Mbango and his party after all?" suggested Peterkin, who wielded his light paddle with admirable effect.

Jack, who sat in the bow, replied that in that case we should have to make the best apology and explanation we could to the niggers, and console ourselves with the consciousness of having done our best.

For some time the rapid dip of our paddles and the rush of our canoe through the water were the only sounds that were heard. Then Peterkin spoke again. He could never keep silence for any great length of time.

"I say, Jack, we'll never do it. If we had only another man, or even a boy." (Peterkin glanced at Njamie's little son, who lay sound asleep at the bottom of the boat.) "No, he won't do; we might as well ask a mosquito to help us."

"I say, lads, isn't one of the crew of that canoe a woman?" said Jack, looking over his shoulder, but not ceasing for an instant to ply his paddle.

"Can't tell," answered Peterkin.--"What say you, Mak?"

"Ye-is, massa," replied the guide, with some hesitation. "Me tink dat am be one ooman's arm what wag de paddil. Oh! yis, me sartin sure now, dat am a ooman."

"That being the case," observed Jack, in a tone of satisfaction, "the chase won't last much longer, for a woman's muscles can't hold out long at such a pace. Ho! give way once more."

In less than five minutes the truth of Jack's remark became apparent, for we began rapidly to overhaul the fugitives. This result acted with a double effect: while it inspirited us to additional exertion, it depressed those whom we were pursuing, and so rendered them less capable than before of contending with us. There was evidently a good deal of excitement and gesticulation among them. Suddenly the man in the stern laid down his paddle, and stooping down seized a gun, with which, turning round, he took deliberate aim at us.

"That's rather awkward," observed Jack, in a cool, quiet way, as if the awkwardness of the case had no reference whatever to him personally.

We did not, however, check our advance. The man fired, and the ball came skipping over the water and passed us at a distance of about two yards.

"Hum! I expected as much," observed Jack. "When a bad shot points a bad gun at you, your best plan is to stand still and take your chance. In such a case the chance is not a bad one. Hollo! the rascal seems about to try it again. I say, boys, we must stop this."

We had now gained so much on the fugitives that we had reason to hope that we might by signs enable them to understand that we were not enemies. We had to make the attempt rather abruptly, for as Jack uttered his last remark, the man in the stern of the canoe we were chasing, having reloaded his gun, turned round to aim at us again. At the same time the rest of the crew suddenly ceased to paddle, in order to enable their comrade to take a steady aim. It was evident that they rested all their hopes upon that shot disabling one of our number, and so enabling them to escape. Seeing this, Makarooroo in desperation seized his rifle and levelled it.

"No, no," said Peterkin, hastily holding up his hand. "Give me your rifle, Mak; and yours, Ralph. Now then, stop paddling for a moment; I'll try an experiment."

So saying, he sprang to his feet, and grasping a rifle in each hand, held them high above his head, intending thus to show that we were well-armed, but that we did not intend to use our weapons.

The device was happily successful: the man in the other canoe lowered the gun with which he was in the act of taking aim at us.

"Now, boys, paddle slowly towards the bank," cried Peterkin, laying down the rifles quickly and standing erect again with his empty hands extended in the air, to confirm the fugitives in regard to our good intentions. They understood the sign, and also turned toward the bank, where in a few minutes both parties landed, at the distance of about two hundred yards from each other.

"Mak, you had better advance alone," said Jack. "If it is Mbango and his friends, they will know you at once. Don't carry your rifle; you won't need it."

"Nay, Jack," I interposed; "you do not act with your usual caution. Should it chance not to be Mbango, it were well that Mak should have his rifle and a companion to support him."

"O most sapient Ralph," said Peterkin, "don't you know that Jack and I have nothing to do but sit down on this bank, each with a double-barrel in his hand, and if anything like foul play should be attempted, four of the enemy should infallibly bite the dust at the same time? But you'd better go with Mak, since you're so careful of him. We will engage to defend you both.--Hollo, Puggy! take the line of our canoe here and fasten it to yonder bush."

The latter part of this remark was addressed to Njamie's little boy, whose name we had never learned, and who had been called Puggy by Peterkin-- not, let me remark, in anything approaching to a contemptuous spirit. He evidently meant it as a title of endearment. We had tacitly accepted it, and so had the lad, who for some time past had answered to the name of Puggy, in utter ignorance, of course, as to its signification.

Mak and I now advanced unarmed towards the negroes, and in a few seconds we mutually recognised each other. I was overjoyed to observe the well-known face of Okandaga, who no sooner recognised her lover than she uttered a joyful shout and ran towards him. I at the same time advanced to Mbango, and grasping his hand shook it warmly; but that good-hearted chief was not satisfied with such a tame expression of good will. Seizing me by the shoulders, he put forward his great flat nose and rubbed mine heartily therewith. My first impulse was to draw back, but fortunately my better judgment came to my aid in time, and prevented me from running the risk of hurting the feelings of our black friend. And I had at that time lived long enough to know that there is nothing that sinks so bitterly into the human heart as the repulse, however slightly, of a voluntary demonstration of affection. I had made up my mind that if the dirtiest negro in all Africa should offer to rub noses with me, I would shut my eyes and submit.

I observed among the crew of Mbango's canoe a female figure who instantly attracted my attention and awakened my sympathy. She was seated on a rock, paying no attention whatever to the events that were occurring so near to her, and which, for aught she could tell, might be to her matter of life or death. Her hands hung idly by her side; her body was bowed forward; her head drooped on her breast; and her whole appearance indicated a depth of woe such as I have never before seen equalled.

I pointed to her and looked at Mbango in surprise. He looked first at the woman and then at me, and shook his head mournfully; but being unable to speak to me, or I to him, of course I could not gather much from his looks.

I was about to turn to our guide, when the woman raised her head a little, so that her face was exposed. I at once recognised the features of Njamie, Mbango's favourite wife, and I was now at no loss to divine the cause of her grief.

Starting up in haste, I ran away back at full speed towards the spot where our canoe lay. Jack and Peterkin, seeing how matters stood, were by that time advancing to meet us, and the little boy followed. I passed them without uttering a word, seized the boy by the wrist, and dragged him somewhat violently towards the place where his mother sat.

"Hollo, Ralph," shouted Peterkin as I passed, "see that you don't damage my Puggy, else you'll have to--"

I heard no more. The next instant I stood beside Njamie, and placed her boy before her. I have never in my life witnessed such a mingling of intense eagerness, surprise, and joy, as was expressed by the poor woman when her eyes fell on the face of her child. For one moment she gazed at him, and the expressions I have referred to flitted, or rather flashed, across her dusky countenance; then giving utterance to a piercing shriek, she sprang forward and clasped her son to her bosom.

I would not have missed that sight for the world. I know not very well what my thoughts were at the time, but the memory of that scene has often since, in my musings, filled me with inexpressible gladness; and in pondering the subject, I have felt that the witnessing of that meeting has given additional force to the line in Scripture wherein the word "love" alone is deemed sufficiently comprehensive to describe the whole character of the Almighty.

Here, on the one hand, I beheld unutterable, indescribable woe; on the other hand, unutterable, inconceivable joy--both, I should suppose, in their extremest degree, and both resulting from pure and simple love. I pondered this much at the time; I have pondered it often since. It is a subject of study which I recommend to all who chance to read this page.

CHAPTER TWENTY FIVE.

I HAVE A DESPERATE ENCOUNTER AND A NARROW ESCAPE.

The happiness that now beamed in the faces of Makarooroo, Okandaga, and Njamie was a sufficient reward to us for all the trouble we had taken and all the risk we had run on their account. Poor Njamie was exceedingly grateful to us. She sought by every means in her power to show this, and among other things, hearing us call her son by the name of Puggy, she at once adopted it, to the immense amusement and delight of Peterkin.

After the first excitement of our meeting had subsided somewhat, we consulted together as to what we should now do. On the one hand, we were unwilling to quit the scene of our hunting triumphs and adventures; on the other hand, Makarooroo and his bride were anxious to reach the mission stations on the coast and get married in the Christian manner.

"Our opposing interests are indeed a little perplexing," said Jack, after some conversation had passed on the subject.--"No doubt, Mak, you and Mbango with his friends might reach the coast safely enough without us; but then what should we do without an interpreter?"

Our poor guide, whose troubles seemed as though they would never end, sighed deeply and glanced at his bride with a melancholy countenance as he replied--

"Me'll go wid you, massa, an' Okandaga'll go to coast an' wait dere for me come."

"Ha!" ejaculated Peterkin, "that's all very well, Mak, but you'll do nothing of the sort. That plan won't do, so we'll have to try again."

"I agree with you, Peterkin," observed Jack. "That plan certainly will not do; but I cannot think of any other that will, so we must just exercise a little self-denial for once, give up all further attacks on the wild beasts of Africa, and accompany Mak to the coast."

"Could we not manage a compromise?" said I.

"What be a cumprumoise?" asked Makarooroo, who had been glancing anxiously from one to the other as we conversed.

Peterkin laid hold of his chin, pursed up his mouth, and looked at me with a gleeful leer.

"There's a chance for you, Ralph," said he; "why don't you explain?"

"Because it's not easy to explain," said I, considering the best way in which to convey the meaning of such a word.--"A compromise, Mak, is--is a bargain, a compact--at least so Johnson puts it--"

"Yes," interposed Peterkin; "so you see, Mak, when you agree with a trader to get him an elephant-tusk, that's a cumprumoise, according to Johnson."

"No, no, Mak," said I quickly; "Peterkin is talking nonsense. It is not a bargain of that kind; it's a--a--You know every question has two sides?"

"Yis, massa."

"Well, suppose you took one side."

"Yis."

"And suppose I took the other side."

"Then suppose we were to agree to forsake our respective sides and meet, as it were, half-way, and thus hold the same middle course--"

"Ay, down the middle and up again; that's it, Mak," again interrupted Peterkin--"that's a cumprumoise. In short, to put it in another and a clearer light, suppose that I were to resolve to hit you an awful whack on one side of your head, and suppose that Ralph were to determine to hit you a frightful bang on the other side, then suppose that we were to agree to give up those amiable intentions, and instead thereof to give you, unitedly, one tremendous smash on the place where, if you had one, the bridge of your nose would be--that would be a cumprumoise."

"Ho! ha! ha! hi!" shouted our guide, rolling over on the grass and splitting himself with laughter; for Makarooroo, like the most of his race, was excessively fond of a joke, no matter how bad, and was always ready on the shortest notice to go off into fits of laughter, if he had only the remotest idea of what the jest meant. He had become so accustomed at last to expect something jocular from Peterkin, that he almost invariably opened his mouth to be ready whenever he observed our friend make any demonstration that gave indication of his being about to speak.

From the mere force of sympathy Mbango began to laugh also, and I know not how long the two would have gone on, had not Jack checked them by saying--

"I suspect we are not very well fitted to instruct the unenlightened mind," ("Ho--hi!" sighed Makarooroo, gathering himself up and settling down to listen), "and it seems to me that you'll have to try again, Peterkin, some other mode of explanation."

"Very good, by all means," said our friend.--"Now, Mak, look here. You want to go there" (pointing to the coast with his left hand), "and we want to go there" (pointing to the interior with his right hand). "Now if we both agree to go there," (pointing straight before him with his nose), "that will be a cumprumoise. D'ye understand?"

"Ho yis, massa, me compiperhend now."

"Exactly so," said I; "that's just it. There is a branch of this river that takes a great bend away to the north before it turns towards the sea, is there not? I think I have heard yourself say so before now."

"Yis, massa, hall right."

"Well, let us go by that branch. We shall be a good deal longer on the route, but we shall be always nearing the end of our journey, and at the same time shall pass through a good deal of new country, in which we may hope to see much game."

"Good," said Jack; "you have wisdom with you for once, Ralph--it seems feasible.--What say you, Mak? I think it a capital plan."

"Yis, massa, it am a copitle plan, sure 'nuff."

The plan being thus arranged and agreed to, we set about the execution of it at once, and ere long our two canoes were floating side by side down the smooth current of the river.

The route which we had chosen led us, as I had before suspected, into the neighbourhood of the gorilla country, and I was much gratified to learn from Mbango, who had travelled over an immense portion of south-western Africa, that it was not improbable we should meet with several of those monstrous apes before finally turning off towards the coast. I say that I was much gratified to learn this; but I little imagined that I was at that time hastening towards a conflict that well-nigh proved fatal to me, and the bare remembrance of which still makes me shudder.

It occurred several weeks after the events just related. We had gone ashore for the purpose of hunting, our supply of provisions chancing at that time to be rather low. Feeling a desire to wander through the woods in solitude for a short time, I separated from my companions. I soon came to regret this deeply, for about an hour afterwards I came upon the tracks of a gorilla. Being armed only with my small-bore double rifle, and not being by any means confident of my shooting powers, I hesitated some time before making up my mind to follow the tracks.

At first I thought of retracing my steps and acquainting my comrades with the discovery I had made; but the little probability there was of my finding them within several hours deterred me. Besides, I felt ashamed to confess that I had been afraid to prosecute the chase alone; so, after pondering the matter a little, I decided on advancing.

Before doing so, however, I carefully examined the caps of my rifle and loosened my long hunting-knife in its sheath. Then I cautiously followed up the track, making as little noise as possible, for I was well aware of the watchfulness of the animal I was pursuing.

The footprints at first were not very distinct, but ere long I came on a muddy place where they were deeply imprinted, and my anxiety was somewhat increased by observing that they were uncommonly large--the largest I had ever seen--and that, therefore, they had undoubtedly been made by one of those solitary and gigantic males, which are always found to be the most savage.

I had scarcely made this discovery when I came unexpectedly on the gorilla itself. It was seated at the foot of a tree about fifty yards from the spot where I stood, the space between us being comparatively clear of underwood. In an instant he observed me, and rose, at the same time giving utterance to one of those diabolical roars which I have before referred to as being so terrible.

I halted, and felt an irresistible inclination to fire at once; but remembering the oft-repeated warnings of my companions, I restrained myself. At that moment I almost wished, I freely confess, that the gorilla would run away. But the monster had no such intention. Again uttering his horrible roar, he began slowly to advance, at the same time beating his drum-like chest with his doubled fist.

I now felt that my hour of trial had come. I must face the gorilla boldly, and act with perfect coolness. The alternative was death. As the hideous creature came on, I observed that he was considerably larger than the biggest we had yet seen; but, strange to say, this fact made no deeper impression upon me. I suppose that my whole mental and nervous being was wound up to the utmost possible state of tension. I felt that I was steady and able to brave the onset. But I was not aware of the severity of the test to which I was destined to be subjected. Instead of coming quickly on and deciding my fate at once, the savage animal advanced slowly, sometimes a step or two at a time, and then pausing for a moment ere it again advanced. Sometimes it even sat down on its haunches for a second or two, as if the weight of its overgrown body were too much for its hind legs; but it did not cease all that time to beat its chest, and roar, and twist its features into the most indescribable contortions. I suppose it took nearly five minutes to advance to within twelve yards of me, but those five minutes seemed to me an hour. I cannot describe the mental agony I endured.

When within ten yards of me I could restrain myself no longer. I raised my rifle, aimed at its chest, and fired. With a terrible roar it advanced. Again I fired, but without effect, for the gorilla rushed upon me. In despair, I drew my hunting-knife and launched it full at the brute's chest with all my might. I saw the glittering blade enter it as the enormous paw was raised to beat me down. I threw up my rifle to ward off the fatal blow, and at the same moment sprang to one side, in the hope of evading it. The stock of the rifle was shattered to pieces in an instant, and the blow, which would otherwise have fallen full on my head or chest, was diverted slightly, and took effect on my shoulder, the blade of which was smashed as I was hurled with stunning violence to the ground. For one moment I felt as if I were falling headlong down a precipice; the next, I became unconscious.

On recovering, I found myself lying on my back at the bottom of what appeared to be a large pit. I must have lain there for a considerable time, for I felt cold and stiff; and when I attempted to move, my wounded shoulder caused me unutterable anguish. I knew, however, that I must certainly perish if I did not exert myself; so with much difficulty I crept out of the pit. The first object that met my eyes, on rising to my feet, was the carcass of my late antagonist; which, on examination, I found, though badly wounded by both bullets, had eventually been killed by the knife. It must have died almost immediately after giving me the blow that had hurled me into the pit. I had not observed this pit, owing to the screen of bushes that surrounded it, but I have now no doubt that it was the means of saving my life.

My recollections of what followed this terrible adventure are exceedingly confused. I remember that I wandered about in a state of dreamy uncertainty, endeavouring to retrace my steps to our encampment. I have a faint recollection of meeting, to my surprise, with Jack and Peterkin, and of their tender expressions of sympathy; and I have a very vivid remembrance of the agony I endured when Jack set my broken shoulder-blade and bandaged my right arm tightly to my side. After that, all was a confused dream, in which all the adventures I had ever had with wild beasts were enacted over again, and many others besides that had never taken place at all.

Under the influence of fever, I lay in a state of delirium for many days in the bottom of the canoe; and when my unclouded consciousness was at length restored to me, I found myself lying in a bed, under the hospitable roof of a missionary, the windows of whose house looked out upon the sea.

And now, reader, the record of our adventures is complete. During the few weeks that I spent with the kind missionary of the Cross, I gained strength rapidly, and amused myself penning the first chapters of this book. Makarooroo and Okandaga were married, and soon became useful members of the Christian community on that part of the African coast. Mbango and his friends also joined the missionary for a time, but ultimately returned to the interior, whither I have no doubt they carried some of the good influences that they had received on the coast along with them.

King Jambai proved faithful to his engagement. All our packages and boxes of specimens arrived safely at the coast; and when unpacked for examination, and displayed in the large schoolroom of the station, the gorillas, and other rare and wonderful animals, besides curious plants, altogether formed a magnificent collection, the like of which has not yet been seen in Great Britain, and probably never will be.

When I was sufficiently restored to stand the voyage, Jack and Peterkin and I embarked in a homeward-bound trading vessel, and taking leave of our kind friends of the coast, and of Makarooroo and Okandaga, who wept much at the prospect of separation from us, we set sail for Old England.

"Farewell," said I, as we leaned over the vessel's side and gazed sadly at the receding shore--"farewell to you, kind missionaries and faithful negro friends."

"Ay," added Peterkin, with a deep sigh, "and fare-you-well, ye monstrous apes; gorillas, fare-you-well!"

###

CPSIA information can be obtained
at www.ICGtesting.com
Printed in the USA
BVHW041017040419
544607BV00018B/790/P